HEART OF
THE STORM

What Reviewers Say About Nicole Stiling's Work

In the Shadow of Darkness

"I really liked this story because it concentrated on the relationship between two women. You get enough of the vampire lore to establish Angeline, and then you're thrust into this mysterious, intriguing and beautiful story of two people wanting love. This is a must read for anyone who's into supernatural romances and anyone looking for an unconventional love story between two lovely women."
—*Lesbian Review*

Secrets in a Small Town

"This was a good story. The mystery of who the stalker was along with the developing relationship between Savannah and Micki had me reading that I didn't realize the end was upon me until I saw 'Epilogue.' If you're looking for a good mystery with a heavy dose of sexual tension, then this one will definitely keep you on the edge of your seats in more ways than one."—*Lesbian Review*

"I really enjoyed this book. The chemistry between Savannah and Micki is believable and the conclusion is sweet."—*poetryandreview*

"The romance was an enemies to lovers one, and I liked how the characters themselves were surprised by it, how fast and how easily it happened. I'm always amazed at the quality of some debut novels… and [I] look forward to the author's next one."—*Jude in the Stars*

Visit us at www.boldstrokesbooks.com

By the Author

Secrets in a Small Town

In the Shadow of Darkness

Heart of the Storm

HEART OF
THE STORM

by
Nicole Stiling

2020

HEART OF THE STORM

ISBN 13: 978-1-63555-789-3

THIS TRADE PAPERBACK ORIGINAL IS PUBLISHED BY
BOLD STROKES BOOKS, INC.
P.O. BOX 249
VALLEY FALLS, NY 12185

FIRST EDITION: DECEMBER 2020

CREDITS
EDITORS: VICTORIA VILLASENOR AND CINDY CRESAP
PRODUCTION DESIGN: SUSAN RAMUNDO
COVER DESIGN BY TAMMY SEIDICK

Acknowledgments

Many thanks to everyone behind the scenes at BSB. I'm so lucky to be a part of this wonderful and supportive family.

To my editor, Victoria—as always, I'm so grateful for your tightening and sharpening and your constant reminders that an em dash and a hyphen are NOT interchangeable.

My wife, my kids, my parents, and everyone else who has helped me slog through the procrastination—I love you all and couldn't do this without you. Thank you.

Dedication

For Uncle Ronnie, a wonderful man and my
favorite lieutenant. Always loved, always missed.

CHAPTER ONE

"Y ou know this is embarrassing, right?"

Juliet Mitchell ignored her son and pulled her SUV into the driveway of his father's sprawling modern farmhouse. She slapped the brim of his baseball cap down over his eyes.

"Listen, Declan. You are my only son, and if I want to sob while dropping you off to go to this godforsaken baseball camp, then I will do it. You can't stop me. Come on, let's go get your dad."

Declan grumbled but followed Juliet up the stone walk toward the front door. Will Bennett opened the door with an apologetic smile. Juliet gave him a once-over and frowned at the suit and tie he was wearing.

"I didn't realize this was a formal occasion." She rested her hand on her hip.

"It was totally last minute, I swear," Will said, running his hand through his hair. His graying temples only added to his stereotypical distinguished businessman persona. "It's for a big client, and I can't miss this meeting. I know it's Saturday, but this was the only day they had available. Dec, will you be upset if I don't go with you guys?"

Declan shrugged. "Not really. I could have just grabbed a ride with Josh and the other guys. Mom's the one turning this into a Hallmark movie."

Juliet glared at Declan, wondering how she'd made it fifteen years without strangling him. "I thought it would be nice for both of your parents to see you off. Next time I'll call you a cab and blow you a kiss from the living room." She turned to Will. "You could have called me to let me know."

"I still wanted to say good-bye in person. Hey, why doesn't Sienna go with you? That way you don't have to make the drive back alone," Will said, seemingly proud of his suggestion.

Sienna walked into the foyer, her eyes wide as saucers. "What was that?" she asked.

"Will, I'm sure Sienna has better things to do than sit in a car with me and Dec for the next three hours. It's fine, really." Juliet didn't want Sienna to think she didn't want her to tag along, but what the hell would they talk about once they dropped Declan off? Sienna was nice enough and they got along fine, but they hadn't shared more than fifteen minutes of conversation in the nine or so years she'd known her.

"No, really. Juliet, I know you hate to drive alone, and Sienna was just saying that she didn't feel like hanging around the house today. You guys will have a blast."

Juliet watched Will's gleefully happy expression fall as both she and Sienna stared at him with uncomfortable, frozen smiles.

Sienna broke the silence. "Okay, then. I'll go get my bag." She walked out of the room slowly, casting one last disdainful look at Will.

When she was safely out of sight, Juliet slapped Will on the arm. "In what world would you think this is a good idea? I suck at small talk, you know that. I would have been fine by myself!" Juliet whispered harshly.

"I just thought it would solve everything. You're pissed that I can't go with you, she's probably pissed that I have to go into work again, and Declan is pissed at the world. It's a win-win. Besides, with everything going on between us, I thought Sienna could use a friend." Will shrugged.

"And you really think I'm the best person for that job? Are we supposed to commiserate about you being an asshole?"

"Okay, that's a little harsh. I'm trying, I really am. You know I don't want my marriage to fail. But being separated isn't helping that."

Juliet looked down. Maybe she had been a little too severe. She knew firsthand that Will wasn't a bad guy, just a little self-centered. "You're right, I'm sorry. I know you're going through a rough patch right now."

"Rough patch. Right."

"Are we ready to go?" Sienna asked, a small backpack slung over her shoulder. "Where's Declan?"

"I think he's in the kitchen raiding the fridge. No surprise," Will said.

"Dec! Time to go," Juliet yelled. She smiled at Sienna. If she was uncomfortable with the idea of being stuck in a car for the foreseeable future with Will's estranged wife, she could only imagine how Sienna must feel.

Will shot Juliet a grateful look and wrapped Declan up in a bear hug. Even though he was fifteen, it was his first full week away from home. Juliet fought the urge to join in.

Pushing the unlock button on her key fob, Juliet ushered everyone out to the driveway. She watched as Sienna slid into the passenger seat, her perfectly coiffed hair bouncing softly on her shoulders. The July humidity obviously had no effect on her. One thing was certain—Juliet had no problem seeing why Will had been attracted to her. She dripped with feminine sensuality, from the tips of her dark mahogany hair to the red toenails that peeked out of her wedged sandals. Juliet looked down at her worn sneakers and felt like a clod next to her.

"Everything okay?" Sienna asked.

Juliet blushed, obviously caught staring at her. "Yeah, sorry. I was just calculating the route in my head and sort of spaced out." Lies.

"Come on, Mom, I don't want to be late. If I'm the last one to get there, I'll get stuck with a shitty roommate," Declan complained.

"Language!" Juliet said, adjusting her rearview mirror.

"Sorry, a shitty *bunk*mate."

Juliet couldn't help but smile as Sienna stifled a laugh.

"Funny guy. Just keep your mouth shut until we cross into New Hampshire, okay?"

The ride was easier than she'd imagined. Sienna and Declan talked about Boston sports, something that Juliet watched from time to time, but wasn't nearly as interested in it as the two of them were. They listened to nineties music while Declan mocked Sienna and Juliet for singing along. By the time they crossed the Eaton town line, Juliet realized she'd actually been enjoying herself.

"There it is." Declan pointed out his window. Up ahead was a huge banner hanging from two telephone poles welcoming baseball players from all over New England. Juliet couldn't remember her broody teenager sounding as excited as he did at that moment in a very long time. It did her heart good.

"Okay, baby boy, this is it. I won't see you until next Saturday. Text me every hour so I know you're okay," Juliet said, meeting him at the back of her vehicle. She promised herself she wouldn't cry, but her eyes filled just the same.

"I'll text you once a day before I go to sleep, okay? Any more than that and they'll call me a mama's boy." Declan hefted his equipment out of the back and swung it onto his shoulder.

"If the shoe fits..." Juliet shrugged.

"Stop. Love you, Mom. I'll see you next week."

Juliet smiled and grabbed Declan's face. It was like looking in a mirror. They shared the same light blond hair, the same hazel eyes, the same lopsided smile that had manipulated more than a few people over the years. "Love you, honey. Be good. Have fun."

Sienna stood next to him with her hands in her pockets. When he turned to her, she opened her arms. "Have a wonderful time, Dec. I'll make sure your dad doesn't raid your 'secret' stash in the kitchen cupboard."

Declan hugged her tightly. "Thanks, Sienna. Thanks for coming along for the ride. Dad's always so busy."

She gave him a sad smile. "Yeah, he is. Now go, before they label you a stepmama's boy at the same time."

Declan smiled and turned toward the front gate. "See you guys in a week!"

Juliet chewed her lip and looked at Sienna. "Do you think we should go with him? Make sure he gets settled in okay?"

Sienna laughed lightly and put her hand on Juliet's shoulder. "Definitely not. He'd be mortified if we walked him in like it was his first day of kindergarten."

"You're right, you're right. Okay, we should just go. Otherwise I'm going to start blubbering and no one wants that." Juliet took a deep breath and got behind the steering wheel once again.

"He's a good boy," Sienna said thoughtfully, while buckling her seat belt. "I know he can be a smart-ass, but you and Will have done an amazing job with him."

"Thank you," Juliet said. "And so have you. It took Will and me a while to find our stride after Declan was born, but we really made it work. Declan is lucky, Will's a great dad. I'm lucky too. This could have gone a whole lot differently if Will wasn't the kind of guy that he is."

Sienna sat quietly. "He never really talked about it much. When I asked him in the past, he'd just say that the two of you had a fling in college and ended up with a baby."

Juliet nodded. "Well, that's the gist of it. I knew I was into women, but I guess I just wanted to be really sure before I closed that chapter of the book of my life entirely. Turns out I was really sure." Juliet shrugged.

"What made you..." Sienna trailed off.

"Decide to keep the baby? Will and I had already split up by the time I found out I was pregnant. We decided that we made better friends, since I was actually a lesbian and all," Juliet said, smiling. "I don't know, really. When my pregnancy test came back positive, all of a sudden I wanted nothing more than the baby growing inside me. I called Will and told him. I also told him he had no responsibility toward me or the baby, but I felt he should know. He was quiet for a minute, and then asked me if we could raise a baby together without being together. I told him I didn't know, but we could sure try. And here we are, fifteen years later."

"That's amazing, really. That you two have been able to maintain an amicable co-parenting relationship after all these years." Sienna looked down at her folded hands.

"It hasn't always been easy, believe me. We've fought hundreds of times over the years, and I'm sure you've heard about them. But we always try to focus on what's best for Declan. And that's the thing that got us through."

Juliet stole a quick glance at Sienna before turning her eyes back to the road. She looked sad, but Juliet was hesitant to bring up the elephant in the room. Will had given her the crib notes version of what was going on between them, but she wasn't sure if Sienna knew that she knew.

"I assume you know?" Sienna asked.

Well, that was that. Juliet sighed.

"Very little."

Sienna nodded and looked out her window. "I don't think Declan knows. Not yet, anyway. But he will when he returns home."

Juliet swallowed. She wasn't sure how much she should engage in the conversation. But Sienna was opening up to her, so Juliet didn't want her to think she wasn't interested or didn't care. Besides, Will said she might need a friend.

"Why, are you planning on having a sit-down with him? Has it gotten that serious?"

"Will has been slowly moving some of his things out to the pool house. I—we—think it would be best if we spent some time apart to, you know, look at things with a clear head," Sienna said.

Juliet hadn't realized it was that strained between them. Will had told her that they were having problems, that the communication wasn't there, that they weren't seeing eye to eye on very much at all. He hadn't given her a whole lot of information, but she'd gotten the feeling that he didn't necessarily see it as all that bad. Juliet had assumed that they would work it out.

"I'm so sorry, I didn't know." Juliet felt the urge to reach over and squeeze Sienna's hand but decided against it. She didn't know her very well, and the thick silence that hung over them was uncomfortable enough. Though she'd known Sienna for nearly a decade, their interactions had mostly been limited to pleasantries and cheering on Declan at his baseball games.

Sienna cleared her throat suddenly. "Enough of that. Will mentioned that you're a fan of horror movies?"

"Yes! I just wish I had someone to enjoy them with. Dec thinks they're corny, Will thinks they're stupid, and my friend Celeste thinks they're too scary. So, I'm usually on my own." Juliet was glad Sienna had changed the subject. She didn't want her to be miserable for the rest of the car ride home.

"I'm actually a huge fan too. I can remember sneaking in to the third *Nightmare on Elm Street* when I was ten or eleven. Scared me to death." Sienna smiled, casting a side glance at Juliet. "Been a fan ever since."

"Come on! That one is actually my favorite of the whole series."

By the time Juliet pulled her SUV into Sienna's driveway, they'd discussed everything from slasher films to psychological horror to post-apocalyptic sci-fi. After spending that amount of time together, Juliet could officially say that she liked Sienna. She'd only wished that she hadn't waited to realize it until Sienna and Will were on the precipice of splitting up.

"Hey, Sienna," Juliet said as she opened the passenger door. "Thank you for coming with me. This would have been pretty boring without you."

"Oh, you're welcome. I'm glad I came. It was really nice getting to know you better." Sienna leaned in, surprising Juliet with an awkward hug. Juliet returned it and gave her shoulder a quick squeeze. She smelled like a heady combination of vanilla and jasmine.

"Please don't say anything to Will about..." Sienna motioned to herself. "You know. I don't want him to think I'm gossiping about it."

"No, no, of course not." Juliet shook her head vigorously.

"Thank you," Sienna said. She smiled brightly at Juliet before shutting the car door and walking up the pathway toward the house. She gave a final wave as she closed the front door behind her.

Juliet sat in the driveway for a minute. Will wasn't back from Boston yet, so she wondered if she should be spontaneous and knock on Sienna's door. Ask her if she wanted to make some popcorn and watch *The Hills Have Eyes,* or something like that. Will had said that Sienna could use a friend, but if they were splitting up, didn't that mean she had to take Will's side? Juliet knew there were three sides to every breakup. But there wouldn't be anything wrong with hanging out with her, changing Sienna's mind for a little bit, would there? They weren't separated yet, after all. She idled in the driveway for a few more seconds and decided there was nothing wrong with it. She could go up to the door and surprise her and they could have a nice afternoon.

Instead, she just drove home. She didn't need the drama.

CHAPTER TWO

S ienna sat on the sofa in the living room, the vaulted ceilings
echoing the empty space inside her. She could see into the
pool house through the French doors, where Will was busy hanging
his clothes in the small closet off of the kitchenette. She wasn't exactly
sad, not in the regular sense of the word, but she did feel an emptiness
she hadn't anticipated. She didn't think, at forty-four years old, she'd
be in this position. She'd purposely held off on marriage or anything
particularly serious for the bulk of her adult life to make certain that
she'd found the "one" before settling down into anything that would
end in unhappiness. The only certainty she'd been able to find was
that she could always rely on a profound sense of uncertainty.

She thought back to when she and Will had begun dating. She'd
been in a relationship with a woman named Lila for about six months
when they'd decided to go their separate ways. Lila had wanted more
than Sienna was willing to offer, and rather than stay in a relationship
that had nowhere good to go, they said their good-byes and promised
to keep in touch. Which they did, for about two weeks.

Not long after, Will had come blazing into the picture with
his good looks and charming smile at the same time Sienna was
celebrating her thirty-fifth birthday. Looking back, she understood that
she'd done exactly what she had railed against for so long: listened
to some imaginary tick of a made-up biological clock. Not that she'd
necessarily wanted any children; that wasn't something she'd ever
felt strongly about either way. But she did feel a pull toward settling
into something that would last. Will seemed to be exactly what she'd

needed at the time, so she'd ridden the wave along with him and held on for dear life.

Things had been good in the beginning. They were easy and simple, and everyone in her life loved him. Declan, just six at the time, had stolen her heart from the jump. She'd heard horror stories of stepchildren hating their stepparents, their jealousy wreaking havoc on an otherwise stable relationship. Thankfully, Declan had never been like that. He'd accepted her from the get-go, and they became fast friends. It was one of the reasons she'd said yes to Will's proposal even though they'd been together for less than a year.

As time went on, Sienna and Will fell into a monotonous sort of routine that had initially worked for both of them. Declan was happy, Will was happy, and Sienna was content. Until she wasn't.

Most nights, Will worked late at his office in the city. A few nights during the week, he didn't even come home, since morning traffic was a nightmare no matter what time of year. Sienna didn't feel neglected or deserted, and she wondered if that was part of the problem. Their lives were interconnected but separate. And for Will, that didn't seem to be an issue. It wasn't really a problem for Sienna either, but in the end, that *was* the problem. She'd grown away from him, and when she'd brought it to his attention, he'd dismissed it as their hectic schedules. Sienna had accepted that for a short time, for herself, for Declan, and for the life that she and Will had created. But the fog of denial had to clear, eventually.

"So, he's really moving out into the pool house? Really?"

Declan broke the silence with his accusatory tone. Sienna focused and looked at him quizzically. Juliet must have just dropped him off. His week at camp had been uneventful, based on his texts, but Sienna hadn't expected him home for at least another few hours.

"Hi, Declan. I wasn't expecting you yet, I'm sorry."

"Well, I just got home and saw Dad making up the bed in the pool house. He told me he was going to be staying out there for a while? While you guys 'figure things out'?" he said, air quotes and all.

"Yes. That's true." Sienna didn't really know what to say to him. She wished Will had come into the house with him, instead of letting her take the lead. Declan was obviously upset and that wasn't fair.

"I love how you guys planned all this while I was away. Cowards," he said, angrily throwing his duffel bag to the ground. "I assume you're getting divorced now?"

Yes. "We haven't set anything in stone yet, Dec. We're going through some things, and we need time and space to decide what we want. What we need."

"What's the problem? Is it because he's never home? Did he cheat on you? Did you cheat on him?" Declan's anger was palpable.

Sienna tried to understand his annoyance without getting agitated herself. But he was straddling the line between appropriate anger and disrespect. "What's going on is between your father and me. He did not cheat on me, and I did not cheat on him. You can put that thought to rest. But this has been brewing for a while. I'm sorry it was sprung on you like this. We'd wanted to sit down and talk about it as a family."

"We obviously aren't a family, Sienna. Dad's out in the guest house and you're in here. I'm pretty sure that's not what families do." He crossed his arms and glared at her.

"Families go through things, Declan. And even if we do end up splitting up, that doesn't mean that we won't be family anymore. I love you very much, and I hope you know that." Sienna felt a lump begin to form in her throat. Was she sure this was what she wanted? Wouldn't it have been easier to just keep going the way things were? No. That wasn't an option.

"I know that. But if you two split up, there would be no reason for you and me to see each other anymore. Unless we run into each other at the mall, I don't see how it would happen." Declan looked at the floor. He looked like a little boy, not a near-man on the cusp of his sixteenth birthday.

Sienna wanted to go over and hug him, tell him everything would be fine, but she knew that wasn't true. "We'd figure it out. I wouldn't leave *you*, Declan."

He cleared his throat. "Whatever. You two do what you want, it's none of my business anyway, right?"

Will walked in as Declan finished. "Hey, don't be all doom and gloom, bud. We're just taking a break. Adults need to do that sometimes. It's not as bad as you think, trust me."

Sienna looked at him incredulously. Why would he deliberately mislead Declan like that? Maybe to ease him into it? Maybe to buy them some time? Either way, Sienna was uncomfortable. She shifted in her seat.

Will walked over to the back of the couch and squeezed her shoulders. "Just because we're going through a rough patch right now doesn't mean we don't love each other. This kind of thing happens all the time."

Her voice had gone missing. Sienna moved away from Will's touch and grabbed her glass of water from the coffee table. The hope on Declan's face nauseated her.

"Okay, thanks, Dad. When I saw you out there in the pool house..." He trailed off, shaking his head.

Sienna stood abruptly. "I'll be upstairs," she said, practically jogging away from them. She went into her bedroom and closed the door, leaning her forehead against the cool wood. Within a minute, she heard a knock.

"Hey, can I talk to you?" Will asked softly.

"I don't really have much to say to you right now." She walked away from the door and started folding the laundry in the basket beside her nightstand.

Will walked in anyway. "Why are you so upset? I didn't want him to think we're splitting up right this second. You never know what'll happen," he said, rubbing an imperfection on the paint above the light switch.

"Will. Why are you acting like this is no big deal? It *is* a big deal. We've taken the first steps toward the dissolution of our marriage. How is that not a big deal?" Sienna willed herself not to cry.

"What do you mean, the first steps? It's not like we've done anything legally at this point," he said, scoffing.

Sienna didn't say anything.

"I mean, we haven't, right?"

"I told you I was going to meet with an attorney, and I suggested you do the same." Sienna swallowed hard, watching the man she'd once loved crumble.

"But you said that during the heat of the moment, when we were arguing about this whole thing. You really went and met with a lawyer?" Will's eyes were wide and his grip on the doorframe white-knuckled.

"I did. Yes."

"I don't fucking believe this." Will rubbed furiously at the back of his neck. "When did this go from taking some space to an all-out divorce? I didn't agree to that. We're better than this, Sienna. Please. Please."

"Will, please don't. I told you that I've been unhappy for a long time. I don't want to hurt you, and I don't want to hurt Declan, but I can't keep doing this. You're a good man, and I will always love you. But I don't want to spend the rest of my life wondering what could have been." Sienna breathed in deeply, surprised, but not really, that he didn't grasp how serious she'd been when they'd had the conversation a few months earlier.

"We can go to marriage counseling again. It was pretty good the first time we went, right? I know I cancelled the last few appointments, because I was busy with work and softball, but I won't do that this time. Promise." Will held up his three fingers in the Boy Scout's honor salute. At one time she would have found it endearing, but those days had passed.

"No. We tried counseling. It didn't help. We've talked about changing and how things would be different, and they're not, Will. They're just not."

"Sienna, I can change. I guess I just didn't see how serious all of this was. I can change." Will's voice seemed to have dropped an octave.

Sienna closed her eyes. "Maybe you can. But I can't. And I just don't want to do this anymore."

The look on Will's face cut her to the bone, but Sienna knew if she didn't make it perfectly clear where she stood that Will would brush it off and they'd end up in the same routine they'd been mired in for the last nine years. It wouldn't be fair to either of them, and she didn't want to look back and be full of regrets. She wanted more.

❖

Sienna and Juliet planned to meet for coffee at the Java Room, but Sienna came very close to canceling. After their ride up north, Juliet had asked if she'd like to grab a coffee before work some morning. Sienna had agreed, and they'd set it up for the following week.

With everything going on at home, she didn't know if meeting up with Juliet, who was so heavily involved in both Will's and Declan's lives, was the best idea. But she'd had a nice time with her, and they really did click, so there was no harm in having a quick breakfast together.

The Java Room was bustling, but she caught sight of Juliet in a window seat booth reading a newspaper. Smiling, she joined her.

"Hey." Juliet put the paper on the table. "How are you?"

"Good, how are things with you?" Sienna pushed her laptop bag against the wall and settled into the cracked leather seat.

"Better now." Juliet's eyes lit up as the server brought over a bacon, egg, and cheese bagel. She adjusted the volume on her police radio.

"How long have you been a police officer?" Sienna asked. She picked apart the Danish she'd purchased when she'd first walked in. They always stuffed it with a little too much cherry filling.

"A long time. This is my...eleventh year. I worked over in Byfield for the first year, learning the ropes, and that kind of thing. Then a position opened up here and I jumped on it. Haven't looked back since."

"Did you always want to do this kind of work?" Sienna asked. She sipped her latte slowly but still burned the roof of her mouth.

"Actually, no. I had my heart set on being an EMT. I took the classes, studied my ass off, and at the age of twenty-one, I went for my first ride along. A kid fell off his bike and had a compound fracture. I took one look at that bone sticking out of his shin and passed out cold. And thus, my career as an EMT ended." Juliet laughed sheepishly. "I wanted to help people, but I didn't have the stomach for it. It's a lot different seeing a picture of it in a book, or even a life-like mannequin. It's a whole different thing in real life." She smiled brightly and took a big bite of her sandwich. "I sort of kicked around for a while after, not sure what I wanted to do. Will suggested that I take the police officer exam, if you can believe it. He knew my ultimate goal was to work with people, in whatever way I could. By day three of the academy, I was hooked. And here I am."

"I love that story." Sienna played with the cardboard sleeve that hugged her coffee cup. "That's the same reason I majored in psychology and social work in college. I wanted to do what I could for people who were in trouble. Did you—"

Juliet's radio squelched and startled both of them. She answered the call and told whoever was on the other end that she'd be there soon.

"I'm so sorry. There was a water main break at the town line. Apparently, we have a geyser situation happening. Can we do this again sometime?" Juliet asked. She leaned over and shoved the last of her bagel into her mouth.

"No problem at all, I totally understand. Definitely. Just let me know when."

Sienna stayed seated in the booth and watched Juliet walk out of the Java Room while texting something on her phone. She hoped she'd see her again soon. It had been a long time since she'd had a friend to hang out with, and someone who knew Will and Declan made it easier to talk about things without explaining everything. At least, it did for now.

CHAPTER THREE

The late August sun was barely cresting the horizon when Juliet pulled up to the Shell Creek Library. The call had woken her out of a dead sleep, but she managed to throw herself together and get to the library within minutes of the call from dispatch. A second cruiser pulled up behind her, lights flashing but the siren off. Juliet nodded a greeting to the chief as he exited his vehicle.

"Chief, that must be the person who called this in," Juliet said, pointing to a woman who appeared to be shivering even though it was close to sixty degrees. "I'll go talk to her."

Chief Quinlan nodded and took out his flashlight. "Looks like Kowalski from here," he said softly. She watched as he walked over to the facedown figure lying in the grass and placed his gloved finger to his pulse points. Quinlan shook his head.

Juliet swallowed hard. She'd had a feeling it was the librarian that the 9-1-1 caller had seen. She'd known Richard Kowalski since her teenage years, when she'd often sit at one of the long tables cramming for an exam. He'd always be the first to volunteer his time and energy to anything the police department or any other community organization had requested. He'd also helped Declan select the right research material for countless projects when he was in elementary school. Juliet's heart was heavy.

"I'm Lieutenant Mitchell." Juliet offered her hand to the woman. She took it weakly. "Thank you for calling us as soon as you saw him. Are you okay?"

The woman shivered again but nodded. "I'm okay. It's Rich, isn't it?"

"I'm not sure yet," Juliet said, although she had a pretty good idea. Juliet took the memo pad from her pocket and clicked her pen. "But we'll get to the bottom of this. I just need a few details from you, if you don't mind. Can I have your full name?"

"Sandra Bonner."

Juliet scribbled in her notebook. "Thank you, Sandra. What were you doing out here so early?"

"I go for my run around five every morning," she said, pointing to her weathered sneakers. "I thought I saw something. As I got closer and realized what it was, well, I screamed and called nine-one-one."

"You did the right thing. Did you see anything while you were running? Anyone in the vicinity or maybe a car nearby?"

Sandra looked alarmed. "Do you think he was killed?"

"No, not at all. We don't know anything yet. Just wanted to ask you the questions while the answers were still fresh in your mind. Did you get close to him?" Juliet looked over at Quinlan, who was taking photographs.

"No. I got about fifty feet from him and then ran in the opposite direction. I didn't see or hear anything out of the ordinary. It's usually pretty deserted at this time of day."

Juliet nodded. "Okay, thank you."

Another police officer had arrived on the scene. Juliet made eye contact with her. "Officer Leland is going to take over from here. She can take down your official statement and get you home."

"I live just down the road." Sandra thumbed in the direction behind her.

"Great. Thank you again for all of your help."

Leland was the best at dealing with the human side of tragedies, so Juliet silently thanked her and walked over to where Quinlan was taping off the area surrounding the body.

"Here," he said, handing Juliet a pair of gloves. "Let's see what we can find. The ME will be here any minute."

"What do you think happened?" She balked at the smell of the latex.

"Could have been a fall when he was leaving last night." Quinlan nodded to the library stairs. "More likely a heart attack or a stroke. He doesn't seem too beat up, and those concrete stairs would do a number on anyone. His wallet was in his back pocket, cash and credit cards still inside."

Juliet leaned down, getting a better view of the victim's face, which was turned slightly to the side. It was definitely Richard Kowalski. Juliet's stomach lurched. "Poor Gretchen. I wonder if she's even awake yet." The librarian's wife had been a town staple just as much as he had been.

The sound of crunching gravel announced the arrival of the county medical examiner. A town as small as Shell Creek didn't have their own resources of that type, so Quinlan had requested that County send someone over. Dr. Kellie McAllister walked over to where Juliet and Quinlan were crouched.

"Hey, Kellie," Juliet said, nodding in her direction. This wasn't the first time Kellie had been sent to Shell Creek, so Juliet knew her well. Not to mention the fact that they had dated casually over the years.

"Hi, Juliet. Chief. What have we got here?" Kellie asked, snapping on her gloves and taking a few tools out of her medical bag.

"Town librarian. Richard Kowalski, late sixties. We're guessing it was some kind of cardiac event?" Juliet said.

Kellie worked quickly while Juliet snapped photo after photo, starting close and panning out slowly from there.

"Can you help me roll him onto his back, please?" Kellie took a thermometer out of her bag.

The three of them carefully turned Kowalski onto his back. Wisps of his hair danced in the light breeze. Juliet felt another pang of sadness, knowing that this kind man's existence had come to such an unexpected halt.

Kellie prodded his ribcage and made a slit in the cotton of Kowalski's dress shirt. Juliet fought the urge to look away as she made a second cut into his skin and slid a thermometer in to check the temperature of Kowalski's liver. "At this point, I don't think this was a fall or a cardiac event. You see the thin blue line across his lips? That points to methemoglobinemia, which is when the blood cells stop holding oxygen." She checked her thermometer and made some notes in her spiral notepad.

Juliet looked closer. She saw the blue line that Kellie was referencing. "What does that mean?"

"We'll obviously need to run tests, but my first thought is a nitroglycerin overdose. Any idea if he had heart trouble?"

Quinlan nodded. "He had angina. Used to pretend to beat on his chest to get the ticker out of A-fib."

Juliet couldn't imagine how he'd have overdosed on nitroglycerin. "If that's the case, could it have been accidental? Like he forgot he took one and took another by mistake?"

Kellie shook her head. "Unlikely. I mean, anything's possible, but a man of his size would have needed at least six tablets to overdose. Probably closer to eight to actually kill him."

Quinlan looked at Juliet and raised his eyebrows. "Could have been suicide, but that doesn't seem to add up. Could be a homicide. But why would anyone want to hurt Richard Kowalski? I doubt he was running drugs from the nonfiction section."

"We'll know more once we fully examine him and run some tests. Based on his temperature, lividity, and rigor, I'd estimate his death between nine p.m. and eleven p.m. Rough estimate, of course." Kellie began to pack up her things as the mortuary technicians arrived. "I'll be in touch as soon as I have some results for you."

"Thanks, Dr. McAllister," Juliet said as she walked away. She made sure to use her professional title in front of the technicians. Kellie winked at her affectionately while Quinlan was measuring something near the body.

"This damned mud should be helpful to see footprints, but it's just a big messy jumble of dirt and grass. We'll need to get footage from the security cameras and canvass the neighborhood to see if anyone saw or heard anything. You think it could have been suicide?" Quinlan asked.

"I didn't know him all *that* well, but from what I did know of him, I wouldn't think so. Not that depression or suicidal ideation is something people wear on their sleeves, but my gut tells me no." Juliet breathed deeply. "Will County send their teams over?" Juliet had presided over many deaths in her eleven years on the police force, but this was the first maybe-murder that she'd encountered.

Quinlan shook his head. "Nah. We're on our own, unless this blows up into something more. As long as things are manageable, investigation and evidence collection are on us. If we find we're in over our heads, we can reach out to County or State. But we're nowhere near that point yet. You ready to dust off all that forensic jargon they taught you at the academy?"

She nodded. "I guess so. Just want to make sure we do right by him."

"We will. Get Leland, Jeffries, and Deagle out here ASAP."

Juliet called in to get the remainder of the Shell Creek Police Department over to the library, speaking softly into the radio clipped to her shoulder. She texted Declan to tell him he needed to go over to his dad's house after school. She didn't know how long the investigation would take, but she wanted to make sure he was taken care of in the meantime. She couldn't seem to shake the butterflies in her stomach. The idea of investigating a homicide had always seemed so intriguing, but the reality of it wasn't nearly as glamorous. The friendly hometown librarian was dead. There was nothing exciting or exhilarating about it. Maybe it would be an open and shut case. She hoped.

Chapter Four

Sienna sat at her desk, going through file after file. She'd wanted to work as a victim advocate so she could help people and make a difference. But it seemed like all she ever did was paperwork. Human interaction was becoming less and less frequent.

She'd decided to take a job in the city instead of in one of the surrounding towns since she figured there would be more to do, and frankly, the pay was better. Not every town had a dedicated victim advocate. It was usually based on population size and budget. In the city, she was one of four. And even that didn't always feel like enough.

She needed a break. It was hard to admit it, but Sienna was burned out. At work, at home, pretty much everywhere. She wanted to decompress, to just be, but there didn't seem to be anywhere she could run to that offered that type of peace.

It didn't go unnoticed by her superiors. She was aware that she'd been snippier than usual and quicker to judgment than she'd ever been in the past. She was still patient and kind to her clients, which would never change, but she was ready to lash out at anyone who needed anything from her. A simple request such as grabbing something off of the community printer prompted a sigh and a temple rub.

Which was why she wasn't surprised when her supervisor approached her desk, looking concerned. She braced herself for an unpleasant confrontation.

"Sienna, I have an assignment for you." Nancy Dixon, the victim services supervisor, sat on the corner of Sienna's desk. Sienna leaned back in her chair.

"Okay?" she asked tentatively.

"It's no secret that something's been bothering you. I've asked you if everything is okay here, and you've told me that it is. I don't want to intrude into your personal life, but I hope you know that if you ever need anything, you can always talk to me," Nancy said. She pulled at the lapel of her suit coat.

Sienna nodded and gave her a light smile. It would have been easier to have a conversation about her personal life with a crocodile than it would have been to have one with Nancy. She was an excellent boss, but a friend she was not.

"Anyway," she continued. "Shell Creek—that's your hometown, correct? They've requested assistance from one of the county advocates. I thought it might be nice for you to take a break from this place and change your surroundings for a bit. And it's in your own backyard, so that will make the commute a hell of a lot easier."

Sienna wondered what had happened at home that a victim advocate was needed. Their small town didn't have much crime to speak of. Of course, she would take the assignment.

"Yes, that would be great. I appreciate you coming to me. Do you know when they need me?"

"Right now. They asked for you to meet up with police at the hospital. The requesting officer said it was urgent." Nancy stood and tapped the desk, her indication clear.

Sienna took the hint, gathered the files she needed to work on later that night, and grabbed her purse from the bottom drawer. A distraction was just what she needed.

Coastal Creek Hospital was located just over the town line in Shell Creek. The hospital was shared by Shell Creek and its sister town, Salt Creek, as well as a few of the other small towns in the area. It was square and nondescript, but it was always clean and inviting. Sienna knocked softly on the door to room 1033 in the intensive care unit.

The door opened and a familiar face greeted her. Juliet looked as surprised as Sienna felt, even though she knew Juliet was on the police department. She hadn't made the connection when Nancy relayed the assignment.

"Sienna, hey," Juliet said and smiled. "Are you the victim advocate that County sent?"

"Yes. Were you expecting someone else?" Sienna asked. She shifted her laptop bag from one shoulder to the other.

"No, not at all. I knew you were a social worker, but I thought Will said you worked with children. I could be wrong, though."

Doubtful. It wouldn't have surprised her if Will didn't know what she actually did for a living. "Same type of work, just a different focus. What's going on here?"

Juliet slipped back into professional mode without hesitation. Sienna hadn't meant to cut her short, but she didn't want to talk about Will and what he thought he knew, either.

"Gretchen Kowalski. Do you know her?"

Sienna recognized the name but couldn't place it. "I'm not sure. Is she local?"

"Yes, she's the wife of Richard Kowalski, the librarian here in town."

The connection clicked. "Oh, right, I do know who they are. I've met them a few times over the years at different functions. Very nice couple."

"Well, we found Richard Kowalski early this morning lying outside the library. He died there at some point last night."

Sienna gasped. "Oh, that's terrible. Do you know what happened?"

Juliet shook her head. "Not yet. We should find out soon, once the medical examiner and the forensics guys finish up. It's a possible homicide."

"Really? Who on earth would want to kill Richard Kowalski? Was it random?"

"We don't know anything yet. But that brings us to Gretchen Kowalski."

Sienna nodded slowly. If Gretchen had had a heart attack or some other type of physical reaction to learning about the death of her husband, that would be awful, of course, but not something Sienna would be called in for. She specifically worked with people who had experienced some kind of crime.

"One of our officers went over to the Kowalski house to notify Gretchen about what we'd found. But she wasn't there. The officer was headed back to the station to get some information when she received a call that there was a vehicle lying in the embankment off of I-22. Sure enough, it was Gretchen Kowalski. She was trapped behind the wheel of her car, drifting in and out of consciousness. Couldn't get to her phone, and she was far down enough that passers-by couldn't see anything out of the ordinary."

Sienna nodded again, but still didn't understand how this involved her. She could tell that Juliet was affected by what was going on, even though she held her cool demeanor. Sienna was skilled at detecting underlying emotion, and the faint lines around Juliet's eyes gave her away.

Juliet toyed with a pen between her fingers. "She's hurt pretty badly, but the doctors think she'll be okay. She was lucid for a while and told us she'd been run off the road. Someone had been following her, flashing their high beams at her repeatedly. She tried to pull over, but they bumped her from behind. She panicked and sped up. So did the car behind her. They pulled up alongside her car and left her no room on the shoulder. She lost control and headed straight into a tree. The airbag deployed, and she couldn't maneuver herself around it. She was heading to the library to bring Richard some leftovers since he was working late. She was driving his car. He had hers because there was a light knock in the engine, and he didn't want her driving it just in case it was anything serious." Juliet swallowed hard and turned toward the bed where Gretchen was lying.

"That's unbelievable. Does she know about…?" Sienna didn't want to mention his name, just in case.

Juliet nodded. "We just told her a little while ago. She broke down and sobbed as much as her body would let her. It was the saddest fucking thing I've ever seen," she said, her voice breaking.

"Did you know them well?"

"Well enough."

"I'm sorry." Sienna placed a hand on Juliet's bicep. "I'll do whatever I can to help her through this."

"I know you will. I'm glad they sent you." Juliet covered Sienna's hand with her own. "She's asleep right now, thankfully. They gave her something to relax her."

"Good. She's going to need her strength," Sienna said. She pulled out her notebook and wrote down everything Juliet had told her. Juliet sat in the empty seat next to her and put her head in her hands, answering any questions Sienna had before she gave her a tired smile and left.

There was nothing left for Sienna to do but wait until Gretchen woke up. She pulled a crossword puzzle book out of her bag and set her thoughts on eight across. Any time spent away from her emotions was time well spent.

CHAPTER FIVE

Will was sitting in one of the lounge chairs in front of the pool house typing away on his laptop when Juliet caught sight of him. She'd rung the bell to the front door, forgetting that he probably wouldn't be in there. It was all so awkward.

"Hey," she said, pushing his lounge chair with her knee. "I'm surprised you're even home."

"Hey. I got your message this morning. What's up? I assume it has to do with Richard Kowalski?"

"Yeah. We don't know anything yet, but I'm going to be spending a lot of time on this, presumably anyway, so I wanted Declan to stay with you in the meantime. I don't want him home alone any more than he has to be. God knows what that kid does when he doesn't have any parental supervision," Juliet said.

Will smirked. "Hopefully, he isn't anything like I was. Of course, that's fine. I've been trying to spend more time at home, for obvious reasons, and Sienna is usually here any time that I'm not, anyway."

Juliet wondered if she should tell Will that she'd seen Sienna earlier in the day, but it wasn't her place to talk about the case, or about Sienna's workload.

"Okay, I'm going to get going. I'll check in with Dec tonight," Juliet said. "Thanks."

"Jules, wait," Will called as she was walking toward the gate. "Can I just run something by you real quick?"

Juliet turned back toward him, her stomach sinking. "Sure."

He looked up at the sky and then back to her. "How am I supposed to fix this? I thought I had it all figured out with Sienna, but obviously I was wrong. She met with an attorney. She really wants this over and I don't know what to do about it."

Juliet sighed. Will had never been great at relationships. She'd seen him with many different women over the years. He started out romantic and interested and easygoing, but quickly slipped into that self-centered place that he liked to call home. He'd always been a better friend than anything else.

"You know I love you, Will, and I'm just trying to be honest with you. I don't know if you *can* fix this. From what I can tell, she'd been pretty open with you about what wasn't working, right? Sometimes you can't undo what's been done."

"That's not helpful at *all*." Will shook his head and pouted.

"The only advice I can offer you is to just give her the space she needs. If you're up in her face twenty-four-seven telling her that you're a changed man, you're just going to piss her off. Talk to her again when the time is right. Show her that you've changed, don't just tell her. Maybe she'll feel differently once she has time and space to look at things from a clearer viewpoint. Maybe not. And if she really does want it to be over, then you need to accept it." Juliet didn't want to hurt Will's feelings by any means, but she also didn't think telling him that sending flowers and chocolates was the way to go either.

Will breathed in deeply. "I don't want to just give up though. We're married. It's not like it's some fling I can just chalk up as a mistake. It's been a sizable chunk of my life. God, I suck at this."

Juliet smiled. "Finally, something we can agree on."

"Real funny. Get out of here." Will gave her a gentle shove on her shoulder.

"Okay. I'll keep you posted as much as possible. Call me if anything comes up."

Juliet slid into her squad car and tightly gripped the steering wheel. In her gut, she didn't think Sienna was interested in reconciling. But stranger things had happened, so she didn't want to dash his hopes completely.

She drove to the library in silence. No radio or phone, just silence. She wanted to collect her thoughts in peace before revisiting the crime scene. Chief Quinlan was standing out front and Officer Celeste Jeffries, who was also Juliet's closest friend, was searching the grounds near the parking lot.

"Find anything?" Juliet asked as Celeste examined an empty nip bottle she found on the ground.

"Not really. Quinlan has the security tapes queued up and Kowalski's assistant is going to open up his private office. She was pretty shaken up earlier when Leland called her. I guess they've worked together for a long time."

"News about his death is already out. Even Will knew. Tough to keep anything close to the vest when word spreads like wildfire like it always does in this place," Juliet said.

"Tell me about it." Celeste bagged the bottle. "When Leland called the Kowalskis' daughter, she'd already heard about it from Sandra Bonner, the lady that found him."

"That quickly? How?"

"No idea. Like you said, wildfire. Maybe she thought it should come from a family friend instead of the police," Celeste said.

"Is she a family friend?" Juliet didn't remember Sandra Bonner mentioning that in their conversation.

"I don't know, you'd have to ask Leland. She took statements from both of them."

"Huh," Juliet murmured. "Okay, I'll go in and take a look at the security footage. Let me know if anything interesting pops up."

Celeste nodded and resumed her bagging and tagging. Juliet greeted Quinlan and went into the library, which was even more somber than usual. Not only was it quiet, but unusually so, and Richard Kowalski wasn't there with his warm welcome and bright smile. His absence would leave a void.

Dust motes swirled above the outdated computer that housed the CCTV footage. Juliet sat in the worn leather chair and tied her hair back into a loose ponytail. The cameras only focused on the front door, the side exit, and part of the bookshelf area of the library. The private offices and children's play area weren't under surveillance, and neither was a large part of the research room. Juliet fast-forwarded until she caught a glimpse of a person on screen. It was Tara Wolfe, the assistant librarian who helped Richard Kowalski with the day-to-day tasks of the library. Juliet couldn't imagine how much work there was to be done in a library of that size, it was a run-of-the-mill small town library, but she admittedly knew nothing about the administration and maintenance that went into the upkeep of a library.

Fifteen minutes later, Juliet had seen everyone who had come and gone for the entire day before Kowalski was found. Nothing of interest stood out. A mother and two children had come in and checked out two books. A college-age kid had used one of the community computers to print something. Kowalski's daughter had brought him something from Dunkin' Donuts, and other than that, it was just Kowalski and Tara. They'd laughed a few times and seemed to get along pretty well. Seeing Kowalski doing mundane things like checking for dust on the front desk and straightening a *Reading is Fundamental* sign caused a lump in Juliet's throat. She wondered what had been going through his head at that moment. Thinking about dinner? Wondering what was on TV later that night? None of it would matter. She swallowed and tried to refocus her attention. Apparently, Wednesdays weren't particularly busy days at the library, even though that was the one night they offered extended hours. Once school started back up again, there would be a lot more foot traffic. It had closed to the public at seven thirty p.m. Kowalski and Tara had presumably cleaned up a bit off camera, or organized books, or whatever it was that they did before closing. Tara had gathered her things and left the building at eight forty-six p.m. Kowalski entered his private office at eight fifty-one p.m. and exited the building at four minutes past nine. Based on what she had seen and what Kellie had said at the scene, Kowalski died shortly after locking the door and leaving for the night. He hadn't seemed in distress, though he did loosen his tie and roll his neck a few times. He had no idea that his wife was just a few miles away, lying in a ditch with a spilled container of chili and a sandwich baggie filled with shredded cheese. He had no idea that the ground outside the library would be the last thing he'd ever see.

CHAPTER SIX

The flashing cursor in her messaging app taunted her. Sienna had started to send a message at least ten times. They'd had one more coffee date after their first, the conversation had been easy and pleasant, and she'd been looking forward to getting together with her again. They'd spent most of their time together talking about Declan and how funny he'd been when he was younger. His teenage years had turned him into a grouch, but sometimes he forgot to be in a bad mood and that sense of humor would shine through. They'd planned on getting together again, but work had gone into overdrive for Sienna, so they hadn't set anything in stone.

The thing was, Sienna didn't know where they stood as friends, with everything that had been going on with Will, and Sienna wasn't the most assertive person when it came to social interactions. She'd always been an introvert, and making friends in adulthood was just weird. The only places she really went with any regularity were home and work. The people she worked with were nice enough, and they had a good relationship at work, but she couldn't see herself hanging out with them after hours. She'd left the friends she'd made when she was younger and when she was in college when she'd moved to Massachusetts at twenty-five, and she hadn't bothered to keep in touch with any of them. Her mother was down in Florida, and Sienna had never really known her father. She talked to her mom every other week or so, but it was usually surface talk. When Sienna had told her that she and Will were separating, her mother had read her the riot act, told her that she was going to ruin her life, and that getting divorced would ensure that she'd become a spinster. She hadn't felt the urge to call her much after that. Her closest friend was her cousin, who was also living in Florida. They chatted on the phone at least once a week, but it just wasn't the same.

Would Juliet just ignore the message if she felt like she had to side with Will in their separation? Or would she text back and say that Sienna was dreaming if she thought she'd socialize with a soul-wrecker like her? Sienna rolled her eyes at her own insecurity. *What the hell.*

Hey, it's Sienna. Talked with Gretchen earlier when she was alert. Not much to report, she was still drowning in grief. Would you like to have dinner?

Sienna hit send before she could change her mind. She immediately wished that texting had an undo button. Unsend. Recall. Send a virus to the other person's phone before they could open the text message. Anything.

It only took a moment for the gray bubbles of response to appear. Sienna braced herself for Juliet's response.

Hey! I figured as much. She's going to be a wreck. I feel so bad for her. Yes, I'd love to get dinner. Did you mean tonight?

Sienna felt her stomach jump, which was an unexpected reaction to Juliet's text. Must have been relief.

Sure, if you're available tonight, that would be great.

Her initial nervousness had subsided, but not by much. When a few minutes passed without a response, the edginess began to creep back in. She heard Declan yelling excitedly about the number of takedowns they'd been able to get in whatever game he and his online friends were playing. Sienna thought about turning the TV on and then decided she wouldn't be able to concentrate. Why she was putting so much thought and angst into a friendly dinner date was beyond her.

The message chime sounded and Sienna dove for her phone like a schoolgirl.

I would love that. Hate to ask—would you mind picking something up and meeting me here at the station instead of going out to eat? I have a mountain of paperwork to get through while we're waiting for the ME results.

Sienna's stomach jumped again. She ignored it.

Of course. Do you feel like Chinese?

Everyone liked Chinese food, didn't they? It was a safe choice.

Always! Get some of those crispy fried wonton things. Delish.

Sienna smiled and responded in the affirmative. It was going to be nice to meet up with a kinda-sorta friend, especially one she didn't have to work for conversation with. Without putting much thought into it, Sienna ran up the stairs to freshen her hair and makeup.

"Is Dad home?" Declan asked, without peeling his eyes from his television. Men dressed in suits and sunglasses dashed from building to building on the screen.

"I don't think so. I didn't hear his car in the driveway." Sienna stopped in front of his open doorway.

"Are you going out?"

"Yes, I'm actually meeting your mom for a quick dinner."

"My mom?" Declan scrunched his eyebrows but didn't turn his attention to Sienna. "Why?"

Good question. "Well, we're working together on something, so I thought it would be a good idea for us to discuss some of the details over dinner." Mostly true, and she wasn't sure why she felt the need to be evasive.

"What are you working on together? Like a family photo album or a police case?" Declan finally looked in Sienna's direction.

"Second one."

That seemed to satisfy him. He didn't ask any more questions and turned back to his game.

"You need anything before I go? Your dad should be home any time now."

Declan shook his head. "Tell Mom I said hi."

Sienna nodded and went into her room. She'd started putting some of the things she didn't use very often into boxes and containers and storing them in her closet. She was sad for the loss of what could have been, for what she had envisioned a life with Will and Declan would be like. Things change, she told herself over and over again. It was hard not to blame herself for where things had ended up. All things considered, Will was mostly the same person now that he was when they met a decade ago. But it wouldn't be fair to him—or to her—to just let things continue as they were. Will *seemed* content enough, but Sienna couldn't imagine that he was truly happy. They barely talked, the intimacy had dried up a long time ago, and they had virtually nothing in common. Their whirlwind romance had seemed like a lasting proposition at the time, but looking back, Sienna saw the cracks in their veneer even then. She put a music box her mother had given her when she was a child into a cardboard box marked "fragile." When things with Will were finalized, she knew that she'd be the one to find a new place. She'd never be able to afford the house on her own, nor did she want to. She hadn't married Will for his money, and she didn't plan on divorcing him for it, either. And she certainly didn't plan on forcing Declan from the home he'd been spending weekends and occasional weekdays in since he was a toddler.

Rain pelted against the bedroom window, which seemed to be a regular occurrence lately. There had been nothing but clouds and humidity and thunderstorms for the last month, or at least that was how it felt. Sienna decided to change out of her business suit and into something more comfortable. She threw on a pair of jeans and a form-fitting V-neck T-shirt. Her hair was still in decent shape, so she just ran her hand through it to bounce up her natural waves. She grabbed a tube of mauve lip gloss and called out a quick good-bye to Declan. She was pretty sure he grunted in acknowledgment, but she wouldn't have put money on it.

CHAPTER SEVEN

Juliet read the email from the medical examiner's office one more time, this time jotting down the important highlights. Kellie stressed that the findings were only preliminary, and the full results could take as long as six weeks to be completely finalized. But based on the initial results, Kellie had been right. Cause of death was noted as methemoglobinemia, likely due to an over ingestion of nitrates. Clinical cyanosis and the presence of brownish blood were also mentioned in the write-up.

Suicide was still an option, but an unlikely one, especially with what had happened to Gretchen Kowalski. Based on all of the records Juliet had been poring through over the last couple of hours, there was nothing in Richard Kowalski's past or present that would have suggested suicidal ideation. Juliet was waiting for a callback from his cardiac specialist to verify his prescription.

While she was in the process of logging into the federal database, Juliet heard the door open and slam shut, as it usually did. She peeked around the corner of her office and saw Sienna standing there, holding a good-sized brown paper bag. She had two bottles of water tucked under her right arm.

"Hey!" Juliet called, smiling at Sienna when she looked over. "Let's go into the conference room. My office is a shithole at the moment."

Sienna smiled back at her, seeming to relax a little. "Sure, that sounds good."

Juliet went to the small kitchen and pulled out a couple of paper plates and some utensils. She tore off a few sheets of paper towels, knowing that duck sauce would inevitably find its way onto her clothing no matter how careful she was.

She stopped in the doorway and watched while Sienna emptied the contents of the paper bag onto the long oval table. She had her hair tucked behind one ear, and her forehead was creased as she ran her finger up the leaking container of lo mein. Juliet caught herself staring and tried to enter the conference room casually. She didn't want Sienna to think she was looking at her like some kind of lecher, but once again, Juliet was taken aback by how attractive Sienna was. For an unsettling moment, she found herself envying Will.

"Can I grab one of those napkins?" Sienna pointed to the leaky container.

"Sure," Juliet said. She cleared her throat. "This all looks amazing. How much do I owe you?"

Sienna waved her hand. "Nothing. My treat."

Juliet was certainly surprised when she'd received Sienna's text message earlier, suggesting dinner, and although it was a little confusing, it was also exciting. She'd enjoyed Sienna's company quite a bit on the few occasions they'd spent time together since the July road trip. Their impromptu coffee date and the times she'd dropped Declan off, they'd been friendly and at ease with one another. She sort of wished she'd gotten to know Sienna better while she and Will were on better terms, but another part of her was okay that she hadn't. It would make more sense to brush this friendship to the side and stand firm with Will even if she didn't agree with his blinders-on mentality. Really, though, would a little dinner or coffee now and again hurt anyone? Of course not.

Sienna handed her the container of chicken fingers when Juliet sat in the creaky seat across from her.

"How was your conversation with Gretchen this morning?" Juliet took a long swallow of her water.

Sienna tilted her head and sighed. "As well as could be expected. She's so consumed by grief right now that she isn't thinking clearly. Obviously. She had her sister come up and her knitting group is coming and going, so at least she isn't alone. She kept asking for her daughter, who still hadn't shown up by the time I left. I hope she's there now."

Juliet looked down at her plate, her appetite gone for the moment. "Me too. Her daughter lives in the next town over, I think. I'm surprised she wasn't there yet."

"She also said that there is no way Richard would have done anything to hurt himself. She was really adamant about that and wanted me to assure her that his death wouldn't be written off as a suicide. She wanted to make sure that the police were taking this seriously. I told her you were." Sienna met Juliet's eyes and nodded slightly.

"Thank you. Ugh, the whole thing is just heart wrenching," Juliet said, shuddering for effect. "How are things with you otherwise?" She needed a subject change, at least for the time being. She squeezed some soy sauce from a packet onto her rice and forced herself to take a bite.

"Fine. Just dealing with everything day by day. You know." Sienna shrugged. "Does Declan ever talk about it? With you?"

"About you and Will?"

"Yeah."

Juliet shook her head. "No, he hasn't said much. But that's not out of the ordinary. He doesn't say much about much. Typical teenage boy. It's like pulling teeth to get him to tell me how his day was, never mind to talk about his feelings."

Sienna chuckled. "He's that way at our house too. If he's not racing a car or shooting at something, it's tough to keep his attention."

"I think he'll be fine though, honestly. He loves you, so I'm sure he's not thrilled with the idea of you two splitting up, but just because you and Will might not be together anymore doesn't mean he'll never see you again."

"No, of course not. And that's what I tried to tell him. I wouldn't be leaving him." Sienna paused. "It shouldn't mean that everyone in Will's life will need to be cut off completely."

"Right, exactly," Juliet said, a little too quickly. "Exactly."

"What about you, are you in a relationship?" Sienna asked, while inspecting her fried wonton.

"Me? No. I've been dating here and there, but nothing to speak of. It's been a while since I've had a full-blown relationship. I'm old and set in my ways." Juliet grinned, but there was truth in it.

"Oh, come on. You can't be more than what, thirty-seven?"

"Thirty-eight to be exact."

"Still a baby," Sienna said, rolling her eyes with a smile.

"Please. How old are you? Thirty-five?" Juliet raised her eyebrow.

Sienna laughed. "If only. Just turned forty-four last month."

"You did not!"

"Really. Though I appreciate the compliment."

"I mean, not that forty-four is old by any stretch, but you really don't look it. I would have thought thirty-five at the *most*. You look amazing. Wow." Juliet took another sip of her water so she would stop gushing. It was about to get weird.

Sienna visibly blushed. "Thank you."

"How did you meet Will? He told me you met at a show or something, but I don't remember the details," Juliet asked, desperate for a shift in conversation. Although as soon as the words were out of her mouth, she wished she could take them back. Sienna perceptibly stiffened. She should have just asked about her job, or about what kind of books she liked to read. Talking about her estranged husband probably wasn't the best topic to discuss.

To her credit, Sienna engaged. "We met at an art show, if you can believe it. I'm not much into art, and neither is Will, but as fate would have it, we were both there that night. My ex-girlfriend had gotten me tickets for my birthday, mainly because *she* was an art aficionado, and I decided that I still wanted to go. My cousin was in town, so we got dressed up and went into the city. And the rest is history."

Ex-girlfriend. Had Will mentioned that Sienna was bisexual? Juliet wracked her brain to try to remember if he had told her that. She was all but certain she would have remembered. She tried to appear nonchalant.

She failed. "An ex-girlfriend, huh? Cool."

Sienna smirked. "Will and I used to joke that he clearly had a type. Can you pass me a fortune cookie?"

"Yeah, sure. Here." Juliet tossed her a fortune cookie and took one for herself. She cracked open the cookie, read her fortune, and then crumbled it up and let it drop onto her plate.

"What did it say?" Sienna asked. She unwrapped her own cookie while eyeing Juliet's tiny slip of paper lying in a scattered pile of rice.

"These things are so stupid. They just recycle old clichés and stick them in a mildly sweet dessert shell."

Sienna snatched the fortune from Juliet's plate before she could slap her hand away. "It can't be *that* bad. Oh. See? It's sweet." Sienna dropped the fortune back onto Juliet's plate like it had stung her, and this time it landed face up. *The love of your life is right in front of your eyes.*

"What does yours say?" Juliet swallowed hard.

"It says 'All things are difficult before they are easy.' Good to know," Sienna said. She popped one half of the cookie into her mouth.

"Might as well say 'Every cloud has a silver lining.' Isn't that usually the gist of these things?"

Sienna laughed. "Yes. Usually." She started cleaning up the table and throwing their trash into the waste bin near the door. "I should let you get back to work. Thank you so much for having dinner with me tonight."

Juliet stood and pushed in her chair. "No, this was great, actually. Just what I needed to take my mind off of things for a little while. Thank you." She walked up to Sienna as she was adjusting the purse on her shoulder. Juliet leaned in to give her a half-hug, not sure if they had a hug good-bye kind of relationship or if a simple see ya later would have been more acceptable, but for some reason, she kind of wanted a hug.

Sienna turned into her hug and embraced Juliet fully. "Thanks again," she whispered, sending a shiver up Juliet's back. When they broke apart, Juliet smiled and rolled her shoulders.

"Okay. Let's do this again?" Juliet said, walking Sienna to the front entrance.

"Yes. Definitely. Call me. Or I'll text you. Or…something. Okay, good night."

Juliet waved as Sienna walked outside to her car. *What the hell was that?* She watched Sienna pull out into the street. It was unlike her to be all goofy around *anyone*, let alone Will's wife. Estranged wife. Separated wife. Soon-to-be-ex-wife? Either way, it was probably best to stuff the strange emotions that were swirling inside her into a black hole where they could never be found again. Ever.

Chapter Eight

Sienna hadn't had a dream like that in *years*. She sat up, breathing in deeply. Her satin pillowcase was mildly damp with sweat. She ran her fingers across her clammy forehead and smiled in spite of herself.

It was mostly a foggy memory now, but she could still remember the basics. She'd been in her bedroom playing guitar, (she didn't even own a guitar, but hey, it was a dream) when someone had walked into her room by mistake. It was Juliet, looking for Declan. Sienna had told her Declan was out, but Juliet didn't leave. She came closer and closer until they were face-to-face. Before she knew what was happening, they were kissing and clawing and ending up in a messy pile of sheets on her bed.

Her stupid alarm clock blaring in her ear had prevented them from going any further. She got out of bed and walked into the bathroom attached to her bedroom. It was big and spacious and everything in it was bright white. What had once seemed so modern and stylish now seemed sterile. Sienna turned the shower on and leaned against the sink while it heated up.

Did she really think of Juliet in that way? She was beautiful, made even more so by the casual way she carried herself. She left her light blond hair down most of the time, only fixing it into a low bun when she was on duty. She was muscular and confident, and her smile was contagious. *Fuck*. Thinking of Juliet as anything more than a friend, or Declan's mother, or Will's past, was an invitation to chaos. But it wasn't like there was any point in putting too much thought into it. People had silly crushes all the time, they didn't mean anything. Juliet was a friend who understood what she was going through, and it was logical that she'd be the one Sienna's mind turned to for comfort. She shook her head, trying to clear out the impure thoughts before she got into the shower. It didn't work.

❖

By the time she'd arrived at the hospital, Sienna had focused herself on Gretchen Kowalski and the tough road ahead of her. Not only would she have to recover from her accident, but she would have to do it without her husband of forty years. Endless physical therapy and emotional setbacks would make healing that much harder, especially under a cloud of grief.

"Hey," Sienna said softly. Gretchen's head was turned toward the window, where she seemed to be staring intently at her view of a brick wall, with a sliver of sky above it. Sienna gently touched her foot.

"Oh, hi. Did the police catch him yet?" Gretchen looked at her hopefully, which caused Sienna's heart to fracture.

"I don't think so. But I know they're working on it. Lieutenant Mitchell has been working round the clock to figure out what happened."

"I can tell you what happened. Someone tried to kill me and then killed Richard. Maybe it was a gang initiation. I saw it on *Crime Files* once." Gretchen sounded monotone and resigned.

Indulging her wasn't a good idea, but neither was shooting her down. Sienna decided sticking to the script was the best way to go. "They'll investigate all angles, I'm sure of it. Right now, we need to focus on you. How are you feeling?"

"Like shit."

Fair enough. She'd still been in shock on their previous visit, so it only made sense that she was feeling a little belligerent once the truth had set in.

"I don't doubt that. Your body has been through a good deal of trauma on top of your tremendous loss."

"The truck was red."

Sienna perked up. "What truck was red?"

"The truck that ran me off the road. I just got a flash of it when it pulled up alongside my car. I didn't remember it until just now."

"That's great, Gretchen. Really helpful information. And you're sure about the color? And that it was a truck?" Sienna asked, writing furiously in her notebook. These were obviously questions for the police, but she wanted to get as much as she could while it was clear in Gretchen's mind.

"Yes, I'm sure, I wouldn't have said it if I wasn't sure. It was a red pickup truck." Gretchen reached for the cup of water on her tray but gasped in pain before she could reach it. Sienna picked it up and placed it gently in her hand.

"Has your daughter been able to make it in to see you?" Sienna asked.

Gretchen looked at her distrustfully. "What exactly is it that you do? When I was first brought here, the policewoman asked if I wanted someone to talk to, to support me through all this. Apparently, I said yes. Are you a cop?"

"No, not a cop. I'm a victim advocate, which is someone who works with victims of crime. It could be any kind of crime, from domestic abuse to sexual abuse to a victim of an attempted homicide. Basically, anyone who has been a victim has a right to an advocate. We make sure that you're not alone in making decisions or confronting your perpetrator." Sienna edged her chair closer to Gretchen's bed. "If you need to go to court for any reason, or meet with a judge, I'd accompany you on those trips as well."

"You sound like a cop. If you are a cop, shouldn't you be finding out who tried to kill me? Why my husband is dead?"

"I'm not part of the police force, but I do work inside a police station. We work closely with law enforcement, so our clients have every opportunity to pursue the justice they deserve."

Gretchen nodded. "What about Rich? What kind of justice does he deserve?"

Sienna said nothing, since it was clearly a rhetorical question. Gretchen wiped at her eyes and pressed the call button for her nurse.

"Are you okay?" Sienna asked.

"I'm feeling things again. It's better when I feel nothing." Gretchen sniffed. "And yes, my daughter came by yesterday for a little bit. So did what's-her-name, that secretary who worked with Rich at the library. I pretended to be asleep when she came in though. Don't like her much."

"How come?"

Gretchen shrugged. "She's sweet. Sickly sweet. I've always felt like she's putting on a show. But anyway, I don't feel like talking right now. We can play *This is Your Life* next time you come by."

A nurse dressed in light green scrubs with a stethoscope around her neck came in to check on Gretchen. Sienna stood and walked to the other side of the curtain while they spoke.

A light knock sounded on the door before it opened slightly. Juliet walked into the room with her hat in her hands.

"Hey." Juliet smiled when she saw Sienna. "You're here. How is she?"

Sienna couldn't help but return her smile, even though her meeting with Gretchen had been less than stellar. "I'm glad you're here. She told me a few things you'll find useful, I think. Otherwise, she's disheartened, as is expected. Angry."

"Is she taking it out on you?" Juliet asked.

"Not really. She doesn't see me as being very helpful at the moment, which I can understand. She wants you to catch who did this to them, but she's not sure who to trust right now. She seems to be in some form of denial, and she's being abrupt and angry because of it. I've dealt with much worse, believe me. I think the nurse is upping her morphine a little to dull the pain. And to let her sleep, which is probably the best thing right now." Sienna sighed as she heard the nurse pressing buttons on one of the many machines Gretchen was hooked up to.

"What did she tell you?" Juliet asked.

"That it was a red pickup truck that pushed her off the road. I asked her if she was sure about both it being a truck and the color of it, and she assured me that she was. Maybe that will give you a place to start, if you haven't found one yet." Sienna internally chastised herself for noticing how shiny Juliet's lips were. She must have applied some type of lip gloss before entering the room. *Not the time or the place.* Damn dream.

"That's huge, actually. We don't have much right now, to be honest. I'm going back over to the library later today to see what else I can dig up. Quinlan talked to Gretchen about their 'enemies,' and not surprisingly, she couldn't come up with any. There were some disruptive kids Rich had thrown out of the library a time or two, but that hardly seems like a motive for murder." Juliet shrugged, seemingly frustrated.

"No, not particularly. Maybe she'll remember more or think of something significant as time goes on. Her life has been turned completely upside down."

"Very true. If she's going to sleep for a while, I'll head back to the station and ask one of the guys there if they can get a list of registered red pickup trucks in the area. How many can there possibly be?" Juliet rolled her eyes.

"Okay, sounds good. I'm going to head back to the house and work out of my home office for a couple of hours. I have a few court cases coming up that I really need to prep for." Sienna wanted to suggest meeting up again in the near future. Not the time or the place, she told herself once again. She gathered her things and gave Juliet a slight wave, and they both mumbled some obligatory parting comments. Juliet seemed to hesitate before walking away, but Sienna didn't want to assume. Damn dream.

CHAPTER NINE

Declan walked toward his bus engrossed in his phone, his wireless AirPods blocking all sound from the outside world. Juliet tried to wave him down with giant, swooping arm motions, but he didn't turn in her direction. She finally hightailed it over to him and grabbed his backpack before he could board the bus, catching him completely off guard.

"Shit, Mom," he said, clearly startled by Juliet's interception.

"Language. Sorry, I called your name like ten times and tried to get your attention, but of course you didn't hear me." Juliet flicked the bottom of Declan's AirPod.

"Is everything okay?" Declan asked, glancing at her squad car.

"Yeah, everything's fine. I just wanted to see my son's smiling face after dealing with so much doom and gloom over the past few days," Juliet said.

"Am I smiling?" Declan ran his hand over his mouth.

"Nah, that was just wishful thinking on my part. I'm meeting the chief over at the library in a little bit, so I thought I'd see if you wanted to grab a quick bite before you went to Dad's. You can stay at home tonight if you want to. I shouldn't be too late. I think Celeste and Brooke are coming over to watch the game. Celeste said the Sox could clinch in the next few weeks." Juliet pulled her sunglasses down over her eyes as they walked across the street toward the Gray Café. The sun wasn't out, really, but it was peeking from behind the storm clouds just enough to make Juliet squint.

"I'd rather just stay at Dad's tonight, honestly. If you don't mind. That's where my Xbox is and I'm supposed to play *Smell of Death* with a few of the guys from school later on. I hate starting school in the middle of summer."

"Oh. Sure, that's fine. It's not exactly the middle of summer. September is in a week. What system do you have at our house?"

"PlayStation."

"You can't just play on that one?"

Declan shook his head, amused. "It doesn't work that way. If everyone is playing on one system, you can't play on a different one and join up with them. Do you want me home for some reason?"

"No, not at all. Just miss your sparkling personality around the house," Juliet said as she opened the door to the café, letting Declan enter first.

"It's been, like, two days."

"Whatever. Just sit somewhere and let's eat," Juliet said.

They grabbed a table near the window. Juliet adjusted her utility belt so her flashlight wasn't stabbing her in the lower back. "The usual?" she asked.

"Yup."

Declan ordered his standard fare: cheeseburger, chips, and a Coke. Juliet echoed his order for herself and was surprised to see Declan smiling at her when she put the menu back into its metal holder.

"What?" she asked.

"How was your date with Sienna the other night?"

"My *what*?" Juliet said, coughing.

"Your date with Sienna," Declan repeated, much slower for effect.

"It was *not* a date. Why would you even say that?" Juliet lowered her voice, realizing that she was nearly shouting. "Why would you say that?"

"She told me she was going out to have dinner with you. Isn't that kinda weird? It's not like you guys are friends." Declan shrugged.

"We are *too* friends," Juliet said, sounding like a five-year-old. "We've kept in touch ever since we drove you up to camp together. She's very nice."

"Well, I'm glad it wasn't a date. I was kidding because that would be way too weird. It would be a lot easier if Dad moved back into the main house and I didn't have to be a kid from a fractured home."

Juliet blanched. "You're already from a fractured home, remember? I've never lived with your dad and you've done just fine."

"Yeah, but that's different. You and Dad were never a couple, so it's not like I was missing anything. I've just gotten used to having Sienna around, I guess. I'm sure they can fix whatever Dad broke." Declan's eyes lit up as the waitress set his plate down in front of him.

"How do you know your dad broke it?" Juliet found it amusing that Declan just assumed it was his father's fault. He'd only been three or four the last time Will had gone through a breakup.

He crunched through a bunch of chips before answering. "Isn't it?"

She wasn't sure how to answer that. Sienna had implied that the fault lay with both of them, for different reasons. She had moved too quickly, Will was content with the status quo. That seemed a little too heavy to get into with her fifteen-year-old son. "Not entirely. Things are rarely that simple when it comes to relationships."

"Still. Maybe they'll just both apologize and realize they've been being stupid. Then things can just go back to normal. That house is so awkward right now."

Juliet nodded but didn't say anything. She concentrated on her napkin and refolded it a few times. She didn't think that Sienna and Will would be reconciling any time soon. And for that inexplicable reason that she refused to address, she didn't necessarily want them to.

Juliet had been friends with Celeste Jeffries since high school. Their paths had always run parallel, and they'd shared the dream of becoming first responders. Years later, when Celeste admitted to Juliet that she had a girlfriend and not a boyfriend, as she'd implied, Juliet had laughed. They were more similar than they'd realized. Celeste had been a wonderful aunt-type figure for Declan, and they were still close, at least as close as Declan would allow without damaging his reputation as a tough guy who didn't need anyone.

"Are the prints guys finished with Kowalski's office?" Celeste swiped a tortilla chip through the melted cheddar and salsa Juliet had put out.

"Yeah, they should be. I'm going back over there tomorrow. Quinlan is going through their house with a fine-tooth comb. Gretchen finally acquiesced earlier today. He didn't want her to feel completely powerless in the matter. She admitted she was afraid that everyone in town would look at her differently if we saw her private things, you know, inside her closets and under her bed. Quinlan promised her that nothing would be broadcast on Channel Five, so she agreed." Juliet flopped onto the couch.

"Leland heard Gretchen telling Will's wife that she didn't know how she was supposed to live without him, how they'd been together for so long—"

"Ex-wife," Juliet interjected, and then cringed.

"They're *divorced*?" Celeste said, her chip only making it halfway to her mouth. "When did that happen? Why didn't you tell me? That's huge news."

"Well, not exactly divorced, but they're separated. I'm pretty sure it's just a matter of time at this point. I didn't tell you?" Juliet busied herself with plastic cups and paper plates.

"No, I definitely would have remembered that. She is *super* hot by the way. I forgot about that until I saw her at the hospital the other day. I'm surprised Will wants a divorce." Celeste resumed her nacho consumption.

"Yeah, he doesn't, exactly. Sienna's the one who filed."

"What did he do?" Celeste leaned in

"Nothing, as far as I know. Nothing specific anyway. Just fell out of love, I guess?" Juliet was getting more and more uncomfortable by the second. It felt strange to discuss Will and Sienna's marriage, when she'd become more than just an onlooker. She didn't want to violate Sienna's trust, even with her best friend. "Would you mind if I invited her over here tonight?" She was more surprised that those words had just fallen out of her mouth than Celeste seemed to be.

Celeste shrugged. "Sure. Wouldn't that be weird, though? Do you guys even talk much?"

"We've started to talk more lately. I've seen her at work a few times, and we had dinner the other night. So, yeah, we're pretty friendly." Juliet smiled tightly and plucked her phone from its charger.

Celeste eyed her. "Why are you acting funny?"

Juliet laughed, but it was clearly forced. "I'm not. What are you even talking about?"

The sound of Juliet's door opening interrupted them. *Thank God.* Brooke Cross, Celeste's long-time girlfriend, walked in holding a six-pack and a bag of Cool Ranch Doritos.

"Ooh, nachos," Brooke said, beelining for the counter with the snacks laid out on it. Hello was passé. "What do you think of this color?" She flipped the ends of her freshly colored indigo hair. She didn't bother to look up from the cheese bowl.

"I like it." Juliet pulled up the last text between her and Sienna.

Having a couple of friends over to watch the Red Sox. You like baseball, don't you? But even if you don't, we have snacks and beer. :) You want to come over?

Juliet put her phone down on the table and cracked open one of the beers Brooke had brought over. She did a cursory look around her house to make sure it wasn't too messy. She didn't think Sienna had ever been inside before. She'd picked up Declan a time or two, but he usually ran out to her car.

The small ranch house was perfect for just her and Declan. Two bedrooms, one and a half bathrooms, and a postage stamp yard for the backyard barbecues they always planned on having but never did. Juliet kept it clean, but she wasn't the best at decluttering. She shoved a pile of junk mail into the trash. If she hadn't needed it yet, she wasn't going to.

Her phone vibrated.

Sure, that sounds like fun. Can I bring anything?

Juliet's heart skipped a beat. She needed to have a long, serious talk with herself about this whole Sienna thing. But later.

No, just you.

Did that sound a little too much like she was planning a secret rendezvous? Juliet quickly added a thumbs up emoji to the text, hit send, and then rolled her eyes. Sienna responded with a smiley face.

"Game's on!" Celeste yelled from the living room. She and Brooke had commandeered the couch, leaving only the loveseat and the floor available.

Juliet considered bringing out a kitchen chair, so Sienna wouldn't feel obligated to sit basically on top of her on the loveseat, but a cold, hard, wooden chair didn't seem like a better alternative. Besides, Juliet was pretty sure all of these strange feelings toward Sienna were one-sided, and on top of that, a side effect of not being intimate with anyone for a while. The last time she'd been with anyone was at least six months ago, when she and Kellie had gone out drinking after a particularly hard death had sent them screeching into each other's arms, and not for the first time.

Fifteen minutes later, a small knock on Juliet's front door barely managed to break through the sounds of Celeste and Brooke screaming at the pitcher. Juliet patted down the front of her jeans, more out of habit than anything else, and opened the door.

Sienna stood there, one hand shoved into the pocket of her light windbreaker, the other holding a to-go bag full of chicken wings.

"I know you said not to bring anything, but I couldn't help myself. I hope you like barbecue and sweet and sour?" Sienna said, holding the bag out for Juliet to take.

"Oh, this is awesome, thank you."

Brooke sidled up next to Juliet, sniffing the air like a dog. "What is that? It smells delicious."

"Sienna brought chicken wings for the game. Sienna, this is Brooke."

Brooke said a quick hi, thanked her, and took the wings back to the living room where she and Celeste dove right in.

"Hey, Sienna," Celeste called through a mouthful of chicken.

"Hi, Celeste, nice to see you again." Sienna shrugged her jacket off. Juliet took it from her and laid it over one of the kitchen chairs.

"Brooke is Celeste's girlfriend. They've been together for fifteen years now. She's a food aficionado." Juliet laughed. "It's her thing."

"It's a good 'thing' to have." Sienna smiled. "Thank you for the invite. Declan is home playing video games and Will was out in the pool house working, I think."

"I'm glad you came. Do you like baseball?" Juliet asked, leading Sienna into the living room.

"I do. I don't get to watch it as much as I'd like, but as soon as they make the playoffs, I'm a die-hard fan. Same with football and basketball. Hockey is too confusing."

Juliet nodded toward the Boston Bruins snow globe Declan had bought her for Christmas a few years back. "That's okay, three out of four is pretty good."

Sienna sat on the side of the loveseat closest to the TV. She didn't look uncomfortable, but Juliet was concerned that she would be. Knowing full well she was probably projecting, she plunked down beside her and made sure their legs didn't touch.

"Smith is so hot right now." Sienna grabbed a handful of chips from the coffee table. Juliet raised her eyebrow and Sienna gave her a mischievous wink in response.

"Yeah, but he always fizzles out when it counts," Brooke said.

"That is *not* true," Celeste fired back, gearing up for one of her favorite pastimes: sports arguments.

Juliet sat back against the leather cushion of the loveseat and smiled softly. She was glad her friends were so quick to include Sienna in their nonsensical debates, and Sienna seemed to be enjoying herself. The comfortable atmosphere allowed Juliet to think about something other than the Kowalskis for a minute, and it was a welcome distraction.

CHAPTER TEN

By the time Sienna unlocked her front door, she was completely exhausted. She'd had more fun with Juliet and her friends than she'd had in a very long time. During the baseball game, Brooke broke out a deck of cards and they played a few raucous games of poker while the Red Sox inched closer to winning the pennant. It was a good night.

"Is this part of the new you, staying out until all hours of the night?"

Sienna jumped at the intrusion and slammed back to reality. Will was sitting in the dark on the couch in the living room.

"You scared the hell out of me."

"Sorry," he said, though he didn't sound sorry at all. "I came in to get some half-and-half and noticed you weren't home. Figured I'd watch something on the good TV instead of the small one in the pool house."

"First of all, it's not even midnight, so I would hardly call this 'staying out until all hours of the night.' Second, what difference does it make if I did stay out late?" Sienna asked, feeling her cheeks flush with annoyance.

Will stood. "I didn't say it made a difference. It's just not like you, that's all. I wasn't trying to pry into your personal life or anything." His voice dripped with sarcasm.

"Okay, well, I'm very tired. So, if you don't mind, I'm going to head upstairs," Sienna said, slipping her shoes off before walking toward the staircase.

"Sienna, wait. Brad called me today. Said he got a call from someone named Lance Cornwell. You know him?" Will asked, leaning on the doorframe to the kitchen.

"I do."

"Brad's been my personal attorney, and friend, for a long time, so hearing it from him was pretty embarrassing, to be completely honest," Will said.

"Not sure what you 'heard' from him that I hadn't already told you. You knew I'd be filing sooner than later." Sienna really didn't have it in her to get into it with Will again, but walking away would just leave everything open-ended. She didn't want that either.

"Did I though? Last I knew, you said you'd met with an attorney. That was it."

"What did you think I was meeting him about? He was going to draw up a separation agreement. Since there is no 'legal separation' in Massachusetts, it's basically a way for us to negotiate an agreement before moving forward." She cricked her neck back and forth. Did she really have to spell things out so clearly?

"Forward with what?"

Apparently, she did. "Divorce, Will."

"So, you're really not going to give me another chance? This is it?"

Sienna could see the sheen covering his eyes. In the beginning, she'd waffled, but the more time that passed, the surer she became. There was no point in trying to revive a marriage that had long been dead.

"I'm sorry. I really am. Being a divorcee was never my goal, I can assure you. But we will never be happy together, not truly. And life is too short, Will. I want to be happy. I want you to be happy. This isn't happiness. This is just…existing in the same space."

Will shook his head slowly. His demeanor turned stoic. "Wow. Okay. I'll call Brad in the morning and we'll get the ball rolling. I'd like it to be all over with sooner rather than later, as you said."

"Okay." Sienna thought about going to hug him, given how sad he looked, but she decided not to in the event that it would muddy the waters she was trying so desperately to clear up.

He went back out to the pool house, the door slamming behind him as he left. Sienna felt warm tears spring to her eyes, and she threw her shoes down on her bedroom floor with force. It was such a fine line, trying to take care of herself and not hurt Will or Declan, who she loved like he was her own son. She'd told herself over and over that it wouldn't be fair to any of them to stay in a marriage she wasn't happy in, and that it would be best to dissolve it before any more time passed.

Sienna grabbed an old T-shirt from her dresser and left the rest of her clothes in a pile on the floor. She covered her entire body, including her head, with her comforter and tried to remember why she'd felt like she was skating on a cloud when she first got home. It was all just a blur.

❖

Gretchen Kowalski was sitting up in her hospital bed. For the first time since the accident, she seemed like she was genuinely recovering. Sienna had been surprised to get an early morning phone call requesting her presence.

"Good morning," she said, placing her bag on one of the vinyl upholstered chairs. "You wanted to see me?"

Gretchen nodded. "I'd like to go home now. I have a lot of things to go through and a lot of tasks to learn. You know, things Rich used to do. He liked to pay the bills. Felt it was cathartic. I don't even know the password to the bank account."

Sienna could see that she was starting to get overwhelmed. Gretchen's eyes glazed over, and she took a deep breath.

Sienna touched her hand. "We can figure all of that out once you regain your strength. I'll call all of your creditors and make sure they know what's going on. You're not alone in this, and that's exactly the kind of thing I'm here for."

"Thank you." Gretchen covered Sienna's hand with her own and patted it a few times. "I have to think about..." She swallowed and closed her eyes. "Funeral arrangements, too."

"I know. I can help you with that too, if you want."

The door to Gretchen's hospital room opened. A middle-aged woman with straight black hair and a scowl entered abruptly.

"Who's this?" the woman asked Gretchen while still looking at Sienna.

"This is Sienna, from the victim helper group," Gretchen said.

Sienna stood and extended her hand. "Sienna Bennett. I'm a victim advocate and I've been working with Mrs. Kowalski. And you are?"

The woman looked down at Sienna's hand before shaking it with a limp fish grasp. "Monique Breen. Her daughter."

"Oh, it's nice to meet you, Monique. I'm very sorry about your father," Sienna said.

"Stepfather, but thanks."

Sienna would have to go through her notes again. She didn't remember Gretchen's daughter being listed as the deceased's stepdaughter, but she may have just forgotten. Either way, he'd been a part of her life for a very long time. Gretchen and Richard had been married for twenty plus years, so Monique had to have been just a child when Richard had come into the picture.

"How much is this costing you?" Monique directed her attention back to Gretchen.

"I don't know, I didn't actually ask that question." Gretchen looked at Sienna with the question in her eyes.

"Nothing," Sienna confirmed. "Advocacy is a service provided by the state."

Monique scoffed. "Paid for with tax dollars, you mean. Nothing is free in this state. I don't even have kids, but my money still goes to schools and silly programs every week."

Well, isn't she pleasant. Sienna didn't want to get into a discussion about the necessities of community support with a woman who clearly wasn't interested in the logic behind it.

"There is no out-of-pocket cost to your mother." Sienna sat back down in the chair next to Gretchen's bed.

"Good. So, what is it that you do?" Monique asked, sitting on the edge of Gretchen's bed.

"She's helping me with some things," Gretchen said. "There's a lot to be done now that Rich isn't around anymore."

"We're going to go over the options your mom has once she's feeling up to it. There are some support groups in the area, we'll go over her bills and finances together, we'll talk about her role in the investigation—"

"I can help her with all that. I don't think a stranger coming in and taking over her finances is a good idea. There are crooks everywhere you turn." Monique paused. "No offense."

Sienna swallowed, reminding herself that she needed to be professional and that lashing out at this woman wouldn't do anyone any good.

"I won't be taking over her finances. My role isn't to make any decisions. It's simply to work with your mom on the options that she has and to help her figure out what works for her. It's about helping her be independent."

"I don't think it's necessary."

"Monique, please. I requested her." Gretchen was singing a different tune than she had a few days ago, just as Sienna had thought she would once she'd had a chance to process what had happened. Sienna was pleased that Gretchen had seemingly changed her mind about her effectiveness. "I want her here."

"Mom, I can do your bills and take you to a support group if you want to go. We don't need anyone intruding into our personal business. No offense."

Fuck off. "None taken, but again, this isn't about intruding into your mom's life."

"Sienna, why don't you come back in a little bit? Is that possible?" Gretchen asked. She looked so forlorn that Sienna wanted to slap the bangs off Monique's forehead.

"Yes, I can do that," Sienna said. She gathered up her things and looked at the clock. "Will an hour be enough time?"

"That will be fine, thanks," Gretchen said.

Sienna nodded at Monique, who was sporting a smug look of victory.

Rather than hang around the hospital for the next hour, Sienna decided a visit to the police station might be in order. She didn't like Monique Breen one bit.

CHAPTER ELEVEN

Juliet stuffed the last bite of the gas station hot dog she'd bought into her mouth as Sienna walked through the front door of the station. For a horrifying second, she thought she might choke, but she was able to swallow it down with minimal effort. She took a long sip of the Great Guzzle she'd bought along with it, because who didn't need a gallon of soda to help them through the day? Then she sorted through the papers on her desk to make herself look busy as Sienna made her way over to her office.

"Hey," Juliet said, acting surprised to see her. "What are you doing here?"

"Hey. I have to be back at the hospital in an hour, but I wanted to check in with you first. What do you know about Monique Breen?" Sienna asked. She dropped her bag onto one of Juliet's chairs and leaned against the wall.

"Kowalski's daughter? Not much, why do you ask?"

"I don't know. She's visiting with Gretchen now. She's actually his stepdaughter, as she made it a point to tell me. She's just really cold about the whole thing. It could just be her way of grieving, I've seen it before, but something just feels off about her." Sienna shrugged.

Juliet pulled up the interview records on her laptop. "Quinlan interviewed her the day it all happened. She confirmed she'd gone to the library to bring Richard a blueberry muffin and a coffee. She told us she did that every once in a while, so it was nothing out of the ordinary. Gretchen couldn't confirm or deny how often it happened, but she did say that Richard had mentioned Monique stopping by a time or two. And Tara Wolfe, his assistant, also said she'd seen Monique around the library before. She doesn't have any sort of record, so we haven't put much stock in her as a suspect." Juliet scanned the records on the screen. "She drives a silver Corolla, so I don't think that could be confused with a red truck, ever."

Sienna pursed her lips. "Okay. Just a feeling, but I've been wrong before. She may not be a psychopath, but she's definitely a bitch."

Juliet smirked. "That I can see. I don't know her well, but she's never been the friendliest person."

Sienna toyed with a pencil and then looked up sharply. "Where's the coffee cup?" Sienna asked.

"What coffee cup?"

"The one that Kowalski was drinking from, that Monique brought to him with his muffin that day."

Juliet knew it had already been dealt with but didn't mind double-checking, if only to put Sienna's mind at ease. "Let me check the evidence log." She scanned the screen and occasionally tapped it with the eraser of her pencil. She stopped scrolling. "They have it. There wasn't enough left in the cup for them to test and the tests on the cup itself were inconclusive."

Sienna relaxed her shoulders. "Good. I don't know if Gretchen could take that kind of betrayal in the state she's in right now. Hopefully, Monique is better to her than she lets on."

"Agreed. We don't have a whole lot of leads right now. I suggested bringing in the big guns from County, but Quinlan is adamant that we don't need them. Not yet, anyway. My fear is that we'll conclude that Richard committed suicide and Gretchen being run off the road was just a terrible coincidence, just so we can close the case, even if I don't believe that scenario is possible." Juliet dropped her pencil onto a stack of paper dramatically and sighed.

"Could it be, though? I don't really believe that either, but sometimes a cigar is just a cigar."

"I mean, anything's possible. But it just doesn't fit. Not here, not in this town. We haven't had a violent crime in Shell Creek for months, and even when we did have one, it was a domestic. I'm having a hard time rationalizing that two people faced this catastrophe on the same day, at almost the same time, randomly," Juliet said. Saying it out loud just confirmed it—there was no way what happened to the Kowalskis was a coincidence.

"I agree with you. Gretchen is so sure Richard wouldn't have overdosed on his pills intentionally. They had plans. Richard was going to retire when he turned sixty-eight, they were going to rent an RV and go see the country. Gretchen even showed me a little pocket-sized map she had in her purse with little circles around each of the landmarks they planned on visiting. I've been in this business a long time, and I've seen a lot of things. Sometimes people do things that don't make sense. But in this case, suicide doesn't seem like something Richard Kowalski had been contemplating. And if he were going to do so, he wouldn't have done it in a place where he'd fall facedown in the dirt." Sienna glanced at the clock and picked up her bag. "I should probably head back to the hospital. Gretchen is on a mission to get discharged today, which I highly doubt is going to happen. I'll talk to you later?" Sienna asked.

"Definitely." Juliet hesitated as Sienna turned to leave. It wasn't her business, but she couldn't help her curiosity. "Sienna?"

"Yeah?"

"Are you...okay?"

Sienna tilted her head, her brow furrowed slightly. "With what?"

"You know, just everything going on with you. At home, I mean." Juliet wished she could just take it back. It sounded caring and supportive in her head, but the words out in the air just sounded weird.

"Oh, right." Sienna smiled tightly in a way that made it seem like she was trying to forget. "I am okay, yes. Strangely okay. This isn't new, or something that just sprung up. It's been a long time coming, and if I'm being totally honest, I feel more relieved than anything else. It's hard, of course, but it will pass, and I'll be fine."

"Good. Good. I just wanted to make sure. If there's anything you need, or you know..." She trailed off without any idea what to say next.

"I appreciate it." Sienna smiled and leaned against the door. "Actually, you know what I need?" she asked after a beat. "I could use a night out. Just to have a few drinks and think about something other than murder or divorce. Any interest?"

"Sure, that sounds great. Tomorrow night? As long as nothing comes up, of course," Juliet said, making a sweeping hand gesture over the paperwork piles on her desk.

"Perfect."

"Will is taking Dec to see the new Star Wars movie, so that totally works out. I'll text you when I'm able to get out of here?" Juliet asked. She hoped she didn't sound as excited as she felt. She didn't want Sienna to get the wrong idea. Or even the right one, really.

Sienna agreed and walked out, giving Juliet one more wave before making her way out to the parking lot.

Juliet sat back down in her chair and covered her mouth with her hands. She liked Sienna, a lot. If circumstances were different, she could see herself developing feelings for Sienna.

I'm a grown woman. She's a grown woman. There is no reason for me to pine away for someone that I could simply have a discussion with. I'm interested in her, she may be interested in me. And also, she's my friend's estranged wife. And my son's stepmother.

Well, that cleared up nothing. If Sienna *wasn't* interested in her in that way, then the awkwardness would be unbearable. They had to work together for at least the next few weeks, and their home lives were intersecting more than ever. Even when the divorce was final, it wasn't as though Sienna would just disappear. Will would probably never forgive her, especially since he had confided in her. Declan would hate her for making things even more difficult than they were currently. Juliet shook her head and tried to bury herself in her work again. It wasn't worth the hassle and emotional fallout. She'd have to settle for having a new friend.

The library was still empty. It was more like an abandoned saloon in an old-time ghost town than an up-to-date resource archive. It was dusty, as usual, and the constant rain outside had made the normally bright reading room gloomy and cold.

Juliet had been through his office a number of times already, trying to find a piece of evidence that would link him to something. *Anything.* Undisclosed debts, a secret family, *anything.* He had an empty calendar on the wall, some knickknacks on the shelves, and a lifetime's worth of reading on how to run a library successfully.

Juliet opened every drawer in Kowalski's office, looking for anything that might have been missed. She sorted through a pile of Post-it notes that he'd crammed into his pencil tray. There were some budget items, a few specific member requests, and a couple of business cards. On impulse, she flattened her hand and ran it along the underside of the drawer. A sharp edge poked her index finger. In the corner of the small drawer was a folded up fluorescent pink note, not visible from the drawer itself. Juliet plucked it from where it had been lodged, unfolded it carefully, and read the single line.

It simply read: *Mr. Restarick.*

She was glad she'd snapped on a pair of cheapie latex gloves before ransacking his office. What did the note mean? It didn't look hidden, it seemed more like it had been shoved down over time through riffling around, and although it could be something as innocuous as the name of someone who'd had a reference question, she couldn't shake the feeling it was more than that. She took a quick spin through Kowalski's Rolodex, which she was surprised he still used with the internet at his fingertips but came up with nothing under R for Restarick.

Juliet pulled off the right glove and lifted her phone from her back pocket. A quick search showed that Restarick was a more common name than one would think. There was a Darren Restarick who had been arrested for a DUI in the area just outside of town the previous year. She sent a quick text to Officer Leland to see if they had anything on him.

"Did you find something, Officer?"

Juliet startled and nearly tipped over in Kowalski's creaky swivel chair.

"I'm sorry, I didn't mean to scare you. Just hoping you found something."

Tara Wolfe, the assistant librarian, stood in the doorway with her rain jacket folded over her forearms.

"What are you doing in here? The building is still off-limits to the public." Juliet tried to angle herself to see behind Tara. She seemed to be alone, but her presence was still unnerving.

Tara gave a fleeting smile. "I know it is. I used my key and came in through the back. I just had a few things I needed from my desk."

Juliet stood. "Can I take a look at the things that you took from your desk?"

Tara hesitated, which Juliet noted immediately. "Uh, sure. But can I ask why?"

"You're not allowed to remove evidence from an active crime scene. If it's just your phone charger and your favorite pen, then I'm sure it will be fine." Juliet walked around the desk, the plastic glove still covering her left hand. Tara opened the plastic shopping bag she'd put her things in and then closed it after a few seconds.

"All set?" she asked.

Juliet had seen a phone charger, fittingly, an unopened box of tampons, and the looping blue nylon of a lanyard.

"Yes. Should be good to go," Juliet said, offering a tight smile. Tara was hiding something.

The relief on Tara's face was palpable. "Thanks. I know I shouldn't be embarrassed by tampons, totally silly. Especially since you're a woman too." She shrugged as though she wanted to appear unassuming.

Juliet laughed with her, forced though it may have been. "Actually, before you go, can I take a quick peek at your lanyard?"

The smile faded from Tara's face, but she quickly plastered it right back on. "For what? I assume they give those out for free at the police station?" She laughed again.

Juliet joined her again. "I know, right? You'd think they would. I just need to see that particular lanyard for a second. No time at all."

Tara opened the bag again. She pulled out the lanyard slowly, exposing the writing on blue fabric. It said, "Majestic AF."

"Cute," Juliet said. She held her left hand out, palm up. "Can I have it, please?"

Tara yanked the lanyard out of the bag and dropped it into Juliet's hand. The lanyard was attached to a flash drive.

"Where did this come from?" Juliet turned it over in her fingers.

"From the children's desk downstairs. I work down there during Saturday reading hour. All that's on it is my personal stuff. Papers

I've written, ideas for engaging children with nonfiction, things like that. Can I go?" Tara asked. Her patience had apparently worn thin.

"I'd like to hang on to this. Don't worry, the tech guys don't care about your personal stuff. We'll just want to see if anything was captured on the drive that might be useful. You know, metadata, that type of thing." Juliet was banking on the fact that Tara wasn't a tech guru, because Juliet sure as hell wasn't. The only reason she knew the word "metadata" was because of her son.

"So, they won't be going through my personal files?" Tara seemed to relax just the slightest bit.

Thank God, she has no idea either. "That won't be the goal. They'll mostly be looking for pertinent information that the computers here gather."

Tara looked skeptical.

Uh-oh, may have gone too far. Juliet kept her expression neutral.

"This flash drive can gather information from every computer it's been in? That seems odd."

"I know, it's so crazy what technology can do these days. Maybe our suspect was messing around on one of the terminals, looking up incriminating information. You just never know." Juliet turned back toward the desk. "I'll get this back to you ASAP."

Tara stood in the doorway for a moment, not saying anything, but not leaving either. "I just need to grab one more thing from the main floor, okay?"

Juliet frowned, liking this less and less. "No, not okay. Nothing else leaves the library. Can I have your key, please?"

"Why? I said I won't use it again."

Juliet smiled that fake smile again. "Because we need to secure the library, and in order to do that, we need to know that people aren't coming and going. The key?"

Tara took the tarnished key off the ring and slapped it into Juliet's hand. "Do you need my key to the supply closet as well? Wouldn't want the pens and paper towels to go missing."

"Okay, you have a good day, now."

Tara hesitated, but slowly started toward the exit. Juliet fought the urge to wave at her sarcastically.

Once Juliet watched Tara walk down the front steps, she locked the door and went back to sorting through Richard's desk.

Juliet pulled out an evidence bag and slid the flash drive into it. She put the strange Post-it Note in a separate bag and continued to flip through every magazine, every book, every notebook he had in the office, page by page. There was something here. She could feel it.

CHAPTER TWELVE

There were too many choices when it came to what a person should wear on a non-date, but also *not* a non-date, when one doesn't want to completely preclude the notion of it being an actual date.

Sienna laughed out loud at the thoughts running through her head. These were the thoughts of a twenty-two-year-old, not someone in their mid-ish forties. But there was also a spark in her belly Sienna hadn't felt for many, many years. Not with Beth, not with Will. Juliet excited her, made her feel alive in a way that she didn't want to let go of. But she also knew that there were so many complications and boundaries between the two of them, anything between them would be too messy. Still, it was a nice feeling, and she wanted to keep it even if nothing ever happened between them.

She decided on a pair of jeans and a pink silk button-up with quarter length sleeves. She'd wanted to wear her chunky sandals, but since it was raining, again, she settled on a pair of black canvas shoes and gave herself the once-over in her full-length mirror. She fussed with her hair a little and applied fresh lip gloss to give her some shine.

"Sienna, I'm leaving," Declan yelled from downstairs.

"Have fun. May the force be with you," she said, laughing as Declan groaned. She tried not to think about the fact that she was getting ready to have drinks with his mother while he was out with his father, whom he wanted Sienna to reconcile with. And that was why it was too fucking complicated. Even just friendship wasn't clear-cut.

She pulled out of her driveway slowly, checking the text that Juliet had sent her the previous evening and setting her GPS. They were going to meet at a little pub right on the ocean that Sienna had never been to.

Neptune's sign came into view just as Sienna opened her window to breathe in the sea air. The rain had finally let up, and there were people sitting on the deck, talking and laughing, and a small band was playing Jimmy Buffet on a riser in the corner. It was still warm for early September, so across the street from the pub a handful of people were running in and out of the waves in the dying daylight. It was fun and peaceful and exactly what she needed right now.

Sienna walked through the main entrance. There was a heavy mahogany bar that was draped with seashells and fishing net. She looked around until she caught sight of blond waves peeking out from behind a menu. She'd recognize those waves anywhere.

"Hey," she said, taking the seat next to Juliet. "Have you been here long?"

"Hey!" Juliet leaned over and gave Sienna a hug, just long enough for Sienna to smell whatever floral shampoo she'd used earlier that day. She didn't want to pull back, but she was afraid if Juliet caught her inhaling her hair, it would come across as creepy. So, she pulled back.

"No, I've only been here for a few minutes," Juliet said, taking a sip of her draft beer. "What are you feeling tonight?"

"Sangria. Lots of it."

Juliet smiled broadly. "That I can do." She signaled for the bartender and ordered Sienna a sangria, preferably in a bucket. The bartender returned Juliet's smile.

An oversized hurricane glass with red wine, peaches, and blackberries was placed in front of her. The bartender included an orange slice garnish, which Sienna promptly pushed into the glass. She took a long swallow from the polka-dotted straw. "Okay, that's amazing."

Juliet was playing with a plastic sword meant for a martini. "Do you ever get the urge to just take something like this and stab yourself in the hand with it?"

Sienna nearly spit out her sangria. She managed to swallow with minimal choking. "Um, no? Do you?" Sienna laughed.

"Of course, I do," Juliet said, joining Sienna in her laughter. "Come on, I'm not making this up. Say you're on a Ferris wheel, and your car is stuck at the top, waiting for the next set of people to get on. You look over the side, and think for a second, less than a second even, 'I might jump,' and then you sit back in the car and pretend like nothing ever happened. That's never happened to you?"

Small talk wasn't on the table, then. She could go with that. "Not that I can think of. I mean, I remember being up on a friend's twentieth floor balcony and wondering what would happen if I fell. Obviously, I'd die, but I was thinking about the moments before. But I wasn't suicidal or anything like that," Sienna said. She licked her lips and took another drink.

"That's totally it. And no, that's the thing, it has nothing to do with being suicidal or wanting to die or anything even remotely like that. It's just some weird impulse we have. Like sometimes when I walk by the constabulary sword Quinlan has hanging in the office, I think about grabbing it and hacking my hand off. I would never, *ever*, do that, because why would I, but the thought is there for a fleeting moment." Juliet grinned and took another sip of her drink.

"That's really weird and strangely relatable," Sienna said. The alcohol was already making her feel a little bit lighter.

"I know. I looked it up a while back. There's even a name for it. *L'appel du vide*. Call of the void. Wild, huh?" She threw a handful of popcorn into her mouth.

"Very."

That strange opening set the tone, and they talked easily about nothing and everything and laughed for the better part of two hours. Sienna suggested splitting an appetizer, to which Juliet heartily agreed. The idea was to soak up the booze so that a buzz was the most Sienna would feel. Continuing to drink at a pretty quick pace while they ate sort of foiled that plan. Sienna wasn't quite drunk, but she was definitely beyond buzzed.

"You want to go outside for a bit? Get a little fresh air?" Juliet summoned the bartender.

"That sounds wonderful, actually." Sienna felt the back of her neck and realized she was sweating. It was hotter in the pub than she'd realized.

Juliet slapped Sienna's hand away when the bill came. She mentioned something about the Chinese food from that night at the station, but Sienna wasn't really paying attention. She was staring at Juliet's eyes, wondering if that mesmerizing shade of grayish-green existed in nature or if Juliet was some kind of science-fiction anomaly.

"Come on," Juliet said, taking Sienna by the hand.

Sienna held on to Juliet's fingers, not breaking contact until they were outside on the deck. Most of the people who had been out there earlier had moved inside; there was a chill in the air that hadn't been there before. There was still one lone person riding the shallow surf on a bodyboard, but aside from him, all the other beach goers had abandoned their activities too. The sun had set, leaving a dull glow on the horizon even as the moon made itself known above them.

They stood at the far end of the deck, away from the noise of music and chatter that drifted outside. The band was packing up all of their equipment a few feet from where they stood. Sienna leaned on the splintered railing, careful not to catch her shirt on a wooden splinter. She watched as Juliet shivered.

"Got cool, didn't it?"

Sienna nodded. She absentmindedly brought her hand up to Juliet's back and rubbed it vigorously. When she realized what she was doing, she took her hand quickly away. "A lot cooler. We're supposed to have another heat wave coming through though." Even the small talk about weather felt natural and easy, not like they were being forced to come up with conversation.

Juliet turned so that her back was facing the ocean and her hips rested against the decking. Sienna just stared out at the water, the waves sliding over the dark sand. The last holdout seemed to have picked up and left as well. Sienna felt hypnotized by the swell and drop of the whitecaps.

"I like you," Sienna whispered, startling herself. She continued to look out at the ocean, though she felt Juliet immediately straighten next to her.

"Yeah," Juliet said, also nearly a whisper. "I like you too."

"I wish you weren't who you are." Sienna's head had mellowed to a comfortable buzz, but she still didn't seem to be able to stop the words from spilling out of her mouth.

Juliet laughed, thankfully. "Nice. What does that even mean?"

"I just meant that I wish there were less...you know, obstacles?" For a terrifying moment, she wondered if Juliet had assumed she meant that she liked her, and wasn't that crazy, because of Will and everything, and isn't it nice spending time with a gal-pal. But she meant so much more than that.

Juliet's gaze told her she understood exactly what Sienna had meant. She was looking at her, *really* looking at her, and Sienna thought she might melt under the weight of Juliet's stare.

"I do know. To tell you the truth, I think about it a lot. Probably too much," Juliet said. "You're funny and genuine and just...beautiful, really. I'm surprised Will hasn't had to fight off both men *and* women trying to get close to you."

Sienna's heart raced. Her head suddenly felt completely clear, as if she'd been drinking nothing but water all night long. So, Juliet had thought of her in that way. If circumstances were different, Juliet would want to be with her. Sienna felt a ripple of elation flow through her. Until she remembered that circumstances *weren't* different.

"Do you think..." Sienna began, then cleared her throat. "The hurdles in front of us are insurmountable?"

Juliet didn't say anything, just looked straight ahead. She seemed overcome with sadness all of a sudden, which Sienna didn't think boded well for her question.

"Probably." She turned toward Sienna, who was leaning on the railing in Juliet's direction. Their faces were inches apart, but neither of them moved. Their eyes were locked, and Sienna found that ethereal light the moon cast on Juliet's face prohibited her from looking away.

Sienna braced herself as Juliet came the slightest bit closer. It was a bad idea, and they both knew it. So why was Juliet staring at her lips, and why was Sienna so ready to pull her closer and never let her go?

A loud beep and buzzing vibration broke the stillness of the moment.

They nearly jumped apart, Sienna fumbling in her pocket for her phone with shaking hands.

"It's Declan," she said, her voice low and scratchy. "He wants to know where I put his case of Mountain Dew, sorry."

Juliet laughed too enthusiastically. "Wouldn't it be in the fridge?" She ran her hand through her hair.

"If it's in the fridge, he'll suck down a twelve-pack in two days. I keep it behind the paper towels in the garage," Sienna said, replying to his message and sticking the phone back in her pocket.

"Makes sense. He's all about those sports drinks at my house."

There was a new tension in the air that hadn't been there previously. Sienna felt awkward, and she was pretty sure Juliet felt the same. She shouldn't have said anything. Now she'd probably lose her friend too.

Juliet broke the silence. "I think I'm fine to drive, but do you want to go have a few waters and play a quick game of pool or something to be sure?"

Sienna nodded quickly, glad the night wasn't over yet. "Yes, that sounds good."

They walked back into the bar, the magic surrounding them earlier completely dissipated. Sienna could barely contain her disappointment about the detour the evening had taken. They played pool, both of them focusing on the game more than each other. Before it was out there, in the open, they could just pretend that it didn't exist and there could be this unspoken chemistry and those unacknowledged sparks between them. Exciting and forbidden and explosive. But she'd opened her mouth, and she feared she'd just ruined everything.

CHAPTER THIRTEEN

I fucked up."

Celeste shot Juliet a questioning look. "What did you do this time?"

Juliet dropped her sunglasses on her desk as Celeste followed her into her office. She nodded toward the door so Celeste would shut it.

"I went out with Sienna last night. We went to Neptune's for a few drinks."

"So?"

Juliet just sighed.

"Did you sleep with her?" Celeste whisper-shouted with wide eyes.

"Shh. No."

"Then what's the problem?" Celeste asked, her hand still resting on the doorknob.

"We talked about…stuff."

Celeste rolled her eyes.

"*Feelings.*" Juliet enunciated the word that felt too strange in her mouth.

"Wait. That night at your house, after the baseball game, you told me there was nothing going on. I even asked you about it point-blank. And you laughed at me and told me I was delusional. I knew it, you big liar. I could tell by the way you looked at her," Celeste said. She was obviously proud of herself.

"There wasn't anything going on. *Isn't*. But okay, I may have denied being attracted to her, because I can't be. She's married to my...whatever the fuck he is. My friend! My son's father. And Declan loves her and wants them to get back together and for them to be a happy little family or some bullshit." Juliet rubbed the back of her neck furiously.

"So, it's a forbidden romance? No wonder you want each other. That shit is hot."

"You are no help at all. It's not a forbidden romance." Juliet used air quotes. "I just realized that I like her, a lot, and it's strange, and we can't be more than friends. That's it."

"Fine, tell yourself whatever you want. But I still don't see how you fucked up?"

Oh, right. Juliet sighed again and stared at the ceiling. "We went out last night and we both admitted that there was something there. Between us. And now this friendship that we were building is in the toilet because we made it weird. Which really sucks, because I like spending time with her."

Celeste pursed her lips. "Isn't this kind of self-imposed, though? Maybe Will would be fine with it. Declan would keep her as a stepmom. Seems like a win-win."

Juliet stared at her, aghast. "What? Will would *not* be fine with it. He still loves her and wants to work things out. And Declan would keep her as a stepmom? That is just...I don't know, I have no words. Both of his parents sleeping with the same woman? That's the kind of stuff that screws kids up for life. What if it didn't work out between us down the line? It's just not a good idea to even entertain the possibility. It couldn't conceivably end well." The more she said it out loud, the more she realized just how inappropriate a relationship between the two of them would be. Which depressed her even more than she had been. She sunk lower in her chair.

"I guess you're right. So, what are you going to do, stop seeing her?"

"I don't know yet. I don't want to. Although, I don't know if she even wants to see me anymore, so I might not have a choice. The whole thing is just fucked." Juliet sighed. She saw Quinlan walk by her office and glance at them through the window. "Okay, you should go back to your desk. I have to figure out who the hell Restarick is and what he has to do with the Kowalskis."

Juliet sat across from Quinlan at the conference room table. Once he finished grumbling about budget constraints and resource restrictions, he sat back and folded his hands behind his head. "What do we have today that we didn't have yesterday?" he asked.

"Not much, Chief. There wasn't much on the flash drive that I got from Tara Wolfe, but the IT guys are going through it to see if anything was missed. And I pulled a note from Kowalski's desk that just says Mr. Restarick. It's probably not even connected to anything, but I can't figure out who Restarick is. I have a feeling it means something, but I might be grasping."

Quinlan continued to stare at the wall. "So, we have a red truck that tried to run Mrs. Kowalski off the road, and Mr. Kowalski died by an overdose of nitroglycerin. They have no known enemies, no unpaid debts, and Rich has no history of mental illness or anything else that might suggest he had suicidal tendencies. The footprints in the dirt were his own, and a search of their house turned up nothing of interest. We have a Post-it Note and a flash drive as our only evidence, and neither one points to anything. Maybe you were right all along, Mitchell. Maybe we should have brought in the big guns, since we clearly have no idea what we're doing."

Juliet looked down. She knew Quinlan was just blowing off steam. His favorite go-to when things weren't going their way was to confirm how terrible they all were at their jobs. Later, he'd apologize and tell them that he was just frustrated. Juliet had been doing the dance with him for a very long time.

"Did Jeffries get you the life insurance info you asked for?" Juliet asked.

Quinlan nodded. "Yep. Rich has twenty-five K and Gretchen has twenty-five K. Not exactly enough to make anyone rich."

"Were they each other's beneficiaries?"

"Yeah," Quinlan said, flipping through some papers. "First beneficiary is each other, second is the daughter. Pretty standard. The daughter's finances don't suggest that she's destitute or in any urgent need. She's rude, but she's been forthcoming so far. She let us into her place without any hesitation."

After a quick knock on the door, Celeste poked her head in. "Sorry to interrupt. The IT guys just sent over some hidden files from that flash drive we sent over. They said it wasn't any kind of high-tech concealment or anything, but anyone who's only semi computer literate wouldn't be able to find them." She looked pointedly at Juliet. "And they were password protected. Anyway, you're gonna want to see what's on it."

Juliet and Quinlan both went over to Celeste's desk, where she had a document pulled up on her monitor. She enlarged the view so they both could see it without squinting. Juliet bent over and read.

Coffee—splash of cream only. He only wears solid color ties. No stripes or designs. He's afraid of the dentist, but he has two crowns, one on a back molar and one on his front tooth. Broke it in sixth grade when he got hit by a baseball. He has to take .4 mg of nitro for chest pain. He wears a size ten shoe.

Juliet stood up straight and looked at Celeste, who was looking back at her expectantly. "It's odd, but maybe he wanted his assistant to know all of these things so she could manage his appointments and fetch his coffee the right way? He didn't seem the type, but you never know."

"Keep reading. It gets a whole lot weirder. Besides, Tara isn't his personal assistant. She's the assistant librarian. Very different, she's like middle management of the library. She shouldn't be fetching anyone's anything," Celeste said.

Juliet leaned back down to continue reading.

That rep from the office supply place came in again today. She flirts with him every single time she's in here, and they smile and laugh, and she touches his shoulder like she has a chance. Laughable. But Rich plays into it and I don't understand why. I think he just doesn't realize it yet. It's me, Rich. It's me! I wish I could wave my arms in front of his face and tell him to look at me, to see me, because once he does, he'll know. Sometimes it seems like he's so close to acknowledging it, like he's finally ready. But then he doesn't say anything, and it must be because Gretchen got into his head or he's afraid that I'll reject him.

It's frustrating, but I'm patient. Real love will wait forever. The sooner you come around, the sooner we can start the rest of our lives. You tell her you love her, but words are just words. I think it's about time I show you what love is.

Quinlan let out a low whistle. Celeste turned her monitor back toward herself.

"Told you," she said quietly.

Quinlan nodded at Juliet. "Bring her in."

CHAPTER FOURTEEN

Gretchen Kowalski stifled a sob as they pulled into her long, gravel driveway. Sienna sat next to her in the driver's seat while Gretchen's daughter, Monique, sat behind them in the back seat. Sienna reached for her hand and Gretchen squeezed it.

"You don't think they made too much of a mess, do you?" Gretchen asked quietly.

"No, I'm sure they put everything back where they found it," Sienna said. She hoped so, anyway. Walking into the house that she'd shared with her husband for the last few decades would be a whole lot worse if the place was flipped upside down. "Do you feel like you're ready to go in?"

"Of course, she's ready," Monique piped up from the back seat. "She hasn't been home in forever. Wouldn't you want to lie in your own bed?"

God, she has absolutely no empathy or tact. Sienna ignored her. "If you need a few more minutes, we can sit here. There's no rush," she said to Gretchen, who was staring at the front door.

"No, I think I'm ready." Gretchen nodded, as though she was confirming to herself that she was indeed ready.

"Okay, then we'll go in." Sienna walked around to the passenger side door and opened the door of her Volvo. She took the walker from Monique who was trying to unfold it but close to breaking it. Sienna had to constantly fight the urge to give her dirty looks.

Gretchen held on to the walker handles, her grip so tight her hands were white as she shuffled toward the front door. Thankfully, there were only three stairs leading up it. Monique used what was presumably her own key and swung the door open. A quick glance inside quelled Sienna's fear that the house was a disaster. Everything looked like it was in its rightful place.

"Smells like feet in here," Monique said, crinkling her nose.

"I'm sure it's just the fact that there hasn't been any fresh air circulating. We'll open some windows once we get settled," Sienna said, this time actually shooting a dirty look in Monique's direction. Monique just shrugged.

"His glasses. His glasses are still resting on the arm of his recliner. He needed them to watch his programs at night." Gretchen stopped to look around the living room.

Sienna watched her closely, though she seemed to be holding up well. It wasn't until she turned toward the kitchen and saw a folded-up newspaper sitting on the kitchen table that Sienna noticed her knees begin to buckle. She reached over and quickly put her arm around Gretchen's waist, preventing her from slumping to the ground.

"Monique, a little help please," Sienna said.

Monique seemed to snap back to reality at the sound of Sienna's voice and put her arm around Gretchen's waist as well. Sienna nodded toward the couch, so they maneuvered Gretchen into a sitting position on the small fabric sofa. Her shoulders lurched as silent sobs wracked her body. Sienna sat next to her, holding her, while Monique stood above them chewing on her thumb.

"I don't really know what to do," Monique said, and that was probably the realest thing she'd said since Sienna had met her. "It's all so eerie. Like his presence is still here, but he's not. And we have the funeral this weekend and this whole thing is just insane."

Monique looked like she was either about to cry or have a nervous breakdown, showing a crack in the facade that made her more vulnerable. Sienna motioned her over and gestured to the seat on the other side of Gretchen. Monique sat down and put her arm around her mother, who leaned into her shoulder. Sienna carefully extracted herself from their embrace and allowed the two of them to cry in each other's arms.

"I'm so sorry, Mom. So sorry," she kept repeating over and over.

Sienna went into the kitchen to give them some privacy. Monique had offered to stay overnight with her mother but couldn't promise she'd be there during the day. Her work schedule was sporadic. They'd set up a visiting nurse to spend the days with Gretchen and a physical therapist to work with her until her legs healed to the point where she could be mobile without as much assistance. From what she'd gathered from Juliet and her time at the police station, there were still no solid leads on Richard's murder or Gretchen's almost-murder. It felt less and less likely that they'd ever find out who'd ripped their world apart so completely.

Sienna pulled out her phone to call the nurse's station, but she stopped to read a text from Will asking her if they could talk later that evening. She didn't have the strength to engage with him at that moment, so she swiped the message away for the time being. A few below his message was the last one she'd received from Juliet, from the night they'd gone to Neptune's. It was just a smiley face in response to something Sienna had texted, but it still filled her with a profound sadness. They never should have crossed that line. *She* never should have crossed that line. She was angry at herself and was about to swipe right on the message to delete the entire chain forever but stopped just before she could press the red delete button. Maybe they could go back to the way things had been before she'd opened her mouth and said it out loud. Maybe it wasn't too late.

The heat wave she'd told Juliet about the other night had made its appearance. Eighty degrees in September wasn't unheard of, but it wasn't the norm either. Sienna wiped a few beads of sweat off her brow before she used the entrance doors into the law offices of Cornwell and Page. She took a deep breath and tried to remind herself that this was necessary. She'd loved Will, she'd married him, and it didn't work out. She wasn't minimizing the importance of their union, but she also didn't want to be unhappy for the next forty years because they'd entered into a legal agreement. It happened, they'd both grow from it, and they'd move on. That was the only choice left.

Lance Cornwell was in the reception area when Sienna walked in. He was a youngish guy who had on suspenders with his expensive slacks and crisp white dress shirt and black tie. He shook her hand.

"Hi, Sienna, nice to see you again. Pam, please hold my calls for the next hour. Shall we?" He motioned into his office, where the door stood open. The entire wall behind his desk was a window. Sienna was pretty sure they could see all the way to Boston from the seventh-floor view. Somewhere in the suburbs between Shell Creek and the city, the leaves had started to take on a dark shade of gold.

"Good to see you as well," Sienna lied, taking a seat across from his desk. It was cold and hard and sterile looking. It fit in well with the office décor.

"Let's get to it. As I said the last time we spoke, I called Will's attorney, and they declined an uncontested no-fault divorce. So, we'll have to move forward with the 1B." Lance clicked something with his mouse and his printer came to life. Multiple sheets started shooting into the catch tray.

Sienna began to feel overwhelmed. Why was it so hot in the office? She'd taken off her jacket, so all she had on was a dress shirt with short sleeves and a pair of black jeans. She'd even worn her sandals, which she wished she could have kicked off. She was just so fucking *hot.*

"What is the 1B again?" she asked, fidgeting with her necklace.

"A contested no-fault divorce. We file that when one of the spouses believes there's an irreconcilable breakdown of the marriage, but the other one doesn't have the same thought process. The divorce can still be a contested no-fault even if both parties think the marriage has ended, but they don't agree on separation of assets, child support, those kinds of things. Very common, don't worry about it." Lance combed through the papers he'd printed and made a few notations with a T-clip Cross pen. Sienna couldn't help but admire his old-school vibe.

"When you say 'contested,' does that mean he doesn't have to agree to a divorce, and it'll be held up in court?" Sienna asked.

"No, the state's not really in the business of forcing unhappy people to stay together. It'll still move forward just like it was an uncontested divorce, but it could just take slightly longer to come to property division agreements if he's belligerent about it. Timeline for everything to be completed is around a hundred and twenty days," Lance said.

Sienna nodded. One hundred and twenty days sounded so long and so short in the same breath. In four months, she would be completely unencumbered and free to move on with the second half of her life. Also, in four months, she'd be a middle-aged divorcee without much of a plan or a support system. And Declan. Always Declan. She hoped beyond hope that he would forgive her and remain part of her life. If Declan hadn't been in the picture, she would have taken this step years earlier.

"Once we file this with the state and we receive our hearing date, it's all pretty quick from there. Depending on how easily the two of you agree on how things should be split, of course. I know you'd mentioned that you don't want to seek alimony. I'm still not sure that's the best course of action. Will would certainly be court-ordered to pay you enough to maintain your current lifestyle."

"No, I still don't plan on asking for alimony. I work full time and I'm capable of supporting myself without Will's assistance." Sienna leaned back in the chair and crossed her legs.

"Alimony isn't a weakness, Sienna. It's about what's owed to you after everything you've put into the household and toward the marriage over the years."

"I know." It didn't matter. She wasn't going to be tied to Will financially for however long that went on. If they stayed friends, great. If not, they could cut ties and be done with it.

Lance sighed. "Okay, once we attend the hearing and the judge signs off on the judgment of divorce, we have ninety days. Then it becomes an absolute, and you will officially be a single woman again. Are you feeling okay with everything?"

Of course not. "Yes, that all makes sense."

"Great. And listen, it's normal to feel sad or unsure, but you just have to remember how you got here. If everything was sunshine and roses, you never would have sought out a divorce attorney. Making something official in this way can sometimes cloud the past and make you wonder if you're doing the right thing. Based on what you've told me and how you've felt for some time now, you are."

"Thank you, Lance," Sienna said, shaking his hand again. "I appreciate all of this."

"You're in good hands. Take care," he said and held open his office door.

Emotions swirled like a tornado and she tried to take deep breaths to steady herself. She had no idea she'd be so conflicted about finally filing the paperwork. She was excited, but also filled with sadness, and she was relieved, but also heavy-hearted. She'd always love Will for who he'd been and for who he'd been *to* her, but she'd been out of love with him for a very long time. It was time for Sienna to focus on what lay ahead. She straightened her collar, rolled her neck from side to side, and walked out to her car like she owned the world. Time was fragile and could slip away in an instant. She just had to figure out what it was she wanted, and then make it happen.

Chapter Fifteen

Tara Wolfe sat across from Juliet, nervously chewing on her index finger cuticle. Her short brown hair was stylish as always, the gray streak deliberate, her makeup impeccable. She wore too much jewelry and was heavy-handed on the perfume, and Juliet could see the anxiety beneath it all. When she'd asked her to come in to answer a few questions, Tara had agreed, sounding resigned. She must have known they'd found her hidden documents.

"Do you know why you're here?" Juliet asked, handing her the cup of tea she'd requested.

"I'm hoping it's because you've made a big break in Rich's murder and need my assistance in some way?"

Juliet knew she was lying based on the way the teacup quivered in her hand. "Not sure if we've made a break or not, but I do want to talk to you about that flash drive."

Tara's eyes widened for a microsecond. She regained a semblance of composure quickly. "Okay, what about it?"

"You didn't mention in your initial interview that you had romantic feelings for Mr. Kowalski."

She flinched. "Why would I? People have crushes all the time, doesn't make them murderers."

"That's very true, but the content on the flash drive doesn't allude to a harmless crush, Tara. You were taking notes about the details of Richard's life, and promising that the two of you would be together someday. I assume you know his wife?" Juliet leaned back in her chair and folded her hands together on the desk.

"I know Gretchen, yes. I never wanted her to get hurt in any of this, she's a lovely woman. She just wasn't good for Rich. And I wasn't stalking him or anything, I just wanted to anticipate the things he wanted before he even knew he wanted them. Like his morning coffee and daily newspaper. In a way, I was being altruistic."

Yeah, right. "How did you know about his medication? The exact dose he takes? I can't imagine there's much altruism in that."

"We talked, you know. Often. You may think the library is a happening place, but there were some days when it was just the two of us for the better part of eight hours. You get to know a person pretty well spending that much time together."

Juliet hadn't for a second considered the library a "happening place." "I have to ask. What was it about Richard Kowalski that would make a forty-eight-year-old woman fall for a near-seventy-year-old married man with health issues? Obviously, looks aren't everything and I'm not implying that they are. But being married as well as two decades older is a pretty big deterrent, don't you think?" Juliet thrummed her fingers on the table while Tara sipped her tea like it could help her find the answers.

"Rich knew me better than anyone else. I told him everything. And he listened. I mean, really *listened.* Better than anyone I've ever known. He knew the parts of me that I kept hidden from the rest of the world," Tara said. Her eyes welled up.

"Did he know how you felt?" Juliet asked quietly.

"Of course not. If I told him before the time was right, it would ruin everything. I was waiting for the perfect moment."

Juliet paused. Had the perfect moment presented itself the night of Richard's murder? Had Tara told him that she loved him, and Richard had rejected her? Would that have sent her spiraling into getting rid of the one thing she couldn't have? Juliet scanned her notes on Tara. She went home after work on the night that Richard had been killed, so no alibi. She drove a black Ford Focus, which in no way could be mistaken for a red truck, although that didn't mean she didn't know someone who owned one. Juliet sighed.

"You have to know this doesn't look good, Tara. You were pining away for someone who was, as far as we know, happily married, and you hid files that you'd composed on him that are, to be frank, creepy.

The fact that you made note of the dosage of the medicine that killed him doesn't help either."

Tara swallowed hard but didn't say anything.

"Can you contradict anything that I've said? Was Richard unhappy in his marriage? Do you have anyone that can corroborate the fact that you were at home on the night of his death?" Juliet spread her hands over the open folder in front of her.

"No. I was alone. I watched TV and went to bed and then went rushing over to the library as soon as someone from your department called me. Rich was my soulmate, for Christ's sake." Tara banged the table with her hand, sending tea flying over the side of the cup and onto the corner of Juliet's folder.

"Who is Mr. Restarick?" Juliet asked, hoping to catch her off guard.

"Who?"

"Mr. Restarick."

"I have no idea. I mean, besides the literary character. Why? Is that someone under suspicion?" Tara asked.

"Literary character?"

"Yes, from *Third Girl* by Agatha Christie. We always joked about how we loved that Poirot book but so many people didn't because it took place in the sixties. It wasn't the usual type of plot, a girl thought she might have killed someone, and a woman was poisoned..." Tara trailed off, seeming to realize the significance.

"Poisoned? How?"

"Arsenic, I think. It's been a while since I've read it and she used all kinds of poisons. It was sort of her thing." Tara dabbed at the spilled tea. She was probably happy that the conversation had shifted.

"That's actually helpful. I'm not sure how yet, but it'll fit somewhere. It usually does. Is there anything else you'd like to tell me about your relationship with Richard? Since he didn't know how you really felt, I assume it's safe to say that it never became physical in any way?" Juliet continued to jot Tara's answers in her small notebook.

"No. Now if you don't mind, I'd like to get back to grieving the life I'll never have. If you could reopen the library so I can get back to work sooner than later, that would probably help," Tara said.

She seemed oblivious to the fact that she likely would never have had her imaginary life at all, which raised alarm bells. "Will you be taking on the role of head librarian now that Richard is gone?"

Tara shook her head. "I doubt it. I've only been doing this for a couple of years. Before I got my degree, I worked in a bookstore. Richard had a lifetime's worth of knowledge. He could recite the location of every classic in that entire place."

Juliet raised her eyebrows at how wistful Tara became when speaking about him. She idolized him, clearly, and that didn't always translate into something healthy. Plenty of people had been killed by their idolizers in order to protect them from something or other. They felt the world was too terrible for the object of their affection to be subjected to its travesties. Or, when their idolizing wasn't returned, they became aggressive. Did Tara fall into either of those categories?

"We'd like you to speak with a therapist that we work with on certain cases that warrant it. Is that something you'd be willing to do?" Juliet asked.

"I'd rather not." She picked up her bag like she was ready to leave.

"It's your choice, of course, but it could help to clear your name, if everything you've told me is true."

"Of course, it's true," Tara snapped. "Fine, I'll talk to your shrink. Are we done here?"

Juliet nodded. "For now, yes. Thank you for your time today."

"Are you going to tell Gretchen? About me and Rich?" Tara didn't meet Juliet's eyes as she pulled her cross-body bag over her head.

"Sounds like there isn't much to tell, at least not at this time."

"Yeah," Tara said and jogged quickly away from the conference room in a scented haze of florals and spices.

Juliet stared after her, wondering if Tara actually wanted Gretchen to know someone else had loved Richard. There was no telling what went through someone's mind when they became obsessed with someone. There was no question, though, that Tara's name was comfortably on the suspect list.

❖

Juliet fiddled with her keyring as she walked outside to the cruiser and a blast of heat hit her in the face like a wall. Fall was supposed to be crisp and cool with sweaters and pumpkin spice and crunchy leaves. Instead, it was about eighty-five degrees and so humid Juliet could feel beads of sweat pooling in the small of her back. Lovely.

A familiar Volvo was parked in the space next to the squad car, stopping Juliet in her tracks. Sienna exited her vehicle, file folders in her arms and a laptop bag swung over her shoulder.

"Hi," Sienna said, clearly surprised at their meeting.

"Hey." Juliet felt an unrelenting tug at the center of her chest, and she ignored it. "Fancy meeting you here."

"Yeah," Sienna said. "Chief Quinlan asked me to come in and chat with him about Gretchen's progress. See if she's remembered anything else, that kind of thing."

"Oh, good. Good." Juliet nodded. Of course, it had to get awkward. What had been so comfortable and so right now felt like a blanket, too thick and too tight and too suffocating.

"Okay, well, I'm going to go." Sienna tilted her head toward the front entrance.

"Okay. See ya." Juliet turned as Sienna entered the building, her hair perfect even with the humidity, her silky sleeveless blouse clinging to her back just a little, Capris hugging her muscular calves, her sandals encasing pedicured feet with pink-painted toenails, and her general air of confidence and warmth filling the space around her.

Trying to push thoughts of Sienna aside, Juliet cranked her radio up and attempted to get lost in the frantic guitar riffs of peak Guns N' Roses. It worked a little and she relaxed into the drive.

Officer Jane Leland was directing traffic on Main Street. The grocer in town had hit a power line during the night and knocked out the electricity for a few blocks. Juliet was glad she wasn't on duty at the time. She'd barely been able to sleep as it was. She didn't need the added stress of telling a sweet little old man that his driving days were likely behind him. Celeste had had the pleasure of that particular task.

"Afternoon, Lieutenant," Leland greeted her as Juliet pulled up beside her. Leland was nothing if not formal. She leaned against the door where Juliet's window was all the way down.

"Afternoon, Officer. Any ETA on the electricity? I'm heading across the street to the library and it looks like it's still out over there too."

Leland shook her head. "The utility guys told me they were working down at the other end of the street first, so they could get the town offices up and running. There are a few doctors' offices over that way as well, so they want to make sure those are on the priority list, too."

"Okay, makes sense. I'm sure I can feel my way around a dark, empty, creepy library with just my flashlight." Juliet smiled.

Leland smiled back. She'd been on the force the longest. She'd been offered promotions over the years, but she felt most comfortable in her role as an officer. Her days with the Shell Creek Police Department had begun around the time Juliet was born. They waved good-bye and Juliet pulled into the library parking lot.

She pulled out the key she'd taken from Kowalski's things and opened the door. It creaked on cue, adding to the haunted atmosphere that gave her the creeps.

"Come on, it's the middle of the day. Don't be such a baby." It didn't help that most of the blinds had been drawn and it really was dark inside. It was almost completely silent. The only sound Juliet could hear was the persistent buzzing of a fly. Otherwise, nothing.

She took the folded-up piece of paper out of her pants pocket and reacquainted herself with its contents. Mr. Restarick, *Third Girl*, Agatha Christie.

When she'd been a kid, reading hadn't been her thing. She'd preferred TV, movies, music—basically, every other medium—over reading. She'd finally grown to enjoy books, especially audiobooks, but when she wanted one now, she'd just buy it. Checking one out hadn't even occurred to her and she had no idea where to begin her search. She felt a little overwhelmed by the enormity of bookshelves in front of her, and the computers meant to guide her in the right direction weren't working. Where were those musty card catalogs she remembered leafing through all those years ago? She pulled out her phone and brought up the site for the Shell Creek Library.

"Of course, the website sucks." It had advertisements for upcoming events and a coupon for ten dollars off a ticket to Six Flags that had expired four years ago. When she clicked on the search bar for "catalog," a little man in a construction helmet appeared, holding a sign that said, "Come back soon, we're working on it!"

With a deep sigh, she started making her way down the aisles. The classics section didn't offer up anything of use. Juliet had just assumed that Agatha Christie would be located with the classics, but apparently not.

She continued to the mystery section, where the carpet in front of the shelves was well worn. Obviously, a popular area of the library, Juliet noted. She slid her fingertips over the book spines as she read the titles. *Jackpot.* She found *And Then There Were None*, and then realized there were about a zillion Agatha Christie books in this particular section.

Bang.

Juliet's head snapped up. It wasn't a loud bang, or a deliberate bang, just a soft thud of two things coming into contact with each other. She rested her hand on her weapon and listened closely for any other sound to interrupt the heavy silence. There was nothing.

Satisfied that it had been an anomaly, Juliet continued to look for *Third Girl*. Her knees creaked as she stood from the crouching position, where a good portion of the Christie books sat on the bottom shelf. As she began scanning the next set of shelves, she finally found what she'd been looking for, a plastic-encased copy of *Third Girl* by Agatha Christie.

Juliet pulled out her latex gloves and put them on, just to be on the safe side and then plucked the book off the shelf. Nothing in particular stood out about the cover, which was just a long shadow of a woman standing in a doorway. She flipped through the pages slowly to see if something had been stashed in the book. A note, a scrawl in the margins, anything. She checked the signature card in the front of the book, which she knew was no longer used, but it was still nice to see. Richard Kowalski had checked the book out in 1983. Juliet smiled to herself and ran her gloved finger along the depression that his name had made. It was still strange to be in this place, knowing that he wasn't going to come around the corner with a book suggestion or a corny joke.

Juliet closed the book in disappointment. She'd been hopeful that something, *anything*, would have been stashed inside it. She pushed it back into its slot on the metal shelf and heard a soft "clink." She pulled the book back out and took the one next to it as well.

A stout bottle of Woodford Reserve Rye, about three-quarters empty, was nestled in the empty slot behind the books.

"What have we here?" Her voice bounced off the tomes around her. She turned the bottle over a few times in her hands but there wasn't anything interesting on the label. She slowly took the cap off the bottle and smelled its contents.

"He didn't like anyone knowing that he drank sometimes."

Juliet nearly threw the bottle into the air. She whipped around, hand on her holster again, and came face-to-face with Tara Wolfe.

"*What* are you doing here?" Juliet asked, unable to mask the anger in her voice. "I thought I made it clear that this place was off-limits. How did you get in here?" She noticed that Tara was wearing ballet slippers, which must have been why she hadn't heard her approaching.

Tara nodded. "I saw your car in the parking lot. I just wanted to get a few more things from my office. Although I see that your crew or whoever it was went through my office. Thanks for that. My notebooks and my computer are missing."

Juliet was furious. "No, Tara. You can't just come and go as you please. I understand that you are an employee here, but that doesn't give you the right to tamper with an active investigation. Is this what you wanted to take last time you were in here? Were you waiting for me to come in again, so you could follow me? What did you come for this time?"

"This." She held up a decorative wooden compass with the library's insignia engraved into the cover. "Rich gave me this a few months ago when I completed my course on library technology. It meant a lot."

"And you couldn't wait until we reopened the library to get it? Are you sure you didn't come for this? After you told me who Mr. Restarick was?" Juliet asked, pointing to the bottle.

"No."

"You are *not* to come in here again. You'll be notified when the library reopens."

Tara rolled her eyes and crossed her arms. "I'm sure I will, Lieutenant Mitchell." She nearly spat the last two words.

"If I see you in here, hear that you've been by, or get a gut feeling that you're lurking around the parking lot, I'll arrest you for obstruction of justice. Got it?" Juliet said, making sure Tara didn't have any doubts about the seriousness of her orders.

"Fine."

"What can you tell me about this situation?" Juliet tipped the bottle of rye toward Tara.

"He liked a little drink from time to time. His wife didn't approve. She told him he might as well swig poison if he wanted to destroy his body. So, he didn't tell her. Probably why he hid it where he did."

"Did he drink often?"

Tara shrugged. "Not really. That same bottle has been back there for months. I completely forgot about it until just now."

She's lying. Her eyes were dodgy, and her demeanor changed. But why? "Did you ever drink with him?"

"No, it's against policy to drink on the job."

"But you had no problem with Rich doing it? Did you ever tell him to stop?" Juliet asked.

"Of course not, he was my boss. Besides, he needed a little bit of freedom from his wife, didn't he? He was entitled to live his own life."

Juliet ignored her indignation. "What if someone had a hankering for a little Agatha Christie? Wasn't he afraid that someone would find his stash?"

"Since my computer is missing and we don't have any electricity anyway, I can't tell you the last time it was checked out. But based on memory, it's probably been at least eight years. So, I'm pretty sure he felt like *Third Girl* was a safe option. If not a little on the nose," Tara said.

Juliet detected a note of wistfulness in Tara's recollection. "Okay. I'll call you if we have any more questions, which we probably will, especially now. We can walk out together," Juliet said, flashing a fake smile.

"Sounds like a dream." Tara sent a phony smile of her own Juliet's way.

When they were safely outside of the building, Juliet locked the door and gave it a tug for good measure. Tara gave Juliet the peace sign with her index finger pointed forward just enough that Juliet got the message. *Well, fuck you too.*

Chapter Sixteen

B y the time Sienna had finished up with Chief Quinlan, it was after four o'clock. She'd updated him on everything that Gretchen had told her about her husband and their life together and who the major players were. She kept everything of a personal nature confidential, of course, but she relayed all of the pertinent facts to him as he'd requested. He'd seemed dejected by the end of their meeting.

"I'm heading over to the elementary school to see my granddaughter run cross-country. Most boring thing you can imagine, but someday she'll appreciate me being there." Quinlan smiled. "Everyone else on duty is out and about, so I'll lock up before we go."

Sienna nodded, slipping her laptop into its bag while Quinlan selected the key he needed from his keyring of hundreds. She couldn't help but wonder what person needed *that* many keys.

As they exited through the front entrance toward the parking lot, Sienna saw Juliet jogging toward them. Twice in one day. Really?

"Oh, hey, you're back. I'll leave you to lock up then," Quinlan said, adjusting his sunglasses. "Hot as a bitch out here."

"Sure thing, Chief." Juliet nodded in Sienna's direction without making eye contact. "Hi, Sienna."

"Good afternoon, Lieutenant," Sienna said. She knew she was being immature, but if Juliet wanted to be professional and detached from her, then she could do the same. She wasn't going to *beg* Juliet to be her friend. Or whatever it was they were. Quinlan called a quick good-bye and walked briskly to his car.

Juliet stopped and looked at her. Sienna met her gaze and raised an eyebrow in question.

"Do you have a quick second, Sienna?"

Sienna checked her watch. "Yes, if it's quick. The cable company is coming over tonight to install some sort of internet booster. Declan promises to pay for it himself."

"With what money?"

Sienna shrugged. "That's between Declan and Will." She looked toward the sky, which was that dark shade of blue before a storm hit. The wind was starting to pick up, sending the few leaves that had fallen from the trees into a cinematic swirl.

Juliet opened the door and held it for Sienna. Sienna kept her bag on her shoulder and her files in her arms while Juliet leaned against one of the cubicle walls in the bullpen.

"Did you get any sense from Gretchen that Richard may have been having an affair?"

Sienna was completely taken aback. "No, none at all. Was he?"

Juliet shook her head. "I don't think so, but Tara, his assistant at the library, was madly in love with him. She had all these ideas and plans for the two of them once he 'finally realized' that they were meant to be together."

"That's…a surprise. If anything was going on between the two of them, I don't think Gretchen knew about it." Sienna tried to remember anything that Gretchen had shared with her that would lead her to believe there was infidelity in their marriage. She couldn't come up with anything.

"That's what I thought. What about drinking? I found a bottle of whiskey hidden in one of the bookshelves. I dropped it off at the county lab before coming here so they could test the contents. Hopefully, we'll get some DNA just to be certain it was his. Did Gretchen ever mention any kind of drinking problem?"

"Nothing at all like that. According to her, Richard was a saint. I take that with a grain of salt, of course, but usually there would be some sign of alcoholism or adultery in the amount of time I've spent with her."

Juliet's phone sounded an alarm. She plucked it from her back pocket and swiped up to see what the message was.

"Severe thunderstorm warning for our area. No surprise. With how sticky it is out there, something has to break the heat. Feels like a slow boil outside."

Sienna frowned. She could see flashes of lightning in the distance. "I should probably get going before it gets too bad. Is that hail?" she asked, listening to the "plink, plink" of something hitting the glass.

Both of their phones began to scream in unison. Sienna dug hers out of her bag and her heart began to race. She unlocked her phone and the public service message appeared on-screen.

*AT 427 PM EDT...A SEVERE THUNDERSTORM CAPABLE OF PRODUCING A TORNADO WAS LOCATED 9 MILES WEST OF SHELL CREEK...MOVING EAST AT 40MPH.

HAZARD...TORNADO

SOURCE...RADAR INDICATED ROTATION

IMPACT...FLYING DEBRIS WILL BE DANGEROUS TO THOSE CAUGHT WITHOUT SHELTER, MOBILE HOMES WILL BE DAMAGED OR DESTROYED. DAMAGE TO ROOFS... WINDOWS...AND VEHICLES WILL OCCUR. TREE DAMAGE IS LIKELY.

TAKE COVER NOW. MOVE TO A BASEMENT OR INTERIOR ROOM ON THE LOWEST FLOOR OF A STURDY BUILDING. AVOID WINDOWS.

HEAVY RAINFALL MAY OBSCURE THIS TORNADO. DO NOT WAIT TO SEE OR HEAR THE TORNADO.

TAKE COVER NOW.

Sienna looked up at Juliet, panic setting in. "What do we do?"

"I don't know," Juliet said. "We don't get tornadoes here. We've had a few watches over the years, but nothing has ever actually happened. I'm sure it's a false alarm."

Sienna stood still, afraid that any movement would set off a natural disaster.

Juliet walked to the entrance door and opened it a few inches. Her hair whipped across her face from the intensity of the gust.

Sienna crept up behind her, trying to see if there was any indication that a tornado was about to hit. The dark blue of the sky that she noticed as she'd walked out of the station had been replaced by greenish-yellow clouds, rotating in a slow circle. Lightning struck somewhere nearby and an explosion of thunder assaulted her ears.

"Okay, maybe it's not a false alarm." Juliet rubbed the back of her neck. "Shit, this is new. We should probably get down to the basement."

"Where's Declan?" Sienna's anxiety nearly overwhelmed her.

"He's at the school until six for some kind of sports assembly. They'll get them to safety." Juliet nodded confidently. She then turned to Sienna and said softly, "Right?"

"Right. Absolutely, they're trained for this kind of thing," Sienna said, swallowing hard. They had to be trained for that kind of thing in a school, right? "I should try to get home—"

"Are you insane? You can't leave! What, are you going to outrun a tornado? Have you never seen *Twister*?" Juliet swirled her finger in the air.

"Well, where is the basement in this place? Does a police station even have a basement?" Sienna asked. The hail had cranked up a notch, hitting the building and the windows with golf ball-sized chunks of ice.

"Come on," Juliet yelled over the din of the wind, grabbing Sienna's hand. She pulled her toward the back of the station, where a wooden door with a skeleton key sticking out of it was situated next to a printer table with a mishmash of paper strewn around it. The police station was an old town landmark that had been updated in a lot of ways, but still had the same bones from the late 1800s when it was originally built. Juliet pulled hard, fighting to release the swollen wood. "Okay, go."

Sienna brushed past Juliet, who put her hand on the small of Sienna's back, ushering her down the stairs. She turned to see Juliet closing the door tightly behind them, pulling hard on the knob so that the door would stay shut. She nearly tumbled down the stairs when the door finally clicked into place.

Juliet stared down at her hand and the doorknob sitting in her palm. "Fuck," Juliet muttered.

"Juliet, come on," Sienna yelled. The howling wind above them had begun to intensify, and a distant growling grew louder by the second.

Juliet moved out in front of her, fumbling for Sienna's fingers as she descended the rest of the stairs. Sienna latched on and followed Juliet into a dark corner of the basement.

"Under here," Juliet instructed, pointing below a tool bench bolted into the stone wall of the basement. She snatched some tablecloths that would have to act as pillows from the shelf beside the tool bench, and she crawled into the small space next to Sienna.

Sienna breathed deeply, trying to avoid having a panic attack. She felt chills crawl up the side of her face, and the pit in her stomach grow larger.

"We're okay," Juliet said soothingly, pushing a piece of Sienna's hair behind her ear. "Declan is with his coaches and about a hundred other kids, so he'll be fine, too. Will is probably at the office, which I'm sure has all kinds of safe spaces. We're all okay."

Sienna nodded, blinking back tears. She knew Juliet was trying to relax herself as well as Sienna, so Sienna held on to Juliet's hand with ferocity. There was no way she was letting go.

"I thought Massachusetts was supposed to be safe from these things," Sienna said. "We had hurricanes in Florida, but at least you had time to prepare for those. I expected blizzards, not fucking tornadoes!"

Juliet covered her mouth with her hand. "I don't think I've ever heard you swear. I'm offended."

"Oh, shut up, Juliet," Sienna said. She gave her a half-smile, but she realized that her air intake was shallow at best.

Juliet smiled back at her and squeezed her hand.

The air outside grew quiet. Still. It had gone from the pounding of hail and the whistling of the wind to near total silence. Juliet looked slightly relieved, but Sienna knew this was probably a bad sign. A very bad sign. Her limited knowledge of weather included the fact that the atmosphere was at its most tranquil before unleashing a raging tempest. But maybe she was remembering wrong. Hopefully.

She wasn't remembering wrong.

Juliet clutched her ears as Sienna's popped painfully from the shifting barometric pressure. They slid closer to each other and Sienna rested her head on Juliet's chest, her arms circling her waist in a tight grip. Juliet adjusted her position and held onto Sienna just as tightly, burying her face in Sienna's hair. Had she not been fearful of losing her life, Sienna probably would have appreciated the moment a little differently. For the time being, she was grateful that Juliet was there with her in what could very possibly be the end of everything.

CHAPTER SEVENTEEN

While she didn't *really* believe they were going to die, Juliet shot off a few silent prayers to whoever might be listening. It was all very surreal; these kinds of natural disasters simply didn't happen in Shell Creek. The fact that she was crouched under a tool bench with Sienna Bennett, wrapped in her arms like they shared the same heartbeat, only added to that feeling of unreality.

The roaring outside became deafening. She'd heard that the sound of a tornado closely resembled that of an oncoming freight train, and she could now confirm that rumor to be true. It was somewhere between a freight train and a jet engine flying way too low.

Wood began to creak and splinter above them. Glass shattered. Thunder continued to reverberate relentlessly. Juliet had been involved in a few dangerous situations in her life, but this particular situation was now at the top of terrifying moments. She could only pray that Dec had managed to get to safety and wasn't nearly as scared as she was right now.

Sienna continued to hold on tightly, and Juliet heard a slight whimper. She rested her chin on Sienna's head and smoothed the back of her hair.

"This is how it ends, huh? You and me, curled up together under a table?" Sienna asked, her heart pounding against Juliet's like a hammer. Her voice shook with fear, and Juliet appreciated her taking a moment to sarcastically state the obvious.

"I could think of worse ways," Juliet said. She was trying to be sweet, but it came off as flirtatious and probably inappropriate. Her eyes widened for a second, but she decided that their predicament overruled any stupid thing she could say. It wasn't like Sienna would remember what they'd talked about when this was all over, anyway. She was too afraid.

The small rectangular windows inside the basement began to rattle like nickels in a tin can. It was pitch-black outside, and a piece of picket fence flew by. A thousand thoughts began to flood Juliet's mind. Maybe this really *was* it, the end. Her breathing began to get shallow, but she closed her eyes and told herself over and over again that they were in the safest possible location. Underground and under a heavy object to protect them. If only her son were with them.

The roaring rumble grew closer and closer. Juliet held on to Sienna and their bodies melded into one another. The noises above suggested that the station above them was shaking and flexing, and Juliet briefly wondered if they would be crushed and suffocated. She had a sudden urge to get up and run toward the stairs, questioning if it would be better to just get sucked into the vortex rather than flattened bone by agonizing bone.

She fought the urge, thankfully. After what felt like hours, the roar began to subside. The thunder had gained some distance, and the growl of the twister sounded more like a loud motorcycle instead of a locomotive.

Neither of them moved for a few long moments. Eventually, Sienna pulled her head back slightly.

"Is it over?" she asked quietly, lifting her head.

Juliet stretched her jaw to unblock her ears. "Maybe. I'll go check."

Sienna tightened her grip on Juliet's shirt, pulling her back down to her knees. "Don't *leave*, for God's sake," she said with a bewildered expression.

"I'm not, I just want to make sure the storm is over. I'll be right back, I promise." Juliet gave Sienna's hand another squeeze in confirmation.

Juliet walked toward the stairs, taking hold of the rickety railing that had probably never been replaced. She got about halfway up when she remembered the doorknob incident. "Shit," she muttered, taking it from where she'd dropped it on the stair. She walked up the rest of the way and tried to force it back on, hoping the other knob hadn't fallen out the other side. It wasn't happening.

"I forgot the doorknob came off. I'll have to kick the door in," she called down to Sienna, who was standing at the bottom of the staircase. Sienna's expression was a cross between desperation and amusement.

"Okay," Juliet said out loud, psyching herself up. She shook out her hands and shifted her weight onto her back foot while still holding onto the old railing.

"UGH," she gasped, as her work boot hit the door with a good amount of force. The door didn't break; it didn't even budge. Juliet faltered from the impact but caught herself on the stone wall before she could tumble down the stairs. "Little harder than I expected. No big deal." She didn't want to admit it, but she was mortified that Sienna had witnessed that.

"Maybe we should go a different route." Sienna held her cell phone up. "I don't have any service right now, but maybe text would work? If we can find some kind of working Wi-Fi connection. I don't want you to hurt yourself."

"We *could* do that, or I could just break this fucker down." Juliet grunted, giving the door another high kick to the middle. When she almost fell again, and the door didn't seem any less stuck than it was before, she relented. "Fine, we'll try your way." She threw the doorknob down the stairs like a child and watched as it bounced on the concrete. So much for heroic moves meant to impress.

"The storm must have taken out the cell tower," Sienna said. She kept pressing send and she kept getting the "call failed" message. She held it up for Juliet to see. "I'll try texting just in case."

No sooner had she pressed send than the telltale exclamation point with the circle around it popped up. Not delivered. She walked from point to point throughout the basement looking for a signal. Juliet watched as she held her cell phone higher and higher in the air.

"No texting either," she said, dejected.

"I'll try mine," Juliet said. "Dammit, I left my phone on my desk." She patted down her pockets again just to make sure.

"Well, this is great." Sienna rubbed at her throat. "What are we supposed to do?"

"Nothing," Juliet said. "We wait. They'll figure out we're down here soon enough, and they'll get us out. Don't worry, we'll be fine."

Juliet clapped her hands together and went to the section of wall in front of the stairs where boxes were stacked nearly ceiling-high. She sorted through the first few and found nothing of interest, mostly just office supplies that would probably never see the light of day again. She pulled out a few dusty bottles of Poland Spring water from the third box and held them up triumphantly.

"These expired...nine years ago, but they should be fine. It's just water, right?" She handed them to Sienna, who took them with trepidation.

"Is drinking water the smartest idea, considering our predicament? What about the windows?" Sienna asked. Juliet detected a mild note of panic in her voice.

"The heavy iron bars could be problematic. It's a police station, after all," Juliet said. She bit the inside of her cheek.

"Yes, I know that. I meant to call for help."

"They face the back lot. I'll see if anyone is back there, but I highly doubt it." Juliet climbed onto an old garden pot she'd pulled over to the window and peeked out one of the two dirt-caked rectangles. The only thing in the back lot was a tree that had fallen. Its still-leafy branches created a blockade from anything beyond the back lot. "No one."

Sienna breathed out slowly. She checked her phone again. "Still nothing."

Juliet removed the pin in the back of her hair to let it fall. The tightness of the twist she'd put it in earlier was giving her a headache. She plucked a few blond strands off her shirt and let them fall to the floor. Something in the far corner caught her eye.

"Hey, come here," she called, waving Sienna over.

"What is it?"

"I mean, it's not ideal, but just in case." Juliet nodded toward a yellowed urinal mounted to one of the makeshift framing walls. It was enclosed by crude borders made of wooden posts to insinuate a modicum of privacy. "This must have been the bathroom back when it was first built."

"I'll hold it," Sienna said, disgust evident in her expression.

"Suit yourself." Juliet gave her a quick smile. "We're lucky to be alive. I'm sure Declan is trying to get ahold of us as we speak, so we should be out of here in no time."

"You're right. Should I try the door again?"

"If you want to," Juliet said. She knew there was no point, but if it made Sienna feel like she was doing something, then there was no harm in it. She took the tablecloths she'd fashioned as soft protection from any possible debris and laid them out against a few large totes labeled "decorations." In all her time on the police force, they hadn't decorated for anything, so she had no idea what was actually contained in the totes. She kicked away a rogue coffee can that had probably been used as an oil collector at some point. Her improvised seating area wasn't perfect, but at least it was clean.

"It's very dark in here," Sienna said. The sliver of light provided by the windows was fading fast. Rain was still beating down on the pavement outside.

Juliet tugged on the frayed pull cord of a single lightbulb screwed into a fixture above her head. She'd hoped that it was just switched off, but no such luck. After several tugs yielding the same result, she let up.

"The tornado probably knocked out the power. We can use the light of your phone if we need to," Juliet suggested, searching for things to say to help Sienna's obvious anxiety.

"I'm only on thirteen percent. Why didn't I charge it on my way here?" Sienna sighed dramatically and sat on the tablecloth; her shoulders slumped.

Juliet sat next to her, cross-legged. "We're okay, really."

"Your optimism is enviable. But don't you think this situation warrants a little panic? I can't rule out an anxiety attack. We just survived some sort of freak storm-of-the-century, and we're going to die in this drab, spider-filled basement."

Juliet rolled her eyes. "So dramatic. Come on, everyone is fine, everything is fine. I'm sure of it. It's not like it was an F5 or something."

"EF5."

"What?"

"You said F5. It's EF5. They don't use the Fujita scale anymore. They use the Enhanced Fujita scale now. The Weather Channel ran a whole special on it," Sienna said.

Juliet shook her head. "Okay, fine. *EF*5. It wasn't that. We don't get those here."

"You also said we don't get tornadoes here."

"Sienna. I'm not a meteorologist. I don't know for *certain* that it wasn't an EF5, but I'm pretty sure it wasn't. Those monsters wipe out whole towns." Juliet couldn't help her exasperation at the minutiae Sienna seemed to be focusing on. It was probably just a coping mechanism, but still.

Sienna looked at the ceiling and wiped away an imaginary cobweb. "Sorry," she whispered, moving closer to Juliet. "I'm scared. Sorry."

"Don't be. We've just been through a…thing. A big thing. I didn't mean to be snappy with you." Juliet reached over and took Sienna's hand, trying to forget about the tension they'd been mired in. She found it interesting that Sienna didn't pull away. Juliet wasn't sure why she was being so touchy-feely all of a sudden, but maybe the brush with death had something to do with it.

"So…how are things with you?" Juliet asked, breaking the silence.

Sienna laughed. "Good, you?"

"Good, good. Thanks for asking."

Juliet cracked open a bottle of expired water and took a long sip. "Ahh. Want some?"

Sienna shook her head.

"Have you, you know, moved forward with the whole divorce thing?" Juliet averted her eyes, looking over at an abandoned bicycle. It was probably none of her business, but she felt compelled to know what direction Sienna and Will's marriage was heading.

Sienna seemed taken aback but engaged nonetheless. "Yes, I have. Our lawyers have been in contact with one another, and at this point I'm just waiting for a hearing date."

"What happens then?"

"Once the judge signs off on it, we wait ninety days and then it's over. The marriage is dissolved. We're single and free to live our lives separately. All told it will take about four months," Sienna said.

Juliet nodded. She was battling with herself about how far to take the conversation. She didn't want to pry, or piss Sienna off, but if they were supposed to be friends, then they should be able to be open with each other. Right?

"Are you happy about it?"

Sienna tilted her head. "I don't think happy is the right word. I know it's for the best. I'll be happier and I'm sure he will be too. I need to start looking for my own place sooner rather than later." Sienna paused. "It could get contentious. I hope it doesn't."

"Last I knew, he was still hoping for reconciliation," Juliet said, still not making eye contact. There was a sudden pit in her stomach that swigging water wasn't helping with.

"I know. I hope you don't think I'm cold for saying so, but that's not going to happen. We've been together a long time, and I've been considering *this* for a long time. I wanted it to work out, I wanted to create a stable family for myself, and for Declan. But I've tried for too long and nothing has changed. This isn't Will's fault. It's not my fault. It just *is*." Sienna looked across the basement, her eyes watery in the dim light. "In my heart, I've been alone for a long time, Juliet. I tried to tell him, over and over, so it wouldn't come as a shock. But it did anyway. I'm sure I could have done things differently. He could have, too. I don't know." She crossed her arms over her stomach. "I'm sorry if this puts you in an awkward position. I know how much you care about him."

Juliet nodded. "I do. He's been a great friend and excellent father. But that doesn't mean that I agree with him on everything. We rarely agree on *anything*. And I know how he can be. Trust me, I don't blame you for what's going on. No judgment. From what I've gotten to know of you, I think Will was crazy not to do everything in his power to make it work. I'm sorry you're hurting."

A faint knocking on the door at the top of the stairs prompted both Juliet and Sienna to jump up from where they were sitting. Juliet took the stairs two at a time to get to the top.

"Hello," she yelled. "We're down here! We're here!"

There was no response, only the soft thud of the continued knocking.

"Is anyone there? We're stuck in the basement. Open the door!" Juliet turned toward Sienna, who was standing on the bottom step. "Quick, shine your light."

Sienna scrunched her eyebrows but complied anyway. "What good is this going to do?" she asked, while waving her phone's flashlight at the door.

"I don't know, maybe they can see it underneath the door?" Juliet pounded on the door again. The persistent knocking made her begin to question if there was a person out there after all. "Hello?" she called again weakly.

"There's nobody there, is there?" Sienna checked the service bars on her phone. She stuck it back in her pocket, so service must have been down still.

Juliet headed back down the stairs. "Maybe it's a tree branch or something. But no, I don't think anyone's there."

Sienna sighed and went back to the wall where they'd been sitting. She slouched against one of the totes and crossed her legs at the ankles. Juliet sat next to her and ran a hand through her hair. Someone had to come. Soon.

CHAPTER EIGHTEEN

Y ou want to play a game?" Juliet fidgeted with the frayed edges of the tablecloth.

"No."

"Sleep?"

"No."

"Do you want me to just stop talking so we can sit in silence and pout?" Juliet asked, nudging Sienna with her shoulder.

Sienna ignored her. "Why haven't they come yet? It's been too long. It's been nearly two hours. Do you think something terrible happened?"

Juliet swallowed. Of course, those thoughts had been going through her head relentlessly, and she was sick with worry about Declan. But she couldn't dwell on it or she'd go crazy. She had to believe that everything was fine, and everyone was working through the damage and would find them shortly. She had to.

"No, I don't. Our doorknob broke off, maybe theirs did too. We could have a whole town of people trapped behind broken doorknobs."

Sienna rubbed her arms as though she was chilled. "Come on, Juliet. I'm serious."

Juliet slid closer to her. "I am too. I mean, obviously we're not in the middle of a doorknob epidemic, but my point stands. There are a million reasons why no one has come yet. Maybe they're out there helping people who are in real trouble. They'll come."

Every muscle in Juliet's body tightened as Sienna closed the slight space between them. Juliet had no idea what was going through

Sienna's mind, but her own heartbeat kicked up a few notches. She closed her eyes as she felt Sienna's head rest on her shoulder. She wasn't sure how to react. The proverbial butterflies fluttered around in her stomach, but Juliet could easily write that off as part of their current situation. She convinced herself that Sienna just needed some reassurance. She was a warm, familiar body, and Sienna just needed to feel safe. In that vein, Juliet slid her arm out and tucked it around Sienna's shoulder, pulling her closer. Sienna offered no resistance. They sat there for a few minutes, in total silence, while Juliet contemplated every breath she took. She didn't want Sienna to move away.

Sienna sighed again but didn't pull back. "Sometimes I think that I should just suck it up and be grateful for what I have. Isn't that crazy? I'm blessed with more than I need, all that I want, and a stepson I love dearly. So what if my marriage is mediocre? Isn't that how most people feel?"

Juliet's eyes widened in the darkness. She wanted to tell Sienna that she was insane, that she deserved to be loved in every way possible, in a way that would fill her completely. Juliet's own experience with women was checkered at best, but it didn't stop her from wondering if Sienna could be the one to fill that void. She'd been in a few relationships that had crossed the one-year mark, but they never made it much further. She'd always concentrated on her son and her work, and if she had anything left to give, she'd fill the time with whoever she'd been seeing at that time, but no one wanted to be the person you spent time with if you didn't have anything else to do. Even knowing who she was and how she'd acted in the past, things were different this time around. Aside from the fact that there was too much baggage and too many hearts involved. She needed to be satisfied with their friendship.

"No, I don't think it is," Juliet said instead. "You should be happy in your relationship. Mediocrity isn't something to aspire to. I've had lots of mediocre relationships over the years. I promised myself a long time ago that I wouldn't settle ever again. You should do the same. You're worth more than that, Sienna."

"Thank you, Juliet," Sienna whispered. "That means more to me than you can imagine."

Sienna pulled Juliet into a hug. Juliet responded, pulling Sienna tight to her chest. She closed her eyes and lost herself in the warmth of Sienna's arms. *Because this is what friends do.*

Sienna pulled away slowly and resumed her position on Juliet's shoulder. Juliet took a drink from her expired water and offered it to Sienna. Seemingly forgetting about the dirty urinal in the corner, Sienna also took a long sip.

"So, what are we doing wrong?" Sienna asked quietly. She sat up and made semicircles with her neck, loosening the muscle tightness that had probably developed from her position on Juliet's shoulder.

Feeling Sienna more than seeing her, Juliet reached out and began massaging Sienna's neck with her thumb and index finger. Sienna moaned in approval, which made Juliet shift a little.

"I don't know." Juliet figured they'd gone back to the relationship question. "I just assumed that since I'm sort of a fuck-up at anything to do with relationships, it's me. I'm a good mom, and a good friend, but I've never been lucky in love, as cliché as that sounds."

"I always wonder if I expect too much," Sienna said. "I haven't been with anyone but Will in a very long time. Maybe that fire and excitement and soul-consuming love that I long for only exists in youth. Maybe I'm yearning for something that I can never have, because it's the stuff of romance novels, not real life."

Juliet stilled her fingers. She let them fall slowly to the middle of Sienna's back, where she turned Sienna toward her slightly. *What am I doing, what am I doing, what am I doing?* No answers came, but that didn't stop her. Juliet brought her hand to Sienna's cheek. She ran her thumb cautiously over Sienna's jawline. "I think that, maybe..." she said, nearly choking on her words, "it *is* real." She inhaled deeply and leaned forward, brushing her lips lightly against Sienna's.

Sienna gasped lightly, taken by surprise. She didn't push Juliet away, as Juliet's chest pounded with about a million feelings. She covered Juliet's hand with her own and tilted her head slightly, parting her lips in what Juliet took as an invitation. The heat within her rose as she explored the warmth and wetness of Sienna's mouth. Sienna ran her tongue along Juliet's bottom lip, teasing her into oblivion. Juliet moved forward again, sliding her hands underneath Sienna, pulling her up and forward so she was straddling Juliet's lap, contact never broken. She felt Sienna grasp the back of her shirt, the material tightening around her midsection. It was messy and heated and desperate. For a moment, self-control became slippery. It had been so long since she'd been so consumed with anyone, and she forced herself to slow down and enjoy the moment.

She almost didn't hear the voice from above until it grew frantically closer.

"Mom! Mom? Juliet Mitchell! Are you in here?" Declan's muffled voice drifted down.

They broke apart immediately, but neither one of them moved. They stayed sitting in the same position as if time had stopped, as still as stone.

Chapter Nineteen

Reacquainting herself with reality, Sienna jumped up off Juliet's lap and tugged her shirt back into place. She carefully wiped her mouth with the back of her hand to remove any traces of errant lip gloss.

"We're down here," she yelled.

Juliet snapped back as well, racing over to the staircase. She straightened herself up in the same way that Sienna did, adding a quick pat down of her hair. "Dec! Open the basement door," she shouted, banging on the door with her fist.

"I'm coming!" Declan yelled back. There was a clamoring of footsteps. "There's no doorknob!"

"I know! Who's with you?" Juliet asked.

"Celeste. What should we do?"

"Is the other side of the doorknob on the floor? You should be able to slide it in and open it that way," Juliet said.

Sienna rubbed her hands together furiously. She joined Juliet at the top of the staircase, listening for their two-man rescue team to let them out. Silence hung in the air like a wet sheet, thick and suffocating.

"I don't see it!" Celeste yelled from the other side of the door. "It's a huge mess out here. I'll just break it down."

Juliet rolled her eyes at Sienna. "Okay, good luck. Declan, keep looking for the doorknob."

Sienna reeled from an immense sense of relief, but also with dread and disappointment. Everything felt different now, and as crazy as it was, she wanted to stay in that dark basement where things had been getting interesting.

"Stand back."

They backed down a few steps to give Celeste room to do her thing. Within seconds, a deafening bang shook the door and it swung open on protesting hinges. Celeste was standing there with an old fire extinguisher in her hands.

"You had a lot more momentum than I did, standing on the stairs," Juliet said.

Sienna gave her a *really* look and rushed over to Declan. She swept him up in her arms and clung to him tightly.

"Thank God you're okay," she said. Her eyes filled with tears.

"Sienna. What are you doing here? I thought you were in your office in the city!" he said, hugging her back just as tight. She couldn't remember the last time he'd been so open to affection.

"Go see your mom." Sienna let him go and Juliet was waiting for him with open arms. Sienna smiled as they embraced.

It took a few minutes for her eyes to adjust to the light, even though it was only a dim glow from a generator-fueled backup system. The station was largely intact, but a fallen tree had broken the glass of the entrance door. The branches had knocked all kinds of files, papers, and office supplies to the floor. It was a mess, but it could have been a lot worse.

Celeste wrapped her up in a bear hug. Sienna was surprised but hugged her back. "Can you even believe this?" Celeste asked. "When the warning came through, I didn't really take it seriously. We don't have tornadoes here. That happens out in Western Mass once in a while, not here. Are you guys okay?"

Sienna nodded. "Yes, we're fine. We got stuck down there when the tornado hit, and we had no cell service at all." She raised her cell to find that she still had no service.

"A tower must have been taken down. None of us have service right now," Celeste said. She turned to Juliet. "We don't have any reports of injuries or…worse, yet. I'm hoping everyone listened to the warning and got to a safe place. We drove by your house first, Jules."

"And?" Juliet asked, raising her eyebrows.

Celeste flinched. "Your roof was ripped clean off. There are about a hundred shingles on your front lawn. I'm actually glad you weren't home."

"Seriously?" Juliet yelled. She rubbed her temples. "Great. I better go take a look at the damage. I'll do that once we take a sweep through the town. I'm glad no one's been hurt, or at least that we know of. Looks like we have a shit-ton of cleaning up to do, though."

"Were you afraid?" Sienna asked Declan, who looked very much like a little boy in the middle of the chaos.

He shrugged. "Not really. I've seen enough disaster documentaries to know what to do. We went down to the custodian's room below ground. Coach just kept smashing us into this tiny little room, but it has no windows, so it was perfect. Everybody was good." He looked between them. "I was just worried about you guys."

Sienna rubbed his arm while Juliet cupped his face. He would normally *never* allow that kind of affection, so they had to take it where they could get it.

"Sienna, can you take Declan home? I'll take the ride with Celeste to make sure everyone is safe and has everything they need." Juliet looked around for her phone. She found it under a pile of paper clips and stuck it in her pocket.

They walked outside where tree branches and debris littered the street. A big blue mailbox was turned on its side; a swing set sat in the middle of the road as if it had been there the whole time. The sky had lightened to a muted gray, so at least they could see, but everything around them looked beaten and battered. The heavy rain had tapered off, but the soft breeze was still carrying the leftover raindrops.

Sienna's car had been spared. She brushed off a smattering of leaves and debris that covered her windshield and unlocked the car. "Come on, we'll go see how the house looks." Sienna waved Declan over to her.

"Jules, you can stay with us until your roof situation is taken care of," Celeste said, standing in front of her own car.

"Is it that bad?" Juliet asked.

"Yeah, it's that bad. I don't want you to be surprised when you see it." Celeste pulled up the collar of her jacket.

"I love you to death and I appreciate you more than you know. But I should really just get a motel room while I have it fixed if it's that bad. Your one-bedroom would be a little tight with me, you, and Brooke," Juliet said.

Sienna was about to offer up their house for Juliet to stay in, but she closed her mouth quickly. She didn't know where they stood or if Juliet was having regrets or if she could even handle her in that proximity.

"You can just stay with us," Declan said, putting the kibosh on Sienna's uncertainty. "It's not like we don't have the room."

Juliet didn't say anything, just smiled and nodded. She shot a quick look to Sienna, who was also silent. *No, we're adults. This is silly. One tiny kiss doesn't change everything. There's no use being all dramatic about it.*

"Of course, you should stay with us." Sienna touched Juliet's shoulder. "It wouldn't make sense for you to spend the money on a motel when we have three spare bedrooms."

Juliet coughed. "Thank you. Maybe Celeste is exaggerating, as usual, and I won't need a place to stay after all."

Celeste smiled and gave Juliet the finger. "I have to go check on Brooke's parents when we're done. I don't think their street was even touched, but I promised her I'd go have a look."

"Thanks again," Juliet said, bringing her hands together in prayer formation. "Love you."

Sienna waited while Declan climbed into her car. She looked over at Juliet, their eyes met, and they both looked away. At some point they'd have to talk about what had happened, but now wasn't the time. Juliet and Celeste drove off, their lights flashing, but the siren off.

Sienna and Declan took a detour by their house, which was completely undamaged. There were some branches strewn around the property, and it looked like one of their wrought iron streetlamps was bent, but other than that, it was untouched by the twister. She caught a glimpse of Will using the net to clear the pool of sticks and leaves. She winced internally at how little she'd worried about him through all this.

"Dad came by the school before he went home, so I knew he was okay. Like I said before, we both thought you were in the city," Declan said. "The whole thing kinda feels like a dream."

"It certainly does," Sienna agreed, looking over at Declan. "We're all very, very lucky."

She pulled up to the curb outside of Juliet's house. It really was as bad as Celeste had said. There were two-by-fours and shingles and bricks from her chimney all over the place.

"You okay?" Sienna asked, noticing Declan's slack-jawed expression.

"Yeah." Declan walked around back to survey the damage in the backyard.

Sienna waited outside, leaning against her car. Declan was picking up small pieces of debris, shoveling sand against the tide, but she wasn't about to stop him. She was chilled, even though it was quite warm out. It was entirely possible that she and Juliet could chalk what happened in the basement up to a stress-fueled reaction to a tragic situation. They could go back to their easy conversations, their flirtatious and then close-then-distant-then-close-again friendship that they'd been engaging in for the last few months. It could be done. It would be a little harder waking up to Juliet in her house for the foreseeable future, but it could be done. What other choice was there?

Chapter Twenty

All hands were on deck. Quinlan and Celeste had just finished hammering a piece of plywood over the broken windowpane of the police station door. When she'd been out with Celeste, Juliet had prepared herself for the worst. Luckily, the tornado had confined the bulk of its damage to property. Life and limb had been spared. Leland and Deagle were out patrolling the community again, making sure that everyone was safe and that the elderly and disabled were taken care of. And Juliet was collecting the paperwork and files that had been scattered everywhere.

"Just hung up with MEMA. They'll be coming first thing in the morning to survey the damage and see what kind of relief we can get. Power crews are already out and about trying to restore the electricity, but that could take up to a few days. Jeffries, what kind of calls have been coming through from the public?" Quinlan pushed his glasses up on his head and sighed. Juliet didn't think she'd ever seen him so fatigued.

Celeste grabbed her notepad. "Could be worse, Chief. Reports of some minor injuries, those people have been taken to Coastal Creek either by ambulance or by themselves. People are upset, of course, but all in all everyone seems to be handling it okay. We've put the word out that electricity may not be restored right away, and that always causes a minor panic. The town council is setting up cooling stations and buffets in the high school gym using their backup generator. If nothing else, this storm will break the heat. We're really lucky, Chief. No deaths and no serious injuries. It seems the worst to come out of this is property damage."

"Great news," Juliet said, along with the chorus of the others agreeing with her. She wished her house hadn't been hit *quite* so badly, but she was still grateful that everyone had made it out of the storm with their lives intact. "We'll need to get that basement door fixed, but I just stuck a wedge under it for now to keep the door closed."

Nobody seemed to care much about the broken basement door, but Juliet decided she'd be sure to put some emergency supplies down there. Just in case.

By the time they'd finished getting everything in some semblance of order at the police station, it was nearly ten o'clock. Juliet was exhausted, but the thought of going to Sienna's worried her. Sienna and *Will's*. But if she didn't accept their invitation, it would open up a whole line of questioning she wasn't prepared to deal with. If she could just get the thought of Sienna's mouth on hers out of her head, it would make the whole thing a lot more manageable. But that was easier said than done. Every time the image of the two of them on the tablecloth in the basement snuck into her mind, her stomach would do flip-flops and her face would flush. This was madness.

Once she was in her car, she shook her head, trying to rid herself of what she was feeling. There was too much going on, too much work to be done to spend time pining over someone she couldn't be with.

She drove slowly up her driveway, not allowing herself to grasp the full impact of the fact that her house was in shambles. She wanted to cry, which would have been a perfectly normal response, but she pushed it down. Her roof was completely obliterated. If anything, Celeste had *understated* the damage. Juliet stepped over a few shingles and shoved open the door. She stood in the hallway, looking up at the night sky. Stars were everywhere now, a cruel erasure of the tempest that had blown through just hours earlier. She hurriedly packed a bag with some clothes, some toiletries, and a phone charger. She took the family photos from where they'd hit the floor and wrapped them in an old T-shirt. She contemplated taking them, along with the lock box that held her passport and other important documents but left them under the bed instead. The house wasn't any less secure than it was when it had a roof, since all the walls had remained intact, and it wasn't like someone was going to scale them to go through the debris inside. She locked the door behind her and cast one last glance at the damage before she drove away. *It doesn't matter. It's just a thing, and things can be replaced. I'm very, very lucky.*

Juliet pulled up to Sienna's house and parked behind her Volvo. She grabbed her duffel bag from the back seat and slung it over her shoulder. She felt like she'd been in the same uniform for a week and she desperately needed a shower.

"Hey, Mom," Declan said as she dropped her bag on the floor near the door. "Look at us, one big happy family."

He was clearly joking, but Juliet could only manage a half smile. "Yeah, look at us."

"Jules, Dec told me about your house. That totally sucks. I called Brian Walsh in Nashua, remember him? He's going to come out tomorrow to see what needs to be done and how quickly they can get it fixed," Will said. He gave her a quick hug before picking up her bag.

Yes, Juliet remembered him. He was a townie who had moved north after college and opened up his own contracting business. She was so ecstatic someone was coming to help she considered throwing her arms around Will and squeezing him until he cried for help.

"That's amazing. Thank you so, so much. I didn't even know where to begin. My brain is complete mush at the moment."

"No problem," he said. "You know you're welcome here as long as it takes."

Sienna came in from upstairs and seemed startled at the sight of Juliet. The feeling was mutual. "I didn't even hear you come in," she said.

Juliet noticed that she had showered and put on comfy clothes, black yoga pants and a baggy yellow tank top. She looked absolutely adorable.

"Yeah, I just got here, actually. You wouldn't know the town was without power," Juliet said. Declan was already flipping channels on the television.

"I'm glad Will had the foresight to have a whole-house generator installed. We thought it would be more for snow than tornadoes, but the end result is the same." Sienna shrugged.

"Definitely. Do you mind if I grab a shower?"

"Of course," Sienna answered. "Follow me, I'll show you to your bedroom."

Juliet swallowed and walked behind Sienna. Her hair was still damp, and her body smelled like a mixture of baby powder and lotion. It was intoxicating.

"I'm sorry," Juliet said when they were well away from the living room. "I know this is awkward."

Sienna turned to her. "It doesn't have to be. What happened down there was a reaction to what was happening around us. I don't want you to feel like I'm some sort of predator who'll be waiting to jump on you at any moment. I'm not. We can talk about it later if you want, or we don't have to talk about it at all. It's completely up to you." Sienna toyed with the hem of her shirt and looked straight ahead. Juliet's heart sunk in her chest.

"I think we should. You know, talk about it. We can wait until a better time, though, that's fine. I know we're both exhausted. I'm just going to get clean and then fall right into bed." Juliet avoided Sienna's eyes at all cost.

"Sure," Sienna said. "The bed has fresh sheets and there's an extra blanket in the closet if you get cold. I'll be in my room if you need anything." She pointed to the far end of the hallway. Sienna hadn't been kidding. She really had put Juliet in the guest room farthest from her.

"Thank you," Juliet muttered as Sienna closed the door behind her. The room was tastefully decorated in earth tones, with a small television perched on the side of the dresser. The attached bathroom had a stand-up shower and a double sink. No wonder Declan enjoyed spending time there. Everything was neat and organized and she'd feel comfortable eating off the spotless floor. It sparkled like floors do in commercials.

And the shower was exactly what Juliet needed. She scrubbed her face with a bar of Ivory, probably a little harder than she needed to. She wasn't trying to remove Sienna from her lips; she was trying to wash away the *feelings* that had welled up inside her when their lips had touched. Her son, Sienna's stepson, was just down the hall. Will, her friend, Sienna's estranged husband, was in the pool house, which could be seen from the bathroom window where Juliet had just pulled down the blinds. There had been a sort of flirtation between the two of them since that day in the car, and while they'd both semi-acknowledged it that night at Neptune's, Juliet had sealed the deal in the basement. It was no longer a hushed secret or an unspoken crush. It was there, out in the open, and they'd both felt something. It would be hard to ignore that going forward. Juliet continued to scrub until her skin was a bright pink.

❖

The following morning, Juliet finished buttoning her uniform and headed out before anyone else was up. She'd slept pretty well considering she was in a strange bed, while a few miles away her own house was in ruins. It was much earlier than she was used to, but she didn't think she had it in her to make small talk.

She drove by her house on her way to the station. Nothing much had changed in the few hours or so since she'd seen it last. Shingles and wood were everywhere. She was lucky her windows had all remained intact. Juliet sighed deeply and continued on to work.

Quinlan and Leland were already there. The smell of fresh coffee was a perfect invitation to begin what would probably be another shit storm of a day.

"Morning, L.T.," Leland greeted Juliet at the Keurig machine. "You're all set with the library at this point, right?"

Juliet frowned. "We've been over everything in the building, yes. Why?"

"It's our biggest public structure that didn't sustain any damage. Town council has set up relief in the school gymnasiums today for those who had their houses destroyed or badly damaged, but we want to get the kids back on their normal routine as soon as possible. The chief gave me the okay to set something up in the library. It's comfortable and spacious and there's plenty to keep small kids and adults alike entertained. And honestly, it's been closed long enough. We have to reopen it." Leland said the last part softly, like she expected Juliet to take issue with it.

She knew it had been closed too long already, and if they were in a city district, it most likely would have been reopened the following day. But since the town was small, and law enforcement was on her side, she had the luxury of keeping the public out of the one place she felt like she'd be able to find a link to Richard Kowalski's murder. The heart medication that had presumably been used to kill him was kept in his desk. Thirteen pills were missing from the bottle. Tara Wolfe's secrecy and Richard's booze and the way he must have stumbled out of there...Juliet shook her head. If the county detectives wanted to come in and close it as suicide, there wasn't much she could do to stop it. She just had to try to work smarter and faster.

"Sure." Juliet dumped a packet of sugar into her mug and stirred furiously. "Just keep Kowalski's office locked up, okay? I don't want anyone in there for any reason."

Leland nodded. "Of course, Lieutenant. We can do that."

Juliet's cell phone buzzed as she sat at her desk. MEMA would be there soon, and she was sure calls would start flooding in once people realized what hazards the storm had left behind.

The text was from Will. *Heard from Brian. Good news. They can have a new roof installed in about a week. I told him to go ahead and get started today. You'll be back home in no time, Jules. We'll figure out the insurance thing after the fact.*

Juliet sent him back a quick thank you with a bunch of hearts while guilt flooded her, hot and uncomfortable. He was a good man, and a good friend, and all she could think about was his wife. She cracked her knuckles and shoved the phone to the side of her desk. She officially felt like a living, breathing, piece of shit.

Chapter Twenty-one

Sienna planned on heading over to Gretchen's house as soon as she was finished with her oatmeal. She'd assumed that a good night's sleep would provide some much-needed clarity, but it hadn't worked. She hadn't slept well, and she still had zero clarity.

It was odd that a tornado in their small town was the secondary news item on her mind. She could easily explain the kiss away if she tried. Moments before, they'd feared for their lives. People always did crazy things when they thought they might be at the end. One last conversation, one last reflection, one last human touch before it all gets swallowed into the darkness. The fact that they were out of danger when the kiss happened had little bearing on the situation. Could have been delayed panic, that sort of thing happened all the time.

There had been nothing concrete said or done that had led up to that moment. Sienna was attracted to Juliet, which had never been in question. She'd been fairly confident that Juliet found her attractive as well, especially after their conversation at the beach. But it didn't matter, because their family dynamic was too enmeshed to allow any sort of romantic entanglement between the two of them. It was an exciting dream, nothing more. A beautiful moment that would ignite the butterflies in her belly and the heaviness in her heart, but Sienna had the good sense to acknowledge it for what it was—a moment.

As she walked outside, Sienna saw Will sitting on one of the chaise lounges speaking to someone on the phone. He held up his hand to wave good-bye, which Sienna returned. Declan had still been sound asleep in his room, grateful for an unexpected day off from school after the terror of the previous evening.

The air was still damp, and clouds covered the sky. It was noticeably cooler than it had been over the last few days, and it finally felt like fall. Sienna grabbed the light sweater on her back seat and draped it over her shoulders.

Gretchen's house hadn't sustained much damage, thankfully. Her chain link fence in the backyard had taken a beating. A few panels were completely flattened by wind and debris, but otherwise her property was in good shape. Sienna was grateful; she didn't think Gretchen would be able to deal with the house she and Richard shared together being ripped to shreds. Monique's car was parked in the driveway.

Sienna put on the sweater she'd been carrying to fight off the chill she couldn't seem to shake. Monique answered the door, apparently surprised to see her.

"Yes?"

"I'm here to see your mom," Sienna said. Duh.

Monique moved out of the doorway, her mouth pursed. All of the blinds were still down, and the living room was dark. The power crews must have been working double time, since the part of town Gretchen lived in had their electricity back already.

"Good morning, Gretchen. You okay?" Sienna asked, seeing Gretchen in her rocker with her eyes closed.

"I'm okay. Never in my life have I seen a storm like that come through. Those are the storms of the South and the Midwest, not the Northeast. I thought I was a goner. I'm thankful the physical therapist was here at the time. He carried me down to the basement like I was a sack of potatoes."

"I'm glad you weren't hurt. It was terrifying, that's for sure. The town's in rough shape, but the good news is that there were no fatalities and only minor injuries. We'll all be fine once the dust settles." Sienna gave Gretchen's hand a pat.

"I would've thought so too. But with everything that's happened lately, I feel like this town has a black cloud over it. Maybe we've done something to anger the gods and we just don't know it yet. Rich was the sacrificial lamb who got the ball rolling." Gretchen still lay back against the recliner with her eyes closed.

Sienna frowned and looked over at Monique.

"She's got it in her head that we're a cog in this grand plan of destruction. I tried to tell her she's being crazy, and Rich's death wasn't some great design. It was just an accident or a random act. But she won't listen."

"Well, she's certainly not crazy." Sienna looked at Monique pointedly before turning back to Gretchen. "I can understand why you feel that way, Gretchen. Something really terrible happened to your husband, and happened to you, and now our whole town was nearly wiped off of the map. Of course it seems like the world is coming to an end. I'd be concerned if you *didn't* feel that way."

"You're a good girl," Gretchen said, nodding slowly.

"I have a question for you," Sienna said. She needed to be delicate. "Did Rich drink much? And did you ever have a problem with it?"

Gretchen furrowed her brow and then chuckled. "Oh, you must have found his secret stash. He thought he was being so sneaky. He knew I didn't like drinking. My father liked the drink and he could be nasty. So, I never encouraged it. In the beginning, I used to balk and complain, but he never did abuse it. So, I let him think I didn't know, but once in a while I could taste it on his lips. Where was it? His trunk?"

"No, it was actually at the library. They're going to run it through some testing to see if there's anything there."

Gretchen pursed her lips. "I thought of something. It's probably nothing, but Charlie Goodman has a truck. I just don't remember if it's red or black."

"Mom, don't—"

Sienna held her hand up to stop Monique. She really seemed to hate her mother having any sort of feelings or opinions that didn't align with her own.

"Who's Charlie Goodman?" Sienna asked. "Should we invite Officer Leland or Lieutenant Mitchell over to take a statement?"

Gretchen shook her head vigorously. "No, no, nothing like that. I don't want to leave a trail of breadcrumbs that ends in nothing but a moldy loaf. They should continue looking for Rich's killer the way they've been doing it."

Sienna knew there were almost no leads and no evidence pointing to anyone in particular. But she obviously couldn't share that with Gretchen. "I think they'd appreciate hearing whatever you have to say. They're not giving up, but I'm sure they've hit a few roadblocks. They always do in these kinds of investigations."

"I'd rather just talk to you, if you don't mind."

Sienna wasn't sure if she'd be allowed to relay a statement from someone else, but she wasn't going to force Gretchen into anything she wasn't ready to do. She held up her phone. "Of course. Do you mind if I record it?"

"I'd prefer that you don't, if it's all the same to you. I'd like to have a conversation without feeling like I'm giving a statement."

"This is silly." Monique picked up the teacups from the coffee table and stormed into the kitchen.

Sienna ignored her. "Okay. Who's Charlie Goodman?" she asked again.

"He's an old *friend* of Rich's," Gretchen said. "I never liked him much. They met at an antique car show and got to talking about business. They kept in touch and Charlie decided it was finally time to go off on his own. He was working at some shop up north. Rich gave him a small loan some years ago to get his garage business off the ground. The plan was for him to be a partner, but it didn't work out. I told him that I didn't trust Charlie, but Rich told me I was too judgmental. Maybe I am. But Rich loved cars. We just never had the disposable income for him to have more than one. He always said he'd have a Corvette in the driveway one day." Tears filled her eyes.

"And you think he might've had something to do with Rich's death?" Sienna asked.

"Not really. But I noticed he'd started calling again. After years without a word. They had a falling out when they couldn't agree on how the business should be run."

"If he runs a garage, doesn't that mean he'd have access to all sorts of cars and trucks?" Sienna asked. She scribbled down his name and the few details Gretchen had provided on the back of an envelope she plucked from her bag. She was afraid if she pulled out her notebook and made it too formal, Gretchen would clam up.

"Yes, he would."

"Did you find him to be suspicious or dishonest?" Sienna asked.

"I didn't get involved with the business. Rich talked to me about it here and there, but I tuned it out. That was his thing, not mine. I don't know exactly what happened between the two of them, but I wouldn't be surprised if he was a questionable businessman. Like I said, I never did like him. But I don't see why he'd come after me. Or Rich, for that matter. It was just a thought."

"He *wouldn't* do that to you or Rich," Monique piped up. "I don't know him very well, but people just don't go around murdering other people because they had an argument a few years ago. That's just nutty."

"Monique, I think your mom is just trying to cover all the angles. She's not accusing anyone of anything."

"Don't you want to know who killed Rich? Who tried to kill your mother?" Gretchen sat forward, her eyes angry in a way Sienna hadn't seen before.

"Mom. I just want you to start trying to accept what most likely happened. Rich forgot he took his pills, took a few more, and by the time he left the building it was too late. And you even said yourself that you were driving slower than usual because of the dark. Maybe it was some kid who was trying to get around you, a punk. That happens a lot."

Monique was on her knees in front of her mother's chair. Her pleading with Gretchen to let go of her theories was the most earnest Sienna could remember seeing her, and it was good to know she could be genuine.

"No," Gretchen said. "He always knew when he took his pills. And from what the lieutenant said, he had enough in his system for about eight doses. He wasn't a fool, Monique. And he wasn't suicidal. So no, I *won't* accept what didn't happen." She paused. "If you two don't mind, I'd like to take a nap. Sienna, I know we said we'd start going over the bills and Rich's online banking thing, but I'm really tired. Monique called a friend over to look at my fence, so she'll be here for a while. At least until the nurse shows up."

"Are you sure? I don't mind staying. We don't have to do the bills today if you're not up for it." Sienna hated the idea of leaving Gretchen in such a state of upset, but it was ultimately her choice.

"I told you I'd help with the bills," Monique muttered.

Gretchen didn't acknowledge her. "Yes, I'm sure. Come back tomorrow."

Sienna gathered her things and said a hurried good-bye to Monique who was outside on the stoop, leaning on the railing. Monique just nodded at her.

Before driving away, Sienna dialed Juliet's number and stuck her phone in the cup holder. At least the damn cell signal had been fixed.

CHAPTER TWENTY-TWO

A nd everyone is accounted for?"
Juliet fought the urge to rub her eyes. She was tired and didn't feel like presenting a facade of solidarity behind the mayor and next to the chief while they spoke with MEMA. It wasn't that there wasn't solidarity; Juliet just didn't want to be there, among the people talking about red tape and making plans around budgets. She wanted to be at her desk looking over files that she'd read through a hundred times, in her own space without having to talk to anyone.

"Yes, everyone is accounted for. We've had some minor injuries reported, but there have been no fatalities. This is Chief Patrick Quinlan and Lieutenant Juliet Mitchell. Chief, Lieutenant, this is Mr. Mullen, the resource unit leader," the mayor told them.

"Good to meet you, Mr. Mullen," Juliet said, shaking his hand. She needed to focus. "Preliminary results put us at an EF2. They estimate that we had winds of about 145 miles per hour. We didn't set up any semi-permanent shelters, as we didn't feel they were necessary. Those that were displaced congregated in the high school gym, and a local motel is offering drastically reduced rates for everyone who needs to assess the damage and plan for repairs the tornado caused."

Mr. Mullen nodded, and Quinlan suggested they move inside the police station to discuss the red tape minutiae. The meeting wrapped up when the final budgetary considerations were finished, and Mullen left to finish surveying the area. Juliet exited Quinlan's office to find Sienna standing near the infamous basement door.

"Hey." Juliet motioned toward her office. "You looking for me?"

"I am, yes," Sienna said.

Juliet hated the way a blanket of tension seemed to be strangling them. She was angry at herself and, irrationally, angry at Sienna. Why did she have to be so attracted to her? Why did she have to *feel things* when she was anywhere in her proximity? Complications weren't part of her plans at this stage of the game. Juliet had decided a long time ago that she'd take life as it comes. And if something didn't feel right, then it was time to walk away. She was happy with her career, her social life, her home. The one constant in her life was her son, and she was perfectly fine with that. Nothing needed to change.

"What's up?" she asked, closing the door behind them.

Sienna filled Juliet in on her conversation with Gretchen about Charlie Goodman. "It doesn't sound like much, but it's someone Richard no longer spoke to who had a pickup truck."

Juliet nodded. "Yeah, doesn't sound like much at all. But I'll go check it out. Was that all?"

Sienna pursed her lips. "Why are you being so short?"

"Am I?"

"Just tell me, what's going on?" Sienna asked.

"I'm not being short. I have a ton of work to do and I have to get a jump on it. That's all." She could feel the petulance oozing out of her and she hated herself for it.

"You've been distant since last night. I get it, but I don't think this is the right way to go about it."

"I haven't been distant," Juliet said.

"Yes. You have."

"Nope, I haven't."

"Damn it, Juliet. Just stop it." Sienna slammed her hand on Juliet's desk, then straightened up immediately. "Sorry."

Juliet was taken aback but quickly regained her composure. "I don't mean to be distant or cold. It's just that everything is weird right now and I really don't want to stay in the house that you live in with Will. Seeing you in the same space makes it even weirder, and more...real, I guess."

"Juliet." Sienna's voice was soft. "What was I supposed to do? Tell him he couldn't come in the house? Don't you think that would have raised a few eyebrows?"

"Probably! And he's being so helpful with my house and he has no idea that I'm a terrible person. Maybe I should just stay somewhere else, like I suggested in the first place. I could take a week off and go spend some time with my parents in Connecticut. Or I could just go to the motel or I could sleep on Celeste's couch. Any of those options would presumably be less uncomfortable than staying at your house." Juliet felt a wave of guilt at the look of hurt on Sienna's face.

"Okay. I get it. Let me know what you decide." Sienna tightened her sweater and whipped her bag over her shoulder.

"Sienna, wait. I didn't mean for it to come out that way. I'm all jumbled inside, and I know I sound more like an eighth grader than a woman pushing forty, but this whole thing is messing with me."

"Do you think it's *not* messing with me? Juliet, I haven't had feelings for anyone besides Will in over a decade. And I haven't even had that with him in...well, a very long time. It's messy and it's unfair and part of me wishes that I could just go back to seeing you as Declan's mom, who shows up now and again and we make small talk about the weather and about Declan's baseball games and that's it. And the other part of me doesn't want that. At all."

Juliet didn't know what to say. She'd been so afraid of the things that she'd been feeling she hadn't given much thought to Sienna's mental state. She sighed and fiddled with the bobby pin keeping her twist in place. "I just think it might make more sense if I stay somewhere else. For both of us."

"I don't want you to go."

"Why?"

"I don't know," Sienna said after a moment.

"You're just a bundle of answers, aren't you? Same as me," Juliet said with a short, humorless laugh.

"Excuse me," Mr. Mullen interrupted, poking his head through the door. "Sorry to bother you, but would you mind giving me a tour of your power facility? Or leading me to someone who can? I can't seem to find the chief or the mayor."

"Certainly." Juliet grabbed a pile of keys off of her desk. "Sienna, can we finish discussing this issue later on?"

Sienna straightened her jacket. "Of course. Will you be coming to my office for the discussion, or will I need to find you elsewhere?"

Her meaning was clear. Juliet made a split-second decision that simply walking away from it probably wouldn't help matters much. "I'll see you at your office."

Sienna was visibly relieved. She excused herself and slipped past Mr. Mullen. Juliet watched Sienna pull out of the station driveway, and a swirling pit of unease settled safely inside her stomach. She led Mullen to the town's electric plant a few blocks over, which served only Shell Creek and Salt Creek. Her cell phone rang, and the caller ID showed that it was from the county lab she'd left the whisky bottle with. She left Mr. Mullen with the plant supervisor and took the call outside.

"Hello, Lieutenant Mitchell. The results have been emailed to you as well, but I saw a note that you'd asked for a call when the results were completed."

"Yes, thank you. What did you find?" Juliet asked.

"The bottle contained a mixture of rye whiskey and sublingual nitroglycerin. There is a trace of gelatin that suggests the nitroglycerin was emptied from capsules."

Juliet closed her eyes. So, someone had emptied Kowalski's pills into his whiskey. So far, the only people who knew about the whiskey were Kowalski and Tara Wolfe.

"Thank you. Were there any viable fingerprints left behind?"

"There were, yes. The deceased's fingerprints were on the bottle, along with another set we've been unable to identify. It's a partial print, and not a very good one at that."

"That's helpful. Thank you again," Juliet said.

"Not a problem and the detailed results are in your inbox. Have a good day."

Juliet ended the call and decided to go find the chief. If Kowalski had wanted to kill himself, he'd have taken a handful of pills and swallowed it down with his whiskey. What would be the point of emptying capsules one by one into the bottle and *hoping* to drink enough for the mixture to be fatal? No, that didn't make sense. Someone had emptied his pills into that bottle and waited for him to poison himself.

She jogged back to the station and opened the email from the lab to see if she could connect any additional dots before asking a few of Richard's family members and colleagues to submit fingerprints. She could always count on work to distract her from the mess of relationships.

CHAPTER TWENTY-THREE

Screams emanated from the television, the pulsing blue light in the darkness providing a much-needed distraction. Sienna shoveled a handful of microwave popcorn into her mouth while Declan sat on the chair across from her, scrolling on his phone.

"This is dumb." He kept looking up at the screen intermittently.

"Come on, this is a modern classic. The first of its kind to do the whole 'found footage' thing," Sienna said. The iconic scene of one of the campers with her face in the camera, nose running and all, was playing. "It's actually terrifying."

"Oh, please," he said, though he didn't look away.

A high-pitched witch cackle came from behind them and caused the two of them to scream. Sienna spilled popcorn all over her lap and Declan threw his phone to the ground.

"Wow, you guys are easy," Juliet said. She was laughing so hard Sienna could see tears in the corners of her eyes.

"What the hell, Mom?" Declan yelled. "You could have broken my phone!"

"Oh, this isn't scary, this is for babies," Juliet mocked him.

"Whatever. It's only because it's dark in here and you surprised me." He gave her an epic eye roll.

Sienna smiled at their interaction. They had a great relationship, and she was glad Declan had such a good support system. "Take a seat, we're getting to all the good parts now," Sienna said. She patted the couch next to her, trying to make it seem like everything was normal.

She sensed Juliet's hesitation, but Juliet sat next to her anyway. She removed her hairpin and let her hair fall over her shoulders. She looked good either way, but Sienna loved it when she wore her hair down. Not that it mattered.

"Give me some." Juliet took her own handful of popcorn. "We should take a field trip to Maryland to see if we can find the Blair Witch ourselves."

"You guys can go. I'm not wasting my time in the woods looking for some made-up witch." Declan scoffed.

Juliet looked at Sienna with wide eyes. Sienna caught her drift and covered her mouth.

"What?" Declan asked, seeming the slightest bit uneasy.

"Legend has it that if you say out loud that she doesn't exist, she comes and *proves* it to you. While you sleep. Why did you have to say that?" Juliet asked. Sienna had to give her kudos for how genuinely shaken she sounded.

"That's bull…crap."

Sienna uncovered her mouth slowly. "Didn't you ever hear about that girl in Delaware? She told her friends it was all a myth and that the Blair Witch could bite her ass. The next day, she was found floating facedown in a pond behind her house. And she *never* went near that pond because she was deathly afraid of water. It was ruled an accident, but everybody really knows what happened that night."

"Stop trying to scare me, it's not going to—"

"Behind you!" Juliet screamed.

Declan leapt out of his chair so fast he knocked it over. Sienna was laughing as hard as Juliet was, and at one point, Juliet put her hand on Sienna's knee. Sienna looked at it but didn't acknowledge it. She didn't want her to pull it away.

"You guys are dicks!" Declan yelled, fixing the chair.

"Language!"

"You deserved it! Go ahead and watch your stupid movie. I'm going upstairs to play *Smell of Death*," Declan said. He stomped away, but Sienna could see the hint of a smile on his lips.

"Keep the light on," Juliet called after him. She smiled again and took a drink of her soda. "It's always fun to scare the shit out of your kid. He's done it enough times to me that I feel sort of vindicated right now."

"Not sure we'll win any parenting awards, but you're right, that was good," Sienna agreed. Their eyes met for a second before they both looked away.

They finished the movie in relative silence, providing commentary here and there. When it was over, Juliet stood and stretched. She was still in her uniform.

"I'm gonna call it a night," Juliet said, bringing the empty popcorn bowl and soda cans into the kitchen. "It's been a very long day."

"Agreed," Sienna said. She followed Juliet up the stairs, taking a left toward her own room while Juliet went into the guest room. "Good night."

"Night."

Sienna changed into a silk nightshirt and turned off all the lights. She went through her nightly skin care routine, tried to read the book that she'd had lying on her nightstand for the last month, scrolled through her phone for a few minutes, and then decided that it was useless. Her brain was too full, moving from one subject to another and always back to the one person she shouldn't be thinking of. She stared up at the ceiling for a few minutes and then threw the covers off angrily.

She sat in the oversized chair near her vanity, still in the dark. Her nightshirt was tucked under her knees, her toes curling and uncurling in response to her indecision. She wasn't sure if she should just burst into Juliet's room and tell her that they needed to talk, or if it would just be awkward and tense for the foreseeable future. The door to Juliet's room was made of both iron and cardboard. Too much, not enough.

It turned out that she didn't need to make that decision. Sienna heard her door snick softly open. She watched as Juliet tiptoed into the room a few feet, presumably assumed that Sienna was sleeping, and attempted to slink back out.

"I'm here." Sienna broke the silence. She didn't bother to whisper. Declan slept like the dead.

Juliet jumped. "Jesus, Sienna. Why are you sitting in the dark?"

"Why are you in here?" Sienna asked, ignoring her question.

"I couldn't sleep."

"Neither could I."

Juliet closed the door behind her and stumbled in the dark until she was sitting on the edge of Sienna's bed. Even in the dark Sienna could tell she was hesitant and uncomfortable.

"Are you angry?" Sienna's voice was softer now.

Juliet chuckled bitterly. "Not for any rational reason, Sienna. I just don't want to sweep this whole thing under the rug and be weird around each other anymore. We can acknowledge it, get past it, and move on. We don't need that kiss to define what we are to each other. Or maybe we do. I don't know."

"We're treading dangerous waters." Sienna tucked her knees under her chin, suddenly feeling chilled.

"I know. But I feel like if I don't tread, I'll drown. We've been dismissing whatever this thing is between us for a while now."

"Okay." Sienna took in a monumental breath. "I've known this for some time, but what happened in the basement confirmed it for me. I'm attracted to you." That was putting it mildly.

"Same."

Sienna rolled her eyes in the darkness. "Good. So, we've admitted that we have an attraction toward each other. Does that clear anything up?"

"You know it doesn't."

"I do know that. Then maybe we shouldn't have to drag it out of each other. Just tell me," Sienna said, though her heart was pounding out of her chest. She was petrified to hear what Juliet had to say; she was even more afraid that she'd never hear it.

"This is hard for me, Sienna. I think, maybe, I mean, I'm pretty sure anyway, that this…is more than an attraction. I like you."

Sienna swallowed. "Okay?"

"Yeah." Juliet fidgeted on the bed. Sienna heard her foot smack against its wooden leg. "So, I think it's been a long time coming. Since that day we drove Dec to summer camp, there was like this little spark, and it wasn't huge or anything, but it was there, and it never went out. And then we went out for coffee and I saw you around a couple times, and it grew a little bit more each time I saw you, but I ignored it. And then we started working together, and it just kind of ballooned into this bonfire I can't control anymore. So…yeah."

Sienna could feel the vulnerability exuding off Juliet, which only made her want her more. Everything Juliet said stabbed her in the heart with an ice pick. She wanted to cry but pushed it down as far as it would go.

"I feel that way too, Juliet," Sienna said. She could barely elevate her voice above a whisper. "I'm trying to be rational about this, in any way that I can. I know a fair amount about the human psyche, and infatuations are common. Especially when the object of that infatuation is off-limits."

Juliet stood. She paced back and forth. "It's not an infatuation. I'm not interested in you because you're 'off-limits.'"

"How do you know?"

"I just know. This isn't my first rodeo, though it probably seems like it."

Sienna didn't want to push. This was the most open they'd ever been with each other, so forcing Juliet to admit something she didn't believe certainly wouldn't help the communication.

"What about Will?" Sienna asked.

"I love Will. I'll always love him, he's a good friend and a good father and we've been through a lot over the years. He would hate me if he knew how I felt. Same question goes for you, what about Will?"

Sienna sighed. "I don't want to hurt him. That has never been my goal. But we're not getting back together. I'll always care about him and he'll always be important to me, in one way or another. But I've let this linger for much too long. I've been ready to move on with my life for years at this point, but I was so determined not to hurt anyone or blow up a 'perfect' life that I just sat idly by and watched the days and nights pass in front of me. I can't do that anymore. I won't."

"And I am one hundred percent not saying you should. But you're not legally divorced yet. Wouldn't that be cheating? Technically?" Juliet sat back down on the edge of the bed and crossed her legs at the ankles.

"I don't know. I don't know the protocol for that kind of thing. It doesn't feel like cheating because it's been over for such a long time. Will would probably feel otherwise. Our hearing is set for December thirteenth and at that point it will be over. I'll be Sienna Carter again, and I don't really know who she is. But I have an idea what she wants." Sienna bit her bottom lip. It was vague, but not really. Juliet wasn't naive.

"Which brings me to my second point. When you and Will are finally divorced, aren't you going to want to go out into the world and see what's out there? Date around, do new things, be Sienna Carter, single woman, for a while? I'm not saying that if you and I...I don't know, but I'm not saying that it's instant commitment or anything, but I've been single for a while and I don't want...that. I know I'm being evasive, and I'm sorry, I don't mean to be." Juliet's leg was shaking as though she was leaning on a nerve.

"I understand where you're coming from," Sienna said. "But I'm not interested in being a serial dater. It's not my thing and it never has been. Remember, I was in my thirties when I met Will, so it's not like I have wild oats to sow."

She heard Juliet swallow hard. "Sienna. What if this is...fleeting? We have this Romeo and Juliet thing going on, and I won't deny it, I've thought about how this could possibly work and what effect it would have on our lives. But you have to understand my hesitation in blowing up everything I've worked so hard for, for a maybe."

Sienna flinched. Juliet was right, but that didn't make the sting any less biting. "Well, that hurt. But I do understand what you mean."

"I'm sorry. I know you love Declan, and I know you don't want to hurt Will any more than he's already hurting. Would *you* be willing to jump into something with me, knowing the damage it would do?" Juliet asked.

Sienna paused. Juliet had a point. What if they decided to give it a try and found they were incompatible after all? Juliet's life would be more difficult, for sure, and Sienna would probably lose Declan forever. "I don't know."

Juliet sighed. "Then I guess we're left with that. We can both acknowledge that there's something brewing between us, an attraction, a spark, whatever you want to call it. But we should probably let sleeping dogs lie. I want you to know this doesn't mean that whatever I'm feeling will just disappear overnight. From the time we've spent together, Sienna, and the way you've treated my son over the years, I can't express just how important you've become to me. I cherish our friendship, and I hope that never changes. I just don't want you to think that you don't mean something to me. Because that's not the case. At *all*."

Sienna nodded, swallowing the lump in her throat. "I feel the same way, Juliet. You've become a welcome fixture in my life and I'm happy with the way things are between us. We'll figure it out. And I do know that you're right. About everything."

Juliet stood. "I should probably go back to my room now. Big day tomorrow. Good night, Sienna."

"Night, Juliet. Sleep well," Sienna said.

Sienna walked past Juliet to climb into her side of the bed. She had so many feelings swirling through her that she felt almost dizzy. As she was about to pull down the comforter, she felt a hand grasp her wrist, sharply tugging her backward. She was about to ask what was wrong, but before she could form the words, she felt Juliet's other hand clasp the back of her neck and pull her forward. Their lips collided in a fury, Juliet wasting no time in thrusting her tongue forward, running it along the length of Sienna's lips. Sienna moaned, nipping at the tip of Juliet's tongue with her teeth. Their entire conversation was erased in a millisecond, and all Sienna could think about was that she wanted more, she wanted all of her, and maybe it was time to pursue what would make *her* happy.

Juliet pushed Sienna down on the bed and straddled her. Sienna grabbed Juliet's shirt in her fist, pulling her down firmly on top of her. She stifled a groan when she felt Juliet's body mesh with her own, her focus obliterated by the heat of their touching skin. Juliet responded, holding both of Sienna's wrists down at her side, while running her lips over Sienna's earlobe, her jawline, and over the taut muscles of her neck. Sienna trembled with a sharp intake of breath. It had been so long, so, so, long since she'd felt this way. Whatever was coursing through her intensified, heightened to the point of no return. Part of her wanted to cry, part of her wanted to scream, and part of her wanted to just melt into Juliet, so close that there was no way to discern where she began or Juliet ended.

Juliet seemed to sense Sienna's excitement, and thrust her hips forward, bringing the two of them even closer. She freed Sienna's hands, which Sienna immediately wrapped around Juliet's back, holding her as though her life depended on it. Juliet smiled into Sienna's lips. The reservations Sienna had had just minutes before were suddenly nonexistent, and she was almost certain Juliet felt the same way. Juliet didn't break contact, but she positioned herself so she could move her hand under Sienna's top, resting on the top button. It was as though she was requesting permission, and without thought, Sienna arched her back to grant it to her.

"Sienna?" called a hushed voice. "Where's Juliet?"

Juliet toppled off Sienna in a flash, nearly falling to the floor. Sienna sat up too fast, an abysmal mix of lightheadedness and sexual energy sending a wave of nausea through her. She cleared her throat in a panic.

Sienna flung the door open, frustration and longing threatening to break her. "What did you say?"

Will stood on the other side of the door, shirtless and tousled. "I couldn't sleep, and Juliet isn't in the guest room. Her car is still here, but I can't find—" Will broke off, noticing Juliet in the background. "Everything okay?"

"Yes, everything is *fine,*" Sienna said, irrationally angry at him. She didn't mean to snap, but at that moment her self-control was nonexistent.

"What are you doing in here?" Will asked.

Sienna saw Juliet's face fall in the sliver of light the hallway nightlight provided.

"She needed an extra pillow." Sienna didn't have enough time to decide if that was believable or not. "Her neck was bothering her, so I wanted to give her something to keep her...elevated." Not her best work, not by a long shot.

"Okay," he said. He looked confused but accepted the explanation. Juliet grabbed one of the pillows from Sienna's bed and patted it for effect. "Jules, I just figured you were still awake and might want to talk. I know it's been a hell of a few days."

Yawning, Juliet swept by Sienna dramatically. "I'm actually really beat, but we can catch up in the morning." She rubbed the back of her neck. Sienna wasn't sure if she was doing that to complement the story or if the stress of the moment had manifested itself into physical pain.

"Okay. Night, Sienna. Night, Jules."

Sienna stood at her doorway and watched as Juliet let Will get a few paces ahead of her before turning back to her. Sienna wanted to grab her by the collar and pull her back into the bedroom. "Good night," she whispered.

"Night," Sienna whispered back. It was going to be a long, *long*, night.

Chapter Twenty-four

Charlie's Auto Body and Repair was still closed. Juliet sat in the passenger seat of Celeste's squad car, sipping coffee. She was exhausted from lack of sleep and an overabundance of emotions and…other feelings from the previous night.

"I'm so confused," Celeste said, twirling the straw in her iced coffee. "You decided that the whole thing would be a disaster and then you kissed her?"

"I didn't say it was my finest moment." Juliet kept her eyes closed as she rested her head against the window. She regretted the contradiction of telling Sienna one thing and then doing the complete opposite…although, she didn't regret it as much as she probably should. "You can't say a word. Not even to Brooke. The whole thing is just so fucked up. I was in *their* house. He came looking for me to see if I was okay, for fuck's sake. I'm a terrible person."

"Oh, stop. It was a one-time thing, right? It happens. People are attracted to each other and it happens. Don't beat yourself up too much." Celeste checked her watch. The garage was set to open in ten minutes.

"Two-time thing. But I get your point."

"Wait, *two*?"

"The night of the storm. It was one of those panicky situations where we thought we were going to die." Juliet focused on a dusty tire outside.

"Oh, that makes sense. Except for the part where you already told me how it all went down, and your life was never in actual danger. Although apparently you left out one really big piece of the story."

"I'm conflicted. You're not helping." She rubbed her temples vigorously. "We should probably just not see each other for a while. I like her a *lot*, Celeste. More than I've liked anyone for a really long time."

Celeste nodded. "That forbidden thing always amps it up a little. What about Kellie? Maybe you could take it to the next level with her."

Juliet frowned. "It's not a swap meet. It's not like I'm going to trade one for the other. I like Kellie, but the connection we have is just…different. We enjoy our time together, but it never means anything. It's more physical and fleeting."

"As opposed to the physical and fleeting connection you have with Sienna?" Celeste asked.

Juliet sighed. "Physical, yes. Fleeting, no. I haven't stopped fucking thinking about her since that stupid road trip to New Hampshire. It wasn't as strong in the beginning, because I had no idea she would ever feel the same, but she's been there ever since. Like a little ghost that fades in and out depending on the background. It's pretty ridiculous, huh?"

"There he is." Celeste pointed to a hulking man with a graying ponytail and scruffy beard kick a rock out of his path and unlock the door to the garage.

"Let's roll," Juliet said, adjusting her radio and tucking her hat under her arm. The sky was cloudy and the chill that had settled in after the tornado remained. She'd worn her long-sleeved uniform and still felt goose bumps on her arms.

They walked into the dirty waiting room where an ancient cash register sat on a counter. A calendar with a barely dressed woman announced the month from the grease-stained wall. It didn't look like a business Kowalski would have attached himself to. "Good morning. I'm Lieutenant Mitchell and this is Officer Jeffries. Are you Charles Goodman?"

"How can I help you?" Goodman leaned back against the counter and crossed his beefy arms, his eyes narrowed.

Juliet's hackles went up. "We just wanted to ask you a few questions about Richard Kowalski."

"What about him? You girls knew him?"

Juliet cast a side glance toward Celeste, whose expression probably mirrored her own. Condescension wasn't new to them, but it still riled them up.

"Can you please tell us about your relationship with Mr. Kowalski? The last time you saw him, how your business arrangement ended, etc.?" Juliet asked.

Goodman threw a handful of peanuts into his mouth. "He was a prick. We had a deal and he backed out. Other than that, loved the guy. Will that be all, ladies?"

"Please answer the rest of the lieutenant's questions, sir." Celeste adjusted her holster, a microaggression Goodman seemed to notice.

"Well," he said, scratching his beard, "Kowalski hasn't been by here in a long time. Maybe a year. Probably more. He was a coward, plain and simple. Didn't want to face me. I needed a little start-up cash, which we agreed to split the profits on. He didn't have a whole lot of money, and neither did I, but we both loved cars. So we gave it a shot. Business was doing pretty well, and Kowalski was making a decent side living. He didn't want to give up his library job, although I don't know why any grown man would waste his time on books. I wanted to expand the business, and he freaked out. Wanted his money back and said that was the end of our partnership. Hell if I know why." Goodman shrugged and popped a few more peanuts into his mouth.

"What did the business expansion entail?" Juliet asked while Celeste took notes.

"Somebody I know wanted in on it, and it was one of those deals that I'd have been stupid to turn down. A guy I knew. Kowalski didn't want to let anybody else in on our two-man gig. Maybe he was jealous," Goodman said, wagging his eyebrows.

Juliet tried not to gag.

"So, you didn't move forward with the 'guy'?" Celeste asked, leaning forward into the word.

"Of course I did, I'm not an idiot. But Kowalski was out after that and he didn't explain why. Not my problem. I got the money I needed to expand and Rich the coward got his back."

"Who is the guy you've gone into business with?"

"Uh...Morris Bright. Cell phone number's shut off though. I'm sure he'll be by again soon, and I'll tell him to hop on over to the police station and look you gals up."

"Do you have an address for him? Or a workplace? Some way for us to get in touch with him?" Celeste asked.

"Nope. When we have business to take care of, he comes to me."

Juliet nearly rolled her eyes. As if he had a partner he couldn't contact. "Did Kowalski have any direct dealings with Mr. Bright?" Juliet asked.

"No, he took off before we had set up anything concrete. I just wanted him to look over some paperwork, calculate a few figures. He wouldn't even do that. He was kind of a pussy."

Juliet nodded, trying not to show her disdain. "Could we take a look at your accounting records?"

Goodman shifted uncomfortably. "For what?"

"We're just trying to fill in the missing pieces. Maybe the income generated from your business after Mr. Kowalski left compared to what was generated before he left could provide some valuable info. We'd also like to see a list of the cars that have been worked on over the last few weeks. Do you have a software program that keeps track of that for you?" Juliet asked.

"Nope."

"You must have records available in order to keep tabs on your customers and to file your taxes, Mr. Goodman."

Goodman uncrossed his arms and leaned on the counter. "I think we're done here, ladies. I don't have to show you shit."

Juliet smiled and looked down at the counter. A take-a-penny-leave-a-penny tray sat empty except for a twisted paper clip. "Yet."

They turned and walked out of the building, Juliet following behind Celeste. She decided to ignore the choice words Goodman was mumbling just loud enough for Juliet to hear.

"You think we have enough to get a warrant for his business records?" Celeste slid behind the wheel again.

"Definitely not. But he answered my question. Obviously, this business partner thing wasn't above board. Kowalski clearly didn't want anything to do with the new guy or what he was offering. There's more to it than Goodman is letting on. We need to look up Morris Bright when we get back to the station." She put on her sunglasses and glanced at a number of broken-down cars and trucks that littered the landscape. Not a red one in sight.

❖

Before heading back to the station, Juliet asked Celeste to detour by her house. The roofing crew was there, which made Juliet breathe a sigh of relief. She didn't think they'd need more than a couple of days to finish it up. Will calling their old college buddy and having them get to work so quickly was truly a godsend. The sooner she could be out of their house, the better, since she clearly had no sense of self-restraint.

They arrived at the station at the same time the glass in the doorway was being replaced. Juliet marveled at how things were being put back together, and soon it would look as though nothing had ever happened. Certainly not a momentous natural disaster. Sitting on Juliet's desk was a small white envelope with Lt. Mitchell scrawled across the front in messy black pen. She picked it up and turned it over, but there was no return address. Inside was a card-stock invitation to an impromptu benefit being held by the Salt Creek Fire Department for the affected citizens of the Shell Creek tornado. For the following night. Juliet sighed heavily and tossed it into her "in" box.

"You have to go, you know," Chief Quinlan said, standing in the doorway of her office. "They're trying to do something nice."

"I get that, but tomorrow night? Some notice would have been appreciated. You know I hate these things."

Quinlan shrugged. "They were going to do a fund me page or whatever the hell that thing is called, but the captain thought they'd raise more money if people could put faces to the stories that have been all over the news. I wouldn't mind helping the Java Room rebuild a little quicker. This swill tastes like dirt." He peered ruefully into his coffee cup.

"I just have a lot going on right now, with the house, and with Declan, and all of that. Not sure I'm in the mood for a party," Juliet said.

Quinlan narrowed his eyes at her. "Showing your face around the community is important, Lieutenant. Not that you need me to tell you that."

Juliet smiled tightly. "No, I don't need you to tell me that. You're right, sir. I'll be there, of course."

"I knew you would be. Make sure Jeffries and Leland show up too. I'll talk to Deagle. Between what happened to the Kowalskis and the damned twister, we could use a little levity around here."

"Will do."

Quinlan walked out of her office, leaving the door slightly ajar. Juliet booted up her laptop and searched the database for Morris Bright. The only hit in a fifty-mile radius was a Morris Brightman, and he was a ninety-three-year-old retiree in palliative care. Didn't seem to fit the profile of the criminal mastermind Juliet assumed she was looking for. Mo Bright, Moe Bright, and every other obvious combination of the name turned up nothing. So, either this guy had concealed his true identity or Charlie Goodman was lying. Neither scenario was out of the realm of possibility.

"Dammit, Rich," Juliet said, out loud and alone in her office. "You couldn't have just had a beer at home? I'm sure Gretchen would have been fine with one beer."

Celeste plowed through Juliet's open door with a piece of paper fresh off the printer dangling from her hand. "That print on the whiskey bottle ended up being too smudged. They couldn't identify a match."

"Of course they couldn't. Goddam it, we can't catch a break. It has to be Tara Wolfe's. Either she poisoned him or drank with him. She knew about the bottle, so there's a distinct possibility she could have moved it, picked it up, cradled it for all I know. Maybe she was just really careful." Juliet leaned back in her chair. She was frustrated beyond belief, in pretty much every area of her life at the moment. "I'll talk to her again. Oh, hey, you have to go to this thing," she said, pointing to the invitation without looking up.

Chapter Twenty-five

The bank's website was fairly intuitive, but Gretchen didn't seem engaged. Sienna showed her again how to add the amount of the bill and click pay. Richard had already set everything up, so it was just the monthly paying that needed to be done. Still, she wasn't having it.

"Gretchen, you can just write out checks if you'd prefer to do it that way. We don't have to do it online," Sienna said, as Gretchen seemed to be inspecting a plant on one of the end tables.

"No, Rich always said this way is easier. I wish I could just pay someone to do it for me. Monique said she'd help me with the money matters, but I hate to put her out. I never realized I was so dependent on Rich. Guess I'm not as modern a woman as I thought I was," Gretchen said. She laughed bitterly. "Nothing like being alone to show you what you can't do."

"It's perfectly normal in every partnership to have 'duties' one partner concentrates on. I'm sure there are many things you do that Rich wouldn't have known how to do. You told me that you were the cook in the relationship. Could Rich have cooked a pot roast?"

"No."

"You kept detailed logs of Rich's blood pressure and chest pain and the medications and doses that he was on. Would he have been able to answer his doctor's questions if you weren't with him?"

"No," Gretchen admitted, looking down at the floor.

"Sometimes you just fall into the things you're good at, or that you enjoy. A lot of people find bill paying and that kind of organization relaxing. I'm not one of them, mind you, but a lot of people are." Sienna gave Gretchen a light nudge with her shoulder.

"Are you going to that benefit thing tomorrow night? One of Rich's buddies at the fire department in Salt Creek asked if I'd be okay with him honoring Rich. He did a lot of volunteer work with them in his younger days," Gretchen said.

"I wasn't planning on it," Sienna said. "I have a lot going on right now, so I'm not really in the mood to be social."

"I'd like to go. But I want to be able to leave if I want to. I don't know if it'll bother me too much to be a part of it. A few friends from my knitting group will be there, but I feel distant from them. Since Rich died, I haven't really reached out to anyone. Monique said she'd go, but once she has a drink or two in her, there's no getting her out of *anywhere*." Gretchen checked her watch. "Speaking of Monique, she should be back anytime now."

Sienna could read the writing on the wall. She didn't want to go to the event, but she didn't want to let Gretchen down either. Getting out of the house for a night could be a positive thing for her, especially if some of her friends would be there. While it wasn't in the realm of her job description, it would probably be the right thing to do. Besides, she didn't want Gretchen to regret missing a memorial for Richard. "Would you like me to go with you?"

"I would, but I don't want you to go if you don't want to."

"No, it's totally fine. I'm sure a night out would do me some good too. Do you want to go in the wheelchair, or do you think you can manage with the walker? Your physical therapist said it's really up to you at this point, however you feel most comfortable."

"I'd like to try the walker," Gretchen said. She stretched out her legs. "The physical therapist said I have to use it or lose it. I told him to mind his own friggin' business," she said and then chuckled.

Monique breezed into the living room from the kitchen where she must have come in through the side door. "Are you two talking about that benefit thing tomorrow night?" She fluffed her bangs with her fingers and raised her eyebrows at Sienna.

"Yes. Your mom would like to go."

"That's fine, I'll take her."

Gretchen shook her head. "Sienna said she'll come too. I'd like her to, just in case it becomes too much."

Monique rolled her eyes. "You do know she's not your therapist, right? Or your doctor? I'm still trying to figure out exactly *what* she is, but I know it's not either of those things."

Sienna fumed silently. It wouldn't do her or Gretchen any good to get into a fight with Monique about her role in Gretchen's life. When she'd trained for her first job as a victim advocate in Western Massachusetts, her mentor had instilled that above all, their job was to help people in need. The job description was just semantics; if they could help a child feel less afraid in court by putting on a stuffed animal puppet show, then they should damn well do it. Sienna had always taken that to heart. She couldn't count how many trips she'd made to the grocery store, or how many games of checkers she'd played, or how many hands she'd held while tears were falling. But she'd helped people. And she was proud of that.

"I don't care what she's supposed to be," Gretchen said, waving her hand in Monique's direction. "She's my friend."

Going home presented a new set of issues. Sienna was equal parts excited and terrified to see Juliet. She still hadn't seen her after what had happened the night before. By the time she got up, Juliet was already gone. Based on Will's conversation with Declan, Juliet's roof would be ready in just a few more days. Sienna had felt like she was watching them through a haze of unreality. Declan had been eating a bowl of cereal and Will had been riffling through the junk drawer looking for a phone charger. Everything was normal. Except that really, nothing was normal.

Juliet's SUV was parked in the driveway when Sienna got home. She felt her stomach flip as she saw her through the windowpane, sitting on the couch thumbing through a magazine. She was wearing a tank top and skinny jeans and her hair fell loosely around her face. Sienna wondered how she'd never noticed just *how* sexy Juliet was before that baseball camp drive.

"Hey," she said, dropping her bag and keys on the table near the door. She could hear Declan up in his room and it didn't look like Will was home yet.

"Hey." Juliet looked up at her, and Sienna noticed the tiniest spark of light in her eyes. It made her stomach jump again.

"Hey." Declan bounded down the stairs two at a time. "What's for dinner?"

Sienna opened the fridge, which was sorely lacking. They hadn't been shopping in a while. "I could make spaghetti?"

"No," Juliet said, jumping up. "You don't have to cook, I'll make something."

"Great," Declan said. He clapped sarcastically.

"Don't you have homework? Study group? Sarcasm practice?" Juliet asked, flipping his baseball cap off of his head.

"Nope. I'm here for your entertainment all night long. Can we just get a pizza?" He gave Juliet puppy dog eyes and then turned them to Sienna. "We just went through a tornado and my dad is living in the pool house and I deserve a pizza."

"Really, Dec? We're going with that?" Sienna laughed. She thrust a menu from the counter at him. "Call it in."

Declan smiled gleefully and walked into the other room with the menu. Juliet smiled and raised her eyebrows in Sienna's direction.

"You're such a softie."

"What can I say? He knows how to manipulate me," Sienna said, shrugging. "When he was eight or nine, he'd throw his arms around my neck and tell me that he'd have nightmares if we made him eat cauliflower. That was always Will's go-to vegetable, so I used to load Dec's plate with rice or mashed potatoes so Will wouldn't notice the lack of cauliflower. It worked."

Juliet shook her head. "He loves you, you know. A lot," she said quietly.

"I love him, too."

"I know you do." They both looked away, focusing on anything but each other. Juliet yelled to Declan at the exact moment Sienna was about to suffocate from the silence surrounding them. "Get me a Hawaiian!"

"Gross." Sienna crinkled her nose. "Did you hear about the benefit thing that the Salt Creek FD is putting on tomorrow night?"

"Yep. I have to go. The chief is making us." Juliet chuckled. "That's super nice of them to do that for us."

Of course, Juliet would be there. "I have to go, too. Gretchen asked if I'd go with her. They plan on saying a few words about Rich. I didn't want to say no."

"That Charlie Goodman tip was actually a good lead," Juliet said, unscrewing the cap off of a Michelob Ultra. "Shady dude. I don't know why Kowalski would have gotten into business with him in the first place and I can understand why Gretchen isn't a fan. Goodman mentioned something about a new business contact that Kowalski didn't like. Supposedly, that's why he left Goodman's garage altogether. Can you see if she knows anything about him? Morris Bright, I think."

"Sure, I'll mention it to her. See if she knows anything else. She's so petrified that the case will be closed as a suicide. She's hell-bent on getting justice for him, which I understand. It gives her something to hold on to as well. The anger and the frustration are a lot easier to deal with than the grief," Sienna said.

"I'm confident it wasn't suicide." Juliet sat at the kitchen table, playing with the label on her bottle. "I'm just afraid that I botched my first murder investigation. I mean, shouldn't we have solved this by now? The chief said that we're following all the procedures and protocols, but Rich was a good guy and I want to do right by him. And I'm scared that I'm not."

Sienna sat across from her and straightened out the placemat. "I'm sure you haven't botched anything, Juliet. It's not like there are tons of leads or really anything that makes sense about this. Richard seemed like a man who lived his life on the up-and-up, and I don't think anything has come out to contradict that. Without a 'why,' it makes it a whole lot harder to figure out who would have done this."

Juliet nodded. "I've watched weeks' worth of security footage, and there's nothing that stands out. Mostly kids. I really wish the camera view extended to the damn mystery section. Would certainly make it easier."

"You'll figure this out. I know how hard you're working on it, and somewhere, I'm sure Richard does too," Sienna said. She checked the time and stood to get her wallet out of her purse. The pizza would be arriving soon. She placed her hand on Juliet's shoulder and squeezed lightly. "You're doing right by him, I promise."

Juliet reached up and clasped Sienna's hand tightly in her own. She brought it down and brushed her lips against Sienna's knuckles. The softness of her mouth made Sienna weak-kneed.

"Thank you," Juliet said.

Sienna swallowed hard as Juliet slowly let her hand go. *We're just friends. Just friends.* She quickly took a few bills out of her wallet and left them on the table for Declan to pay the delivery person. She told Juliet she had to go respond to a few work emails before the food got there, which was a lie, but she had to get out of that kitchen for a minute. Being in Juliet's airspace was proving harder and harder as time went on.

HEART OF THE STORM

CHAPTER TWENTY-SIX

Morris Bright didn't exist. At least not the one that Charlie Goodman had been referring to. Juliet looked through hit after hit in her database, all the way to California and back, and there wasn't anyone who fit the person Goodman had been describing. She'd hoped that would be enough for a warrant, but Quinlan had shot her down. There wasn't enough probable cause; it could have been a nickname, Goodman may have botched the pronunciation, that kind of thing. They were going to need to take another trip out to his garage. Maybe they wouldn't be as nice this time.

Celeste walked into her office and dropped a box of pastries on her desk. "Here, have a Danish. Also, Kellie is here to see you."

"Why?"

Celeste shrugged. "You're the lieutenant and she's a medical examiner, so I assume she has something to discuss with you? Or maybe she's here for a little physical, fleeting action? Hard to tell."

"Ugh, get out of here. Take the box with you. Wait, leave me a chocolate croissant," Juliet said. She looked up as Kellie walked through the door with a manila folder.

"Morning, Lieutenant Mitchell." Kellie greeted her with a sweet smile. They always used their professional titles in public, even when it was just the two of them. It was mostly a type of foreplay, but Juliet wasn't feeling it that morning.

"Good morning, Kellie. What can I do for you?"

"No, no, it's more what I can do for *you*." Kellie wiggled her eyebrow. "But in all seriousness, I have the official results from the Kowalski case. It was as we expected, methemoglobinemia is the cause of death. There were no signs of a struggle, or anything that would allude to one, so it's unlikely that he was physically forced to take the pills. Wish I had more answers for you."

"Thanks, Kel. Me too."

"Are you going to that benefit thing tonight? I heard some of the guys in my office talking about it, but I'm on the fence."

Juliet nodded. "Yeah, we're all going. All town officials need to show up as a sign of solidarity. You know, so no one feels like they're alone in this."

"Makes sense. I might swing by, I'll have to see," Kellie said. "Maybe if you're free after we can hang out." Her smile made her meaning clear.

Celeste poked her head into the office again. "Juliet, the victim advocate is here to see you as well. You're a popular woman today." She widened the door so Juliet could see Sienna standing behind her.

"We're just about finished here, anyway," Juliet said, her pulse quickening at the sight of Sienna, and a weird sensation of being caught with her hand in the cookie jar running through her.

"I have to head over to the city in a few minutes," Kellie said. She gave Juliet one last private smile before turning to leave. "Maybe I'll see you later."

Juliet gave her a tight-lipped smile and nodded.

Sienna turned to watch Kellie leave, before whipping back around toward Juliet. "Did she just make eyes at you?"

Juliet blushed. "No."

"Uh, she absolutely did."

"Maybe...I don't know. We've gone on a few dates, so I guess..." Juliet trailed off, feeling more than a little awkward.

"Thought so." Sienna smirked

"Why, you jealous?" Juliet asked, leaning back in her chair.

"Yes."

Juliet's stomach dropped at Sienna's directness. She didn't know what to say and words failed her entirely.

Sienna seemed to pick up on that. She closed Juliet's door lightly and sat across from her. She straightened her hair with her hand while Juliet watched her with fascination. She seemed so put together and so undone at the same time.

"Did you ask Gretchen about Morris Bright, by chance?" Juliet asked, focusing too hard on the pencil cup on her desk.

"I did. The name didn't mean anything to her. She said she'd think on it, but she couldn't remember ever hearing about him."

"Okay. Thank you. It's like searching for a ghost."

Sienna apparently wanted to cut right to the chase. "You snuck out early this morning. And yesterday. I hope you don't feel too uncomfortable at the house. According to Declan, you're not exactly a morning person."

Truth. "I just figured I should get an early start. And if we're being totally honest, it could be a little problematic, being a part of your morning routine, while things are so tense between us."

Sienna sighed. "Which brings me to my next point. It's complicated, which I realize is an understatement, but I thought maybe I should," Sienna paused, clearing her throat, "apologize. For the other night. What happened was—"

"Why are you apologizing? I kissed you, not the other way around. And I'm not apologizing for it. It was real, it was honest, and to be frank, it was amazing," Juliet said. She noticed a hint of color rising in Sienna's cheeks. They shouldn't have kissed, but there was no use lying about it.

"It was, I'll grant you that. But it certainly didn't help matters. We both agreed. There's too much at stake," Sienna said.

Juliet sighed and looked up at the ceiling. There was a small water spot on the drop tile that probably felt better than she did. "So, that's it? We just pretend like nothing ever happened and go on with our lives? I'm not sure I know how to do that."

Smiling sadly, Sienna plucked a piece of lint off of the chair she was sitting in and watched it fall to the floor. "I'm not saying we pretend it never happened. We both know it did. And I can honestly tell you that *I* won't forget that it happened any time soon. It was... well, you know. But anyway, we can try not to be uncomfortable around each other for the time being. That's probably the best I've got."

"Me too. And my house will be ready for me in a few days, which will make it easier." Juliet had a lump in her throat, as though their imaginary relationship was coming to an end, and she had to deal with the grief of it. Which, in a way, she supposed it had.

"I'll see you tonight," Sienna said. She walked out the door and didn't look back.

❖

The very last thing Juliet wanted to do was go to a party where she had to pretend to be happy. She rummaged through her drawers, even though they were covered with heavy plastic. The construction crew had covered as much as they could while her roof was still a gaping cavity. She was grateful they were almost finished. They hadn't even brought up compensation, so Juliet assumed Will had taken care of it. She'd have to pay him back as soon as she received the insurance check. Although everything was so chaotic at the moment, Juliet had no idea when that would actually be.

She selected a pair of black slacks and a silky lilac dress shirt. She had no idea how anyone else would be dressed, but she knew the chief wouldn't want them to look too casual. He was strict about the department maintaining a calm and professional exterior no matter what was going on around them. At first, she'd thought he was being a hard-ass for no reason, but as time went on, she'd seen the merit of that concept firsthand. Impressions mattered, both in and out of uniform.

Declan was going to the benefit with Will, though he had put up a fight about attending at all. Even with all of his teenage bravado, if Will gave him the "look," Declan backed down pretty quickly. Juliet had to bring on the tears to achieve the same effect, which was wholly unfair.

She drove in silence to the Salt Creek Country Club where the benefit was being held. She'd fiddled with the radio, listened to a little politics, got exasperated, played about three minutes of an audiobook she'd been trying to get in to, and finally landed on an eighties station playing "The Weakness in Me" by Joan Armatrading and decided she hated the radio and every song ever made.

The parking lot was full by the time Juliet pulled in. She checked her phone and it was still ten minutes to seven. She thought she'd be early, but it seemed like the entire town had already arrived.

The hall was impressive. There were hundreds of twinkling lights strung from the rafters, and bright flowers decorated the center of every table. A buffet station was set up near the dance floor, where a DJ was hooking up her equipment. The Salt Creek Fire Department had really outdone themselves.

Her breath halted in her throat when she caught a glimpse of auburn hair, but it wasn't who she was looking for. False alarm. She relaxed a little. And anyway, she really shouldn't be so fixated on when and how Sienna arrived. Their conversation had closed the chapter on the two of them and whatever it was they were feeling toward one another. It was the right thing to do.

Juliet felt a tap on her shoulder. She turned to see Officer Deagle behind her, looking sharp in his full-dress uniform.

"Evening, L.T.," he said, straightening his tie. "Chief wanted me to make an appearance. I thanked everyone from Salt Creek and grabbed a plate from out back. The chicken, broccoli, and ziti is amazing, try it. I have to get back to the station to hold down the fort, in Chief's words. I'm sure there'll be at least one noise complaint, since we're supposed to get a thunderstorm later tonight."

Juliet laughed. They'd always get someone calling in about an explosion or fireworks, and they'd have to explain that thunder sometimes happened during the warmer months. It was a running joke at the station. "To be honest, I wish I was going with you. I'm not really in the mood for a feel-good community get-together at the moment."

"Your roof coming along?"

"It is, yeah. Should be done soon," Juliet said. She was thankful he led with that. She should have just wished him a good night and been done with it, but she'd felt the need to share her frame of mind for some inexplicable reason. "I'll be fine."

Deagle nodded. "Stay for a little bit and then sneak out the back. Chief will never notice once he gets a few G&T's into him. See you tomorrow."

"Hey there, Lieutenant," a sultry voice from behind said. "You look amazing."

Juliet whipped around to see Kellie standing behind her, looking flawless in her black business suit. "Oh, hey, Kellie. You made it after all. You look nice."

Kellie narrowed her eyes. "Have you been distracted lately? I texted you a few days ago and never heard back."

"I am so sorry, I completely forgot. There's definitely a lot going on. The case, family, fixing my house, you know the drill. Maybe we can catch up at work next week," Juliet said. She wasn't interested in getting together with Kellie in their usual way and didn't want to leave that possibility dangling.

Kellie seemed surprised but composed herself quickly. "Okay, we can do that." Her air of professionalism returned. "I have to go say hello to the chief, so if you'll excuse me."

Juliet sighed. She wasn't trying to make Kellie feel minimized, but letting people down was something she could comfortably add to her résumé at this point.

Juliet took a seat at one of the round tables, the white tablecloths making her nervous as she placed her wine glass in front of a place setting. She heard a familiar laugh and looked up to see Will standing at the entrance, shaking hands with Chief Quinlan and reintroducing him to Declan, even though Declan had met the chief at least fifty times in his short life. Juliet felt a surge of pride at Declan's appearance. The kid cleaned up nicely. His sandy hair was combed back, and he had on a black dress shirt with pressed jeans and a pair of black dress shoes. She wondered if Sienna had assisted with that. Declan had never ironed anything in his entire life. Will was impeccably dressed in a suit, of course.

She was about to walk over to say hello when the side door, the handicap entrance, opened slowly. Gretchen Kowalski and her daughter, Monique, walked in, Gretchen taking small, slow steps up the ramp while using a walker. Behind them, Sienna carried Gretchen's coat and purse.

Juliet swallowed hard, unable to look away. Sienna looked like she'd walked straight out of an expensive perfume commercial. Her hair was styled perfectly, with tiny wisps blowing gently in the breeze, her makeup was subtle but accentuated her features like she'd been airbrushed, and her scarlet A-line dress wrapped around her body elegantly, the soft chiffon swaying with her every move. She looked directly at Juliet, who realized she'd been openly staring. She dropped her phone and startled as it clanged loudly to the parquet floor. This was going to be a long night.

CHAPTER TWENTY-SEVEN

Seats were filling up fast. Sienna scanned the room for an empty table, but they mostly had at least a person or two saving a seat with a purse or a jacket. She looked over and saw Juliet standing next to a table, her gaze almost predatory, and her stomach jumped. The way Juliet's waves, the color of sunset, draped over her shoulders and accentuated the hollow of her neck made Sienna smile. The night just got a lot better, and at the same time, a lot harder.

Juliet seemed to notice that Sienna was looking for a place to land, so she waved her over while Gretchen was thronged by everyone in attendance with a mixed bag of condolences and encouragement. Sienna looked at Gretchen to see if she was okay, if she needed help, or if she just needed to sit down. She appeared to be doing fine, and Monique was standing a few feet behind her. Sienna crossed over to Juliet's table and put Gretchen's purse and jacket over the back of one of the chairs.

"You look beautiful," Sienna whispered, as she passed Juliet on her way to the hors d'oeuvre table. She felt Juliet follow behind her until they were in lock step.

"So do you. I'm glad we had that talk earlier today, because I don't know if I'd be able to contain myself otherwise," Juliet said while she smiled at a firefighter across the room who gave her a wave.

Sienna's pulse quickened. "That's not helpful," she said, unable to contain a smirk. She took a few crackers and some cheese squares for herself, and a couple of spanakopita triangles for Gretchen.

"Hello, ladies." Will joined them at the buffet table. "You both look lovely. What's a respectable time to bag out of here?"

Sienna stayed silent while Juliet laughed and chided him for being a terrible member of the community. He nudged Sienna with his elbow.

"That is *not* true. We ran the dunk tank in 2015, remember?" he asked, smiling softly at Sienna. "You collected the money and I went for a swim. Many, many times."

She smiled back at him, but the mixture of emotions that churned within, being sandwiched between Will and Juliet, was too much. "Yes, I do remember that. Declan saved up his allowance for weeks to take a shot at you."

"Big deal. I had to go to that carnival every single year and watch the mayor make an ass of himself at the water gun game and then come up with fifteen excuses as to why he didn't win. It's like *Groundhog Day* at that thing." Juliet popped a pepperoni into her mouth.

More than anything, Sienna suddenly wanted to get away. She felt like an intruder in a relationship that had overcome so much and had been so uncomplicated until she'd seen Juliet in a new light. Since then, she'd seen nothing and no one else. She breathed deeply and excused herself, nearly jogging over to Gretchen and Monique.

Music started playing loudly, and people began to flock to the dance floor. If nothing else, the Salt Creek FD threw one hell of a party. She had to shout over the din for Gretchen to hear her.

"I'm just going to grab some air, okay? I'll be back in a few minutes," she said.

Gretchen nodded. "You were right, I'm glad I came tonight. The captain showed me a picture of a beautiful bench they're donating to the library. It has a plaque dedicated to Rich, and on each side of it, a book is engraved. Isn't that wonderful?"

Sienna smiled genuinely and rubbed Gretchen's shoulder. "It is. I'm sure it will get a lot of use too, which is exactly what Rich would want."

Gretchen patted her hand affectionately and turned to a few women from her knitting group who were waiting to speak to her. She seemed to be the belle of the ball even though the benefit didn't have much to do with what had happened to her and Richard. Still, Sienna was happy for her. It was a much-needed distraction from all of the horrible things she'd been through.

The sun had fully set, and a light breeze had taken hold. Sienna wished she'd worn a jacket of some sort, but she hadn't planned on being outside. She rubbed her arms and walked toward the veranda where an ornately decorated archway stood at the entrance. The ocean was crashing along the rocks, the steady hum of the tide providing the perfect soundtrack to the evening. Sienna wondered why she didn't seek out the solace of the ocean more often. One of the hazards of living in a coastal town was taking the sea for granted.

She sat on one of the built-in wooden benches, her legs crossed, and focused on the choppy waves. She had to move out of the house. It was time. Lines were blurred and she was tired of avoiding Will. Declan was still blissfully ignorant, and she didn't have the heart to tell him that it was really and truly over, that the family unit they'd created was about to splinter. As much as Sienna had told him that things wouldn't change between them, the reality was that things *would* change. Maybe not in their hearts, but their day to day lives would never be the same again.

"Hey," a voice said from behind her.

Sienna would know that voice anywhere. "Hey," she said, not turning around. She didn't know if she could face Juliet at that moment. There was too much, and it was all at the surface, threatening to spill over.

"The party is actually pretty great," Juliet said. "Really well done for such short notice. And the wine is flowing a little too easily." She swished the wine in her glass from side to side.

Sienna didn't think she could deal with small talk. "Yes, it is."

Juliet sighed heavily. "Okay, I guess I'll go back in then. You probably came out here for some alone time, anyway."

A fast dance song was playing inside the hall. They heard a loud "whoop" come from the dance floor. Sienna turned to see if she could catch a glimpse through the window, but it was just a big blur of dancing and laughter.

"You don't have to go in," Sienna said. "I should get back to Gretchen anyway."

"No, I'll go. I just hate that we're being all weird around each other. I miss being able to talk to you. It's all so confusing." Juliet ran her finger over the design on one of the pillars.

Anger suddenly welled within Sienna. She knew it probably wasn't sensible, but she couldn't stuff it. "Where is the confusion? We put an end to our little charade earlier this afternoon."

Juliet stepped back, seemingly baffled by Sienna's abrupt tone. "Our little *charade*? What the hell is that? I don't know why you're snapping at me, but that is totally unfair."

Sienna stood quickly, just inches from Juliet's face. "*That's* what's unfair? What we've been doing to each other for the last couple of months isn't unfair? How *fair* is it that I think about you every second of the day? I'm a middle-aged woman acting like a fucking teenager. How *fair* is it that I look at Will and I'm disgusted by the sight of him, because it means that I can't have you? How fucking *fair* is any of that?"

The air hung heavy between them. Juliet opened her mouth to speak and then closed it immediately. "It's *not* fair, Sienna. None of this is fair." Juliet hesitated. "You think about me all the time?"

Sienna laughed bitterly. "Yes, Juliet, I think about you all the time. I think about what your lips taste like, and how good you felt pressed up against me. I think about the constant roller coaster of emotion you trigger inside of me. I think about how the two of us actually being together would cause a huge rift in everyone's life and turn everything even more upside down than it already is, and that's what makes this *so hard* because it's all I want!"

Juliet stood stock-still, her eyes wide. Sienna didn't know what else to say, and she'd already said too much.

They heard a loud knock on the glass and turned to see Celeste motioning for them to come in.

"Well, of course," Sienna said. Time to pretend everything was A-OK again.

Juliet shook her head. "They can wait a few more minutes. Come here for a second." She extended her hand.

Huffing in frustration, Sienna clasped her hand and followed Juliet to a small area next to the building where decorative trees obscured the lights shining over the promenade. "The Way You Look

Tonight," the Tony Bennett version, was playing, and though it was slightly muffled, it served its purpose.

"We are so totally fucked up right now." Juliet closed her eyes. "You're always in my head too. No matter what I'm doing. I have this weird pit in my stomach that's filled with all these different things— guilt and excitement and fear and *possibilities*. That's the one that I can't escape. The one that scares me and electrifies me the most. The possibilities."

Sienna tried to fight the hot tears pricking her eyes. "Juliet, someone is going to come looking for you. Every police officer in a twenty-mile radius is inside—"

"Shh," Juliet said with a soft smile. She pressed her index finger to Sienna's lips, and then dropped her hand to take Sienna's hand in her own. She put her other arm around Sienna's waist and pulled her close.

Sienna began to protest. There were too many people nearby and there were too many sensations and too many emotions that could bubble over at any moment, and Sienna was afraid that if she let herself plummet into what Juliet was offering she'd never recover. But it was too much to resist. Sienna let herself melt into Juliet, swaying softly in the evening breeze, their bodies moving as one. She breathed in, the scent of Juliet more intoxicating than any glass of wine. Juliet dropped her hand lower, resting it just above Sienna's panty line. Sienna didn't know if she was trying to tease her, taunt her, but it was working. Sienna trailed her fingers up Juliet's back, eliciting a shiver when she touched the bare skin beneath Juliet's hair. Though everything inside her blared alarms and raised an infinite number of warning signs, Sienna kissed Juliet's neck softly. Juliet leaned into her, tightening her hold on Sienna's back.

"They're about to do the toast for Mr. Kowalski," Declan called out, trudging along the stone path with his phone in his hand.

Sienna and Juliet sprung apart as if they were polarized magnets. Sienna turned to see Declan staring straight at them. "Um, Mom?" he asked, sounding very much like a child.

"Yeah!" Juliet answered, a little too loud and a little too enthusiastic. "Hey, Dec. I was adjusting Sienna's dress. Her dress. There was something weird with her...dress. We should go back in. Gretchen will want you there for the speech." She nodded to Sienna.

"Definitely," Sienna agreed, her heart beating so fast she wondered if it was possible it could burn itself out.

They walked quickly toward the door, Declan still staring at them. His eyes were accusatory, but Sienna didn't know if he'd actually seen anything, or if he was just questioning what he thought he saw. She hoped it was the latter.

They managed to avoid each other for the rest of the night, even though they were sitting at the same table for half of it. Sienna was able to partially focus on the benefit as support for Gretchen. She'd been in and out of tears since Chief Quinlan had started the toast, and at least half a dozen other people had spoken up to express their respect, sadness, and confusion at the loss of Richard Kowalski. Even Monique brushed at her eyes a few times. It ended with the Salt Creek Fire Department presenting Gretchen with the bench in Richard's honor, and the captain announcing the impressive totals collected toward offsetting the damage inflicted by the tornado. Aside from the gnawing havoc eating away at Sienna's stomach, and the anxiety and tumult within her chest, it was a good night.

Chapter Twenty-eight

Before the twister had torn the roof off her house, Juliet had no idea how long it would take to replace a roof and make a house suitable for living once again. She knew the answer now: too fucking long.

She walked into the house later than everyone else. Sienna had left with Gretchen. Will and Declan had taken off in Will's car, and Juliet had stayed behind with the rest of her team. She was thoughtful and quiet, but she didn't want to come off as uncaring. But she also couldn't face getting back to the house and having to talk to anyone, so she stayed to help clean up even though she didn't need to.

Trying desperately not to wake anyone, Juliet took off her shoes and carried them quietly up the stairs to her room. She threw her shoes into the corner before flipping the light on. She nearly jumped out of her skin when she saw Declan sitting on the edge of her bed.

"Mom."

"Jesus, Declan, are you trying to give me a heart attack?" Juliet asked, placing her hand on her chest.

"You weren't fixing her dress."

Damn it. She thought he might have seen something, but he didn't bring it up again at the benefit, and patience wasn't Declan's strong suit. She cautiously assumed he hadn't seen anything suspicious. It appeared she'd been wrong.

But maybe if she kept up the pretense, he'd question what he'd seen. She didn't want to gaslight her son, but neither she nor Sienna were prepared to have this conversation with their fifteen-year-old.

"If you must know, her underwire was poking into her, and I was just trying to—"

Declan shook his head. "Mom, stop. You weren't 'fixing' anything. You were dancing. Like married people. I saw you."

Juliet rolled her neck back and forth. Just how much was she willing to lie to her son? She'd always prided herself on being open and truthful with him. And now she was destroying all she'd built with him.

"Listen, honey, it's not exactly what you think. We were out by the ocean and neither of us felt like going in. The music was playing and it was all romantic, so we thought it would be funny if we danced together." Juliet swallowed the lump in her throat.

Declan frowned, shaking his head. "There was nothing *funny* about it. I saw you. Why are you doing this to Dad?"

"Come on, Dec. You're overreacting. Sienna and I are friends."

"Really? You're friends with Celeste, would you dance like that with her? You're friends with Officer Deagle, would you put your hand on *his* ass?" Declan asked, his voice raising an octave.

"Of course not!" Juliet answered, much too quickly. "That's different, they're both..."

"Both what? Friends?"

"Declan. You need to watch your tone. I understand that what you saw tonight was confusing, but that doesn't give you the right to interrogate me." Juliet was fighting a losing battle, but she didn't know how to stop the bleeding.

Declan continued to sit on the edge of the bed, his calmness and detachment both disturbing and a little intimidating. He knew what he knew, and Juliet didn't think she'd be able to change his mind.

"You're right, it was confusing. Because I'm pretty sure I saw you dancing, romantically or whatever, with Dad's wife."

Juliet covered her mouth with her hand and rubbed her cheek. "You need to talk to your dad about what's going on between him and Sienna. It's not my place."

"Not your place? You're my mother. What the hell is happening?" Declan said, finally allowing his emotion to get the better of him.

Juliet sighed. "They're not getting back together. She cares about him, he cares about her, but they'll be better off apart. It happens, sweetie." Juliet sat next to him, trying to decide how much she should tell him and how much she should withhold. She didn't want to destroy her entire family with a few unchecked words.

"I don't understand. Dad said it wasn't a big deal and the whole thing would blow over and he'd be back in the house in no time. Now you're saying that, what, it's over between them for good? Like they're getting a divorce?"

"I really need you to talk to your dad about this, Dec. He's going to be very upset with me if all of this comes secondhand." Juliet touched his knee, but he pulled it away from her angrily.

"Well, Dad is obviously a liar. So, both of my parents are liars and my stepmother is purposely keeping me in the dark. Boy, I hit the jackpot, didn't I?"

He was angry and hurt. Juliet knew he had every right to be angry and hurt. She just wished she could make it go away. "I'm so sorry, Dec. I know this is hard. I'll talk to your dad in the morning, okay? I'll make sure he has an honest conversation with you, so you don't feel like you're being blindsided. I'm sorry."

Declan nodded, but he was clearly still upset. "If Sienna's cheating on Dad, it better not be with you. That would just take all of this to a whole new level. I don't know. Just...don't." He walked out of the room like he couldn't stand to be in her presence for a second longer.

Juliet fell back onto the bed and tried to get her emotions under control. It didn't work, and she cried harder than she had in years. The last thing she remembered before sleep enveloped her was the sound of her own sobs. They'd both known better and had ignored the warnings. Now they'd have to pay the price.

❖

"Here are the reports on Charlie Goodman," Celeste said, dropping a few documents on Juliet's desk. "A DUI and a petty theft conviction, both in the eighties. He was arrested for being involved with a bookie in the early nineties, but nothing came of it. Squeaky clean for the last two decades. Another dead end?" She flopped dramatically into one of the chairs in front of Juliet's desk.

"Not necessarily. Probably, but not necessarily. You think Kowalski could have been a runner for him? Something like that?" Juliet chewed on her pen cap. She didn't believe that scenario for a second, but they had to explore every possible situation.

"No. According to his wife, he was either at the library or at home. I know spouses lie, but she seemed to have a good pulse on his whereabouts. He didn't have any drugs in his system, or anywhere else that we've found, so it's not like he was an addict that got involved with the wrong people. I think we should look at the assistant again," Celeste said.

"Tara Wolfe? She's odd, for sure, and totally inappropriate, but the timeline of Rich's death and Gretchen's accident don't make sense with her as the culprit. Unless the two things are completely unrelated, which is possible, but really freaking unlikely, we can't finger her for it. She seems pretty isolated except for a few acquaintances around town, so I can't come up with an accomplice. She could have paid someone to take care of Gretchen, but until we find out who was behind the wheel of the red truck, we have nothing. Did you keep an eye on her during Kowalski's honoring at the benefit?"

"I did," Celeste said. "She laughed and cried at the right times. She did seem to watch Gretchen and Monique an awful lot during the speech. Could have been watching for their reactions, or maybe she was feeling guilty. Hard to tell."

Juliet sighed. "I think it might be time to tell the chief that we've hit a wall. I really didn't want to do that, and I feel like a complete failure. But based on everything we know, I don't know where else to turn. Everybody in Kowalski's orbit either has an alibi or covered their tracks well. Maybe the county detectives can find something that we missed or that we haven't thought of, since they'll be looking at it with fresh eyes. If I read Tara's love letters or look at the DNA results of that whiskey bottle or try to search for Morris Bright one more time, I'll go insane. There's something there, something we're just not seeing. Was he hiding anything else? It sucks that we can't help our old friend."

"Don't throw in the towel yet. We'll set a firm date. If we don't have anything else to go on by, say, next Monday, we'll turn it over to County. Let's go talk to Goodman again, and maybe Gretchen has a few more tidbits that she can think of. Four days. That's it, and then we step back completely. Let someone else take the reins," Celeste said. She spread her hands out on the desk like she was a dealer at a blackjack table.

"Okay. Monday," Juliet agreed. Celeste was a good friend. She knew how badly Juliet wanted justice for Kowalski, and she knew that it would taste even sweeter if they could uncover the killer in their own front yard. But Juliet was realistic. She'd never investigated a murder before, and if she'd been in a bigger town with a bigger police force, maybe she'd have been given more tools, or learned other things that would have helped. She'd received a loud and clear answer to a question she'd never really asked. She was happy with her position on the small town force. She didn't need to be a detective or a flashy investigator to be happy. This was an aberration, not a career path. She considered it a privilege that she'd been afforded the opportunity to seek justice for a man who didn't deserve what he got.

Celeste left her office. Juliet began searching for all car-related crimes in the general vicinity of Shell Creek. Any mention of a red pickup or stolen vehicles. Something. Anything. It didn't surprise her when nothing seemed to fit; chasing shadows seemed to be her MO these days.

CHAPTER TWENTY-NINE

S ienna knew something was wrong when Declan brushed past her that morning without saying hello or good-bye, or even giving her his usual grunt as he headed toward his bus. Juliet was already gone, so she couldn't ask her. She peeked outside to see Will making his way toward the house.

"You have any OJ?" he asked, dropping his newspaper on the kitchen table. "All I have in the mini fridge is tomato juice and some sort of margarita mix."

"Yes, there should be some left." Sienna looked at the clock and saw that she had a little bit of time before she had to leave. She straightened her cuffs. "Have you had a chance to sign the papers?"

Will stopped abruptly in front of the refrigerator and turned toward Sienna, leaving the door open. "No, I haven't. In a rush?"

She ignored his sarcasm. "Can I ask what you're waiting for? My attorney said that everything in the agreement is standard, and I'm not asking for alimony, so I'm not sure what the holdup is."

Will scoffed. "When did you become so cold? You're acting like this is a business deal gone wrong. We've been married for nine years, Sienna. Don't you think we owe it to ourselves to see if this can be fixed?"

Instead of acquiescing to his apparent need for yet another rehash, Sienna felt her cheeks burn with anger. "No, Will. I don't. I have tried to make it clear, perfectly fucking clear, that we are no longer in a viable marriage, and rather than keep delaying the inevitable, it would be better for both of us to just rip off the Band-Aid."

"Wow. I don't even know what to say to that. I thought I meant more to you than making a decision like this on a whim." Will's expression was still defiant, but he flinched after the last words exited his mouth. He knew.

Sienna had to restrain herself from flying into a rage. It mostly worked. "A *whim*?" she yelled. "Did you really just say *on a whim*?"

"Sienna, I—"

"No, no, you don't get to say anything right now. I have been telling you for *years*, and I mean *years*, that something needed to change, that I wasn't happy, that we needed counseling...this is as far away from a whim as you could possibly get. We have nothing else to work on, we cannot fix it because it's no longer broken. It simply doesn't exist anymore." Sienna crossed her arms, feeling her wrath begin to temper. She was harsh and maybe a little more antagonistic than she needed to be, but there was no more room for confusion.

Will just stood there looking dumbfounded. He looked more like a wounded child than the powerful, charismatic businessman he was. His face clouded over, and he slammed the refrigerator door, the juice forgotten.

"I don't understand you," he said. "I've given you absolutely everything. Look around you, Sienna. What's missing?"

"Is that really what you think this is about? That I want more *things*? That I'm so shallow and vapid that I'm throwing a fit to get you to pay attention to me? Fuck you, Will. Fuck you."

"That isn't what I said. You're always twisting my words around to make me look like the bad guy."

Why couldn't she get through to him? "I told you from the moment we had the conversation about separating that this wasn't your fault, that you weren't to blame, and it was just the natural progression of who we are and who I want to be." Sienna paused and stared at him indignantly. "Although, now I'm reconsidering that line of thinking. If you'd actually listened to someone for once, instead of being the self-centered prick you've obviously become, you'd have heard what I've been saying all these years."

His face morphed into a mask of fury. "It's time for you to move out," he said coldly. "I'll sign the papers today and get them over to Brad ASAP. Don't be here when I get home."

"Will," Sienna started, but he stormed out of the house. She shook her head as she heard him peel out of the driveway. It wasn't a reasonable request for her to pack up her things and be completely moved out by seven p.m. She leaned against the counter and finished off the last of her coffee.

The truth was, she probably should have moved out months ago. But something inside her wanted to hold on to those last vestiges of the life she'd known for so long, even if the biggest part of that life had been making her unhappy. She loved her home and her stepson and the comfort that had developed over the years, but it wasn't baseline contentment she wanted for the rest of her life. She wanted passion, excitement. She chided herself for sending mixed messages to Will, and ultimately, Declan. If she'd been gone, there wouldn't have been any room for confusion or hesitation. That would have truly ripped off the Band-Aid. Sienna checked the clock one more time before heading into the city to check in on her abandoned office. Getting some distance seemed like the best idea.

❖

There were very few apartment listings in Shell Creek. Sienna scrolled through listing after listing, trying to find anything remotely close to her home. It wasn't like she had tons of friends, or an office located in town, or even family she wanted to stay close to. But Shell Creek was her home, and she didn't want to leave it. Not because she had to, anyway. If she was going to pick up her life and move out of town, she wanted it to be on her own timeline.

She looked down at her cell phone when her text alert went off. It was Juliet.

Do you want me to pick up dinner? Heard from the construction guys that they're going to finish up today, so I'll be ready to go home later tonight. Dec is going to stay with you for a bit longer. He's got some big gaming tournament thing that my internet apparently can't handle. Thank you again for being so gracious.

Sienna shook her head at how formal Juliet was being. Nothing had been solved and everything was still a giant question mark between them, even though they'd repeatedly said that nothing could happen, and they were both okay with that and they'd just be friends. Evidently, they'd both lied.

Don't think I'll be home tonight. Got into it with Will and I'm desperately looking for a place at the moment, as he asked me to go. I'll probably stay at the Salt Creek Inn until I find something. Declan loves the pad Thai from Jasmine's if you feel like something different.

It was so strange, talking to Juliet as though their lives hadn't been teetering on the edge of implosion. Maybe space was what they needed.

Sienna, you don't have to stay at a motel. You can stay with me. You let me stay with you, and I'd like to repay the favor.

Sienna's breath caught in her throat. That was probably the worst idea she'd heard in her entire life. Her and Juliet, in close quarters, alone, without any distractions. What could possibly go wrong?

That's probably not the best idea.

It pained her to type out those words.

I can control myself, you know. Just know that the offer is there. Besides, we're friends, remember? It's what friends do.

Maybe Juliet had a different definition of friendship, but Sienna was pretty certain that what they shared was *not* friendship.

Thank you.

The little text bubbles appeared, disappeared, reappeared.

Of course.

Sienna tossed her phone on her desk and went through her casefiles, making sure she hadn't neglected anyone or anything with all of her time spent with Gretchen. Thankfully, her supervisor had given the more time-consuming cases to the other advocates in her office. Sienna suspected that had something to do with how she'd been acting before being assigned to Gretchen's case. She was grateful, but also embarrassed that she hadn't been able to keep her home life from spilling into her work life.

Sienna called the Salt Creek Motel to reserve a room. The clerk answered the phone on the fourth ring, sounding out of breath.

"Yes, I'd like to book a room for a few nights, please."

The clerk chortled. "We're booked out for the next four days. Everyone whose house was damaged by the twister is staying here, and that $25,000 Sand Castle Challenge they're broadcasting on NBC is taking place up in Gloucester. Good luck finding a room within a thirty-mile radius."

Sienna opened her mouth to ask if there was any possibility of a cancellation, but the clerk ended the call before she had a chance. She called around to a few hotels in the area, and everyone she spoke to echoed the clerk at the Salt Creek Motel.

She checked her watch and saw that it was almost eight o'clock. She was excited to find one lone room available at the Courtyard, about ten miles outside of town. She pulled out her credit card and then audibly swore at the computer. They wanted six hundred and forty dollars for one night, based on absolutely nothing but price gouging.

She needed to get out of her head. With everything going on around her, it wasn't a fun place to be. Sienna picked up a training manual in her inbox and started to leaf through it. Anything to put off making a decision about staying at Juliet's, although it looked like that was the best option, at least for one night. She plucked a highlighter out of her pencil cup and sat back in her chair, ready to immerse herself in the untainted world of policies and procedures.

Chapter Thirty

Obviously, telling Sienna to stay with her was a colossally bad idea. On just about every possible front. But Juliet didn't know what kind of fight Sienna and Will had gotten into, and if he was serious about her leaving the house, then Juliet wanted her to know she had a friend. Besides, she was sure Declan would want to stay with Will for the time being, so his room would be vacant. There was no reason they couldn't cohabitate for a few nights like platonic roomies.

Celeste opened Juliet's office door and nodded to the front entrance. "Tara Wolfe is here for your meeting. She looks upset."

Juliet rolled her neck a few times. "Wonderful. Send her in, please."

Tara Wolfe walked into Juliet's office and gave her hair a toss. She sat in the seat across from Juliet and placed a tote bag on the other chair.

She raised her eyebrows defiantly. "Aren't we going to go into the interrogation room? So you can handcuff me to a table and withhold cigarettes as a way to get me to talk?"

Juliet raised her eyebrows. So that's how it was going to go. "We can certainly move into the interrogation room if you feel more comfortable playing out a scene from a TV crime show. I don't see a need to handcuff you to a table, but if you feel like you might get the urge to get up and run, I can do that too. I wasn't aware that you smoked, but this entire building is smoke free, so I'm afraid withholding cigarettes wouldn't be a viable tactic to get you to open up." Juliet folded her hands on her desk.

Tara rolled her eyes and leaned back in the chair. "We can talk here, that's fine."

"I just wanted to recap the timeline of events from the night Richard Kowalski was killed. Based on the surveillance footage, you left the library at eight p.m. You said you went straight home from there, correct?" Juliet asked.

"Correct."

"Your fingerprints were found on Mr. Kowalski's bottle of nitroglycerin, as well as many other items in his office. Did you take the pills from his desk at any point?"

"Oh, for fuck's sake," Tara said, exhaling loudly. "I've touched everything in that library about a billion times. I know you all think I'm a weird stalker because I had feelings for Rich. Well, I'm here to prove that it wasn't one-sided."

Juliet perked up. She'd found nothing to imply that Richard had been unfaithful to Gretchen or had reciprocated Tara's feelings. "I'm listening."

Tara took an item out of her tote bag and placed it on Juliet's desk. It was a greeting card of some sort.

"Here's the first thing. It's a Valentine's Day card."

Juliet took the card and opened it. The front cover showed a woman's hand, writing a note, with a cup of coffee and a laptop in the background.

"Happy Valentine's Day, Co-worker. Thank you for letting me steal your best pens. And then he signed it 'Rich.'" Juliet shrugged. "I don't see where this indicates any kind of inappropriate feelings."

Tara scoffed. "Really? Who gives their co-worker a Valentine's Day card? And that's just the beginning."

Juliet sat back again while Tara went for the next item. Her smugness filled the room.

"Look at this. He left this on my desk a few months ago for absolutely no reason at all."

She plunked down a mason jar with a yellow ribbon tied around the cover. There was a packet of peanut M&Ms inside, and a pre-printed note attached to the ribbon. It read, "A little something to brighten your day." with a bright yellow sun underneath the words.

Juliet looked at the jar but didn't comment on it. She assumed there would be some romantic love letter or diamond ring coming out of that bag, because so far, the items amounted to nothing.

Tara seemed to sense Juliet's disinterest, because she immediately went back into her bag. She pulled out a bobblehead made in her likeness. It was holding a cell phone in one hand and a laptop in the other. She put it down forcefully on Juliet's desk so that the little head rattled back and forth.

"What do you make of this?" Tara asked. Her demeanor appeared to soften as she followed the sway of the bobblehead with her eyes.

Juliet watched her closely to see if Tara was playing some kind of game. "Not much. Why do you think this signifies that he reciprocated your feelings? It's a business gift. Was his gift-giving making you uncomfortable?"

The anger returned. "Of course not! But you don't think it's strange to have a bobblehead of your co-worker on your desk?"

Maybe. "So, he kept your bobblehead on his desk? Was yours the only one?"

Tara bristled. "No. He kept it next to his." She pulled out the Richard bobblehead, complete with a book in one hand and the other giving a thumbs-up. The inscription on Tara's said, "Reading is…" and Richard's showed "Fun-damental!"

Juliet sighed softly. "Tara," she said, deciding on a different approach. "There is nothing here that would make me think differently about the relationship you shared with Richard. He obviously appreciated you as his co-worker. We've been through all of his things, both in his office and at home. We went through his car. His phone. There wasn't anything that gave us the assumption he was interested in another woman."

Tara's eyes filled up, which Juliet hadn't been expecting. "I know you think I'm crazy, but sometimes you just feel things. You just *know.* I could tell by the gentle way that he spoke to me, and the softness in his touch. He was trying to figure out a way to tell Gretchen. And then my entire world just exploded into a million pieces."

Juliet handed her a tissue. "I need you to be honest with me, Tara. Did Richard ever tell you he was planning on leaving Gretchen? Did he touch you in ways that a co-worker wouldn't?"

"He didn't need to. What don't you get about that? What do you want from me, anyway? To admit that I killed him? That I killed the one person in this world that made me feel like I was the most beautiful creature on earth? Fine, I killed him. Are you happy?" Tara shouted, rubbing her forehead with her thumb and index finger.

"Tara," Juliet said, her pulse quickening. She didn't intend to come off as stern as she did, but she needed Tara to understand the gravity of the situation. "You just confessed to murder. Is that what you came here to do?"

"No. I don't know. Maybe I did do it. Everything about that night is a blur. I know I didn't mean to do it. I wanted him to have a drink that night, to loosen up, so I could decide if it was the right time to tell him I knew how he felt and that I felt the same. I suggested that we share a little whiskey."

Unprofessional, definitely, on both their parts, but not indicative of anything more sinister. "Did you drink with him?"

"I pretended to, or at least I thought I did. I took a small sip, I think, so maybe I blacked out. I didn't even think Rich drank that much. I decided it wasn't the right time. But can you imagine if I'd stayed? He'd probably be alive right now." Tara dabbed furiously at her eyes and crumpled the tissue into a ball. "Does his wife know? About us, I mean."

Juliet's head was spinning. There was nothing concrete in what Tara was telling her. Tara was clearly delusional based on her belief that they were carrying on a hot and heavy affair when absolutely nothing pointed to that notion as a reality. And taking a drink from a poisoned bottle didn't equate to her putting the poison *in* the bottle.

"Listen, Tara, I think at this point it would be best if you spoke with a friend of mine from the county police force. Her name is Dr. Marron, and she should be able to help you remember some more details about that night. Is that okay with you?" Juliet asked, as she waved Celeste in through the glass partition. Sending Tara to the police psychologist for a clinical interview seemed like the best course of action.

"You don't need to speak to me like I'm insane, Lieutenant. You're being condescending and I don't appreciate it. Don't minimize what we had. Just because he couldn't be open about it doesn't mean it wasn't real," Tara said. She turned when Celeste walked in.

"Officer Jeffries, would you or Officer Leland take Ms. Wolfe to talk with Dr. Marron? Clinical interview. I think it would be helpful to piece together some of the missing information from the investigation," Juliet said, giving Celeste a subtle nod.

Celeste knew what to say. "Of course. I'm sure the others involved with Mr. Kowalski have already had their interviews with Dr. Marron. And if not, they'll be happening shortly."

"So, everyone talks to this doctor? Not just me because you think I'm a psycho?" Tara clutched the Valentine's Day card to her chest.

"Nobody said you were a psychopath, Tara. We just want to be sure we're exploring every possibility. And since you said there are parts of that night you don't remember, it would be helpful for us, and for you, to have some answers," Juliet said.

Celeste took her to the lobby to sit with Officer Leland and went back into Juliet's office. "What's up?"

Juliet shook her head. "I don't know, honestly. She said she might have killed him accidentally because she encouraged him to have some whiskey, but she didn't say anything about putting the meds in the bottle. She's completely convinced they were having an illicit affair, even though it appears that Kowalski had no idea he was a part of it. He may have noticed her flirting, but he didn't seem to play into it, based on what I've seen. I swear to God, anybody looking at this from outside in must think I have Bumbling Cop Syndrome."

"What the hell is that?" Celeste asked.

"You know, on every cop show ever, where the lead investigator misses evidence or overlooks obvious clues or chases cold leads into oblivion where the cop ends up getting shot in the leg and some super sleuth swings in and solves the case in fifteen minutes. *That* syndrome," Juliet said. She pointed to the bobblehead dolls still sitting on the edge of her desk. "Get rid of those, would you? I'm sure Tara wants them back. Those things are creepy as hell."

"You think she did it? Setting up the blackout as a temporary insanity defense?" Celeste asked, poking at one of the dolls with her pinky.

"I have no idea. Unless she fabricated a breakup in her head and didn't tell me about it, the 'relationship' was still going fine, according to her. Maybe Dr. Marron can shed some light on it. Maybe this whole thing is a long con, but I still can't fathom what she'd get out of it."

"Are we going to Goodman's this afternoon?" Celeste asked.

"Deagle said his shop is closed today. He's been low-key watching the place for me. Nothing too exciting yet. He's not there a whole lot for someone who's self-employed," Juliet said. "Deagle went by his apartment earlier, but he wasn't there, either."

"Wow. It seems like we have a lot more weirdos in this town than we thought. Makes Sam the Supermarket Screamer look like a civil engineer." Celeste looked down at Juliet's cell phone, which was buzzing with text messages. "At least you can sleep in your own bed tonight. You don't have to sleep twenty feet away from Sienna and pine for her all night long."

Juliet opened her mouth to tell Celeste that her pining for Sienna was about to get a whole lot worse but decided against it. It would devolve into an entire conversation Juliet didn't have the strength to participate in. She just smiled and nodded and pretended like everything around her wasn't on fire.

Though it hadn't been very long, Juliet looked around her house as though she hadn't been there in months. Everything looked the same, but it felt different. Declan wasn't home, and not just because she was busy, but because he was angry with her. She couldn't imagine how he would have reacted if he'd known the full truth instead of just basing it on his instincts. What he'd seen had told him plenty. The fact that Sienna had texted her not long before telling her that she'd be over around nine had only heightened Juliet's anxiety. *It will be fine.* They had two options. They could either cut each other out of their lives completely or learn to be friends. The third option, Juliet's preference, wasn't really an option at all. One big happy family.

She found the invoice for the new roof in her mailbox. They'd given Will a hell of a deal and she reminded herself to thank him again the next time she saw him. She tried to push away the guilt gnawing at her stomach, at least for the time being. She was thrilled with the quality of the work and the amount of time it had taken to complete it. She was grateful for how lucky she'd been.

Without knowing if Sienna had eaten or not, Juliet decided it was better to be on the safe side. She grimaced at the state of her refrigerator. Thankfully, she found a frozen lasagna that hadn't passed the expiration date yet, so she threw that in the oven along with a few frost-bitten dinner rolls.

Juliet's heart dipped as she heard an engine cut off in her driveway. Moments later, she heard the clicking of shoes on her front porch. What seemed like a long time after, a slight knock on the door. It startled her even though she'd been expecting it. Juliet took a deep breath and opened the door.

On the other side, Sienna stood on her front stoop, laptop bag in one hand and a backpack slung over her shoulder. Juliet smiled at her nervously and decided that Sienna looked nervous too. It would be the first time they'd been alone together without the fear of getting caught or having to explain themselves to anyone.

"Hi," Sienna said quietly, wiping her feet on the doormat.

"Hi," Juliet echoed, opening the door wider. "Come in."

Sienna stood awkwardly in the living room, still holding her bags. Juliet smiled again but felt droplets of sweat bead on her forehead. She probably should have second-guessed the light sweater she'd been wearing. Fall hadn't completely set in just yet.

"Wine?" She headed toward the kitchen to get herself a gallon of it.

"Definitely, thank you. Where should I drop these?" Sienna asked.

"Oh, you can drop them in Dec's room. Fresh sheets on the bed and I stuffed all of his crap that was on the floor into a box in his closet. So, it actually looks clean in there for once," Juliet said. She poured them each a full glass of wine.

"Something smells delicious." Sienna sat on the far end of Juliet's couch and took the glass of wine eagerly.

"Don't get too excited. It's a frozen lasagna. I haven't been shopping in a while, sorry."

"I am totally on board with frozen lasagna. I think just about anything would hit the spot tonight," Sienna said.

Their eyes locked for a brief moment before they both looked away.

"Have you heard from Will?" Juliet asked.

Sienna shook her head. "I don't expect to, either. He was pretty angry this morning when I pushed him to sign the papers. Which I get, I really do. I shouldn't have stayed in the house as long as I have. Even with him out in the pool house, it's still *our* house, and that's unfair."

"Okay, but you can't really blame yourself. You made it clear that it was over. He chose to ignore it. That's not on you."

Silence overtook them. Juliet didn't think she was alone in her anxiety and unease. She stood and went to the kitchen to take the food out of the oven.

"Would you mind if we ate out here?" Sienna asked from the living room. "I wouldn't mind just kicking back and watching something while we eat. It's been a very long day."

Relief washed over Juliet. That was preferable to an uncomfortable dinner at the kitchen table, asking each other to pass the salt and wondering if the rolls were overcooked. "Great idea. See what's on."

The television roared to life on the Weather Channel. Juliet plated their sad looking lasagna and brought it over to the coffee table.

"Ooh, *Final Destination* is on. You up for it?" Sienna asked, sounding more interested in something than Juliet had heard her in a while.

"Always."

"I didn't want to fly for about a year after I saw this movie for the first time. I kept checking the tray table lock and I refused to turn the air on." Sienna took a small bite of the pasta. "This is actually pretty good."

"Have you seen the second one? To this day, I switch lanes if I'm behind a truck carrying giant tree logs. I refuse to be decapitated while I'm driving down the highway," Juliet said.

"Oh my God, I do the same thing. Every time I pass a store window, I check to make sure there are no phantom bus reflections in it. I don't care what anybody says, this franchise is in my top three."

A twinge in her stomach made Juliet pause before taking another bite. She watched Sienna for the briefest of seconds, as she tucked her hair behind her ear and took a sip of her wine with a slight smile on her face as she watched the movie.

"Do you want any more?" Juliet asked, standing up with such abruptness that Sienna physically jumped. "Sorry, I just needed a refill." Juliet held up her empty glass.

"Oh, okay. Sure, I'll take a refill, too. Thank you."

Juliet stood at the counter, grounding herself. She picked up her phone and texted Declan good night, even though it was barely ten o'clock. She needed to distract herself. Of course, Declan didn't respond. Still mad. Juliet's heart was heavy.

"Juliet, come sit down for a minute," Sienna said. She turned off the television.

Juliet felt her heart pick up speed as soon as the words were out of Sienna's mouth. What could she need to talk about that warranted turning the television off? Maybe she was moving out of state. Maybe she decided that she was going to give Will another chance. Maybe she didn't feel something for Juliet after all and wanted to let her down easy. Maybe, maybe, maybe.

Without responding, Juliet handed Sienna's freshly refilled glass to her. Sienna took a long sip before placing it on the coffee table.

Sienna turned so that she was facing Juliet dead-on. "I don't know what to do," she whispered. "I've always been in control. I've always had a plan. This is new territory for me." She chewed on her bottom lip. "I know how this looks. That I'm so afraid to be alone I'm jumping to a new ship before the other one has docked. I can promise you that is *not* the case."

"I didn't—"

Sienna held up her hand. "Let me finish. Please. Before I lose my nerve."

Thunder rumbled in the distance. Juliet sat back on the couch while Sienna stood, pacing the room, her wine glass in hand. Juliet's heart continued to beat at twice its normal rhythm.

"It's embarrassing, really. Look at me. I'm a woman in my forties pining for my soon-to-be-ex-husband's ex-girlfriend. My stepson's mother. I'm like a bad Lifetime movie at this point. But that doesn't change the facts. I know there are obstacles in our path. I don't want to be the cause of your relationship with Will turning to shit, and I certainly don't want to be a strain on your relationship with Declan."

A flash of lightning illuminated the dimly lit room. Juliet sat forward, clutching her glass, white-knuckled. Where was Sienna going with this?

Sienna continued to pace. "Sometimes, fate is cruel. I wonder if my fate is to see that there isn't an easy road. I tried to settle down with someone who was safe and pragmatic, and it didn't work. I've known it wasn't working for a long time, and as much as he doesn't want to admit it, I'm sure Will knew something was off, too. I have a lot of guilt over this thing between us, and I know you do, too. After a lot of thought, a bit of spontaneity, and a good amount of wine, I've decided that I'd like to give us a chance. If you don't want to, I understand and respect your decision. You don't have to answer me now. But I don't think relationships should be a struggle, and for me, it's never come easier than it has with you." She paused and took in a large breath. "That's it."

Juliet swallowed. That was a lot. She'd never seen Sienna look as vulnerable as she did at that moment, as though she needed reassurance that she wasn't alone, floating on an inner tube in the middle of the ocean. Juliet set down her glass and sighed heavily. She walked over to where Sienna had turned to the window, watching sheets of rain drifting down the street as the trees blew side to side in the autumn thunderstorm.

Juliet put her hands on Sienna's hips and looked out the window over her shoulder. Sienna's body stiffened at the contact and Juliet heard her breath catch. "You have no reason to feel guilty," Juliet whispered. Her chin rested on Sienna's shoulder as she continued to hold her from behind. If that didn't send a horde of mixed messages, nothing would. "You tried your best, you wanted it to work, and it didn't. That's life."

Sienna turned her head so their faces were just inches apart. "No reason to feel guilty?" Sienna asked, curling her index finger around a strand of Juliet's hair.

Her heart fluttered like a hummingbird and her mouth felt dry. "Well, not about *that* anyway. Not about leaving him. This," Juliet said, breathlessly. She motioned between the two of them. "This is a whole different story."

"We can't do this anymore," Sienna said quietly, her lips ghosting over Juliet's.

Juliet wavered, but dug for her resolve. "No, we can't."

"It isn't fair to Will or Declan."

"No, it isn't."

Sienna sighed. "We should probably say good night, then,"

"Yes. We probably should," Juliet said. Her paper-thin determination was fading quickly. She was feeling too many things to be able to think clearly, and making any kind of decision was plainly out of the question. With Sienna so close, her head was dazed, and her body cried out for more.

"Okay," Sienna whispered, before slowly pulling away and turning to face Juliet. "I'm sorry, Juliet. I didn't mean to put you in such an awkward position."

Juliet reached out, enveloping Sienna in her arms. She closed her eyes and told herself that she needed to think, she needed to really dissect the possible outcomes of the two of them being together.

Sienna broke away first and let her fingers linger against Juliet's arm for a second before turning toward the bedrooms.

"Sienna, I just need a little time to figure things out. Is that okay?" Juliet asked.

Nodding, Sienna gave her a slight smile. "Of course it is. Take whatever time you need. I'm not going anywhere."

Juliet exhaled. There were a million reasons to walk away, to go to her bedroom, fall into bed, and stick to the plan. She'd been over and over them, so many times that her brain revolted at the thought of rehashing them. She looked at Sienna, who was so ready to do whatever Juliet asked her to do. Emotion welled inside her, and she was going to burst if she stayed in that position for a second longer. "Oh, fuck it."

She pushed her up against her bedroom door. She covered Sienna's mouth with her own, and her body was on fire. Sienna immediately melted into her, returning the kiss with fervor. Sienna pulled her in tighter, and they slowed their kiss to a tender exploration. Juliet's mind had abandoned all reason and all she could think of was how much more she wanted.

Before long, their breathing grew ragged and their hands were beginning to roam. Sienna bit down softly on Juliet's lower lip, and at Juliet's moan, Sienna pushed her away.

"We have to stop. If we don't stop now, I'm not going to be able to. Seriously," Sienna said. She was still out of breath. "We have to go slow."

"Says who?" Juliet reached forward to pull Sienna back into her.

"Uh…you did. We did. We've been saying all along that this is a bad idea and could never work. And about ten minutes ago, you agreed that we should just say good night." Sienna pushed the hair out of her face, her forehead glistening.

"I say stupid things sometimes. Don't listen to me," Juliet said, wrapping her arms around Sienna's waist.

Sienna backed up against the wall again. "I can't even begin to tell you how much I want you. I really fucking *want* you. I can't even breathe right now. But I don't want you to feel like we rushed into anything, especially after we keep saying the same things over and over. Don't you think we should wait?"

Sure, it made rational sense to wait. But Sienna had made her intentions clear, and as selfish as it might be, Juliet wanted her. That was it. The crux of it all. Juliet wanted her. As though an epiphany had erupted, Juliet knew. She wanted Sienna and she would fight for her. There had to be a way to make this work.

Juliet stood back, straightening her shirt. She looked directly into Sienna's eyes, leaving no question where her head was at. "I've been waiting months to finally experience what you feel like, what you look like, and what you *taste* like. I think we've waited long enough."

Sienna lunged forward, bringing their mouths together once more, all pretense abandoned. Their lips melded together, full of want and need. Juliet felt a rush of warmth from her scalp all the way to her toes. All the oxygen in the room had suddenly disappeared, and Juliet didn't mind that she was suffocating. It was worth it.

Sienna pulled back a fraction of an inch and whispered into Juliet's mouth, "Tell me to stop."

Juliet shook her head, pushing Sienna up against the door again. "I can't. I don't want to."

Sienna tilted her head, inviting Juliet in, fully. Juliet had control, or at least the illusion of it, and it turned her on even more. She held the back of Sienna's neck and kissed her deeply, the magnetism between them threatening to explode into a million tiny sparks. It wasn't just chemistry. It was preordained magic.

When Sienna's moans began to increase in volume, Juliet pulled back slowly. She had never been so attracted to someone in her life. Sienna's eyes were lidded, her breathing was erratic, and her lips were pale and swollen.

Sienna realized that Juliet was watching her, and bit down on her bottom lip. "You're pretty good at this, you know," she whispered, and tugged on Juliet's hair.

"You're really fucking beautiful, you know," Juliet answered, as Sienna looked down and blushed. For someone as classically attractive as Sienna was, she didn't seem to grasp it. To Juliet, it wasn't even a subjective opinion. It was simply a fact.

Sienna responded by taking Juliet's hand and leading her toward the bedroom. Juliet licked her lips, a sense of anticipation mingled with nervousness overwhelming her. She'd been thinking about Sienna nonstop for the last few months, knowing it couldn't happen, and then to have her, so open and ready, was almost too much to handle.

Rain battered against the window, providing them with their very own soundtrack. Juliet swallowed hard as Sienna sat on the edge of the bed, looking up at her expectantly. Once they were in the bedroom, the mood tempered slightly at the reality of what was about to happen.

"I'm nervous." Juliet ran her finger along Sienna's jawline.

Sienna smiled and tugged on the hem of Juliet's shirt. "I am, too."

Juliet leaned in and kissed her again, this time softer, gentler. Sienna lifted Juliet's shirt over her head and let it fall to the floor. She glided her hands up and down Juliet's back, making Juliet shiver in response, and then she slipped her finger beneath Juliet's bra and unhooked it, letting that too fall to the floor.

Feeling exposed, Juliet pulled Sienna to her and covered her with her body. She wanted Sienna on top of her, beneath her, and inside of her all at once. She settled for kissing her again, letting her tongue run over the shape of Sienna's perfect lips. Sienna dipped her head and kissed Juliet's neck, driving her to a near frenzy of need.

"You are gorgeous," Sienna murmured into Juliet's shoulder. "I have never wanted anyone the way I want you. Never." She slid her fingers lightly over Juliet's breasts while she continued to kiss her neck. Juliet groaned reflexively as Sienna grazed her nipple, her body tightening with want.

"Come here," she said, her voice thick and full. She pulled Sienna back up to her lips, kissing her fully as she removed Sienna's shirt, keeping it crumpled in her hand while unfastening the hooks of Sienna's black lace bra. She undid the button of her pants with a quick flick and pushed them down as far as she could with her thumbs tucked into the waistband. Sienna wriggled out the rest of the way, pressing herself against Juliet. "Oh God." Juliet moaned, unsure if she could handle what was surely coming next.

The rest of their clothing came off quickly, the craving of feeling each other outweighing the desire for a slow seduction. Juliet savored Sienna's body, her lips, her tongue, her hands roaming freely. Sienna's head was on the pillow, her eyes closed, and her head tilted toward the headboard.

"It's been a long time," she whispered.

Juliet paused and lifted her head to meet Sienna's eyes. "Are you okay?"

Sienna nodded quickly. "Yes. Better than okay. I just got emotional. I'm sorry, I didn't mean to ruin the moment."

Juliet put her finger against Sienna's lips. "You didn't ruin anything. You couldn't. I know it's been a while, and I know how intense it must be to give yourself to someone new after such a long time. I'm so grateful that you chose me."

Sienna responded by tipping Juliet's chin toward her, and she kissed her slowly while holding her body tightly against her own. Juliet couldn't help squirming above her as Sienna began exploring with her hands again, her touch teasingly light. Sienna turned, and Juliet dropped onto the mattress with one fluid motion, so that Sienna was on top of her, kissing and teasing every inch of her. Juliet reveled in the attention of Sienna worshiping her body so languidly, so adoringly.

She writhed passively beneath Sienna's touch, wanting more, but Sienna paid no attention to her silent pleas. Juliet arched as Sienna's palm glided smoothly down her stomach. Juliet bucked as Sienna slid her finger along the wet length of Juliet's sex, in that same unhurried way. Juliet clawed at the sheets beneath her, her body undulating with Sienna's leisurely rhythm. Bringing their lips together again, Sienna nipped lightly at Juliet's bottom lip as she slowly inserted her finger into Juliet, eliciting a gasp from the uninhibited pleasure that she was creating.

Juliet let out a string of incoherent words, though she didn't know what they would be or why she was trying to say them. Sienna began stroking her in restrained circles, matching the cadence of her gentle thrusts. Juliet inched closer and closer until every ounce of her was throbbing with an ache for release. Sienna reached for Juliet's breast, seeming to sense how close she was. Juliet could hear her own breath coming in rapid waves, her whole body electrified. Her climax washed over her, crashing through every limb and nerve ending and setting her on fire. As she slowly made her way back to earth through the haze of bliss surrounding her, her body went limp. Her body was sated, but her heart ached for the uninterrupted comfort of Sienna's touch. She reached down and squeezed Sienna's hand.

Sienna slid up beside her, placing soft kisses on her shoulder and chest. Juliet stirred, still a bit weak, but Sienna's constant kisses were bringing her around again. She sat up and pulled Sienna up to straddle her. The blankets were strewn around them and Sienna pushed a pillow that had dared to come between them to the floor. Juliet licked hungrily at the hollow of her neck, her collarbone, while Sienna moaned in approval. Juliet pulled Sienna tightly to her with one hand and used the other to slide into her wetness.

"My *God,*" Juliet whimpered, dizzy with want. She concentrated on Sienna's breathing, and when it started to become ragged, Juliet withdrew, grabbed her by the waist, and lifted her so she could lie her down.

"You're pretty strong," Sienna said. Her voice was thick, and her eyes were filled with lust. Juliet's body reacted immediately.

Juliet positioned herself so that she was on top, trailing her lips softly against her skin until she stopped at Sienna's hip, kissing her while caressing her everywhere. Sienna dug her nails into Juliet's wrist as Juliet circled her breasts, running her palms lightly over them to make Sienna want her even more. Sienna moaned deep within her throat, and Juliet could almost hear her body cry out for relief. Juliet slid her tongue across Sienna's hip, across her pubic bone to the other hip, and drew a trail down her thigh.

"Please," Sienna whispered, clutching a handful of Juliet's hair in her trembling hand.

Juliet smiled and made her way between Sienna's legs, where she ran her tongue lightly up the length of her, confirming just how much Sienna wanted her. It was better than an invitation. Juliet spread her slightly and descended upon her with abandon. Sienna arched her back, pushing herself even farther into Juliet's mouth. Juliet breathed appreciatively, her warm breath on Sienna's sex causing her to tighten her muscles in anticipation. Juliet began to trace circles with her tongue in the spot where Sienna needed her most. After a minute at most, Sienna cried out and clutched her thighs tightly around Juliet's shoulders. Juliet held on to her forcefully, so the contact between them wasn't broken. When the sensitivity became too much for Sienna to handle, she gently coaxed Juliet back up to her. Their bodies intertwined, and Juliet rested her head on Sienna's chest, blissfully spent.

"That was...I don't even think I can put it into words," Juliet said, chuckling at the flashes of light dancing behind her eyelids.

"Mmm," Sienna agreed, placing soft kisses on the top of Juliet's head. "We didn't even make it one night. I promised myself when I knocked on your door that nothing was going to happen."

"I made the same promise. Clearly, promise-keeping isn't our forte when it comes to staying away from each another," Juliet said. She ran her finger along Sienna's arm, watching the skin erupt in goose bumps beneath her touch. She couldn't remember the last time she felt so at ease. So comfortable. "You really haven't been with a woman in ten years?"

"Yes. Maybe even a little longer." She played with the ends of Juliet's hair and scratched her nails lightly down her back.

"Well, it must be like riding a bike. Because *damn*, woman," Juliet teased her, squeezing Sienna's hand.

Sienna scoffed, but it wasn't enough to hide her smile. Juliet laughed and bit down gently on her stomach. She wished they could just stay the way they were, happy and content and at ease with each other.

As if reading her mind, Sienna sighed. "So, what happens now? I don't mean to get heavy, but we've deviated from our plan. Yet again. Do we just go back to promising that it won't happen?"

Juliet didn't see how that was an option. Connecting the way they had, all the feelings she'd been pushing down had exploded to the surface. She was pretty sure she wouldn't be able to stuff them any longer.

"I don't know," she answered honestly. "I don't think I can promise that anymore. I'd be lying to myself. I really hope this doesn't scare you, and if it's not where you're at right now, I totally understand. I'm falling for you, and I know it's not ideal, but there it is. Does that scare you?"

Juliet closed her eyes and braced herself for Sienna's response. She knew Sienna had feelings for her, but was she ready for something so raw and intense? The ink hadn't even had time to dry on the divorce papers.

"Yes, it does." Sienna wrapped her arms tightly around Juliet, bringing her even closer to her. "But it scares me because I feel it too. I haven't been in love in a very long time. And now I remember what it feels like."

Before she allowed any of the guilt, fear, and anxiety to set in, Juliet reveled in the pure joy that flowed through her. She kissed Sienna's stomach again and closed her eyes, trying to hold on to the moment for as long as humanly possible.

Chapter Thirty-one

M mm," Sienna murmured, somewhere between sleep and arousal. She was aware of a pleasant sensation, a burning deep within her stomach. As her eyes fluttered open, she felt a velvet tongue sliding over her. She craned her neck slightly and groaned as she saw Juliet's hair splayed over her stomach. She brought her hands to Juliet's hair, curling her fingers in the soft mess while she moved closer to the brink, her body responding as intensely as it had the night before. She writhed beneath Juliet's mouth, muttering nonsense, until her muscles tightened and she came. When the aftershocks subsided, Sienna laughed quietly as her head hit the pillow, and she rubbed her hands over her face. Juliet placed sweet kisses up the length of her thigh, her stomach, her chest, and her neck, until she'd made her way back up Sienna's body. Juliet rested on her forearm and raised her eyebrows.

"Good morning," she whispered seductively.

Sienna laughed again, suspended somewhere between heaven and earth. "Yes. Good morning."

"It's really early," Juliet said. "Go back to sleep."

She turned on her side and pulled Sienna's arm around her so that they were spooning. Sienna held on to her tightly, the feeling of being entangled with Juliet so new, but so familiar, so exciting, but so comforting, that anything she'd felt prior to that morning didn't hold a candle to the electricity that crackled in the air above them.

After drifting in and out of sleep for the next hour, Sienna opened her eyes when she heard the rattle of a doorknob. She patted Juliet's leg to wake her, but Juliet just rolled over. Sienna sat up and furiously tapped Juliet's arm.

"What?" Juliet asked. She was clearly still in the haze of sleep.

"Someone's at the door," Sienna shout-whispered.

Juliet jumped up, taking the sheet with her. Sienna heard the deadbolt turn over and scrambled to pull her yoga pants on without tripping over the leg and falling headfirst into Juliet's dresser.

"I need my cleats," Declan called out. When he wasn't met with a response, he announced himself a little louder. "Mom? Are you here?"

Juliet ran her hand through her hair, but it didn't do much considering how messy it was from their late-night activities. Sienna stifled a laugh even though Declan walking in at that moment was decidedly unfunny. Seeing Juliet completely frazzled was quite amusing.

"I'm here," Juliet yelled. She straightened the hem on the sweatshirt she'd pulled out of the closet and took a last look at Sienna. "Do you think he'll be able to tell? Should you hide?"

Sienna shrugged. "I don't know. Maybe. Probably. No, I'm not going to hide! Just act natural."

Juliet walked out of the bedroom and Sienna followed her a minute later. She'd hoped Declan wasn't looking in the direction of the bedrooms.

No such luck.

"What are you doing here?" He froze midway through putting his shoes into his backpack.

"Well, your dad and I had a disagreement, and we thought it would be best if we spent the night apart. Your mom was kind enough to let me stay here. There aren't any hotels in the area with rooms available, at least for a few days," Sienna said, unable to meet Declan's eyes. He seemed so angry and on edge, and that wasn't the boy Sienna knew. He'd always been so easygoing and affable, even when his teenage moodiness had kicked in. It broke her heart to think she'd been one of the biggest contributors to his unhappiness.

"Because the pool house and your room weren't far enough apart?" He shoved the shoes into his bag. "Not sure why you needed to sleep in my mother's room. I wasn't here, my room was free."

"Dec, no one said that I slept in your mother's room. I was in there—"

Declan shook his head. "Don't. I'm not stupid, Sienna."

Juliet walked out of the kitchen and stood next to Sienna. "I'm not really a fan of your tone right now, Declan. We can have a conversation, but please be respectful."

"I'm not really a fan of you lying to me, and I'm not really a fan of Sienna being a cheater."

"Okay, that's enough," Juliet said.

Sienna had never heard her speak to Declan so sternly before. "No, Juliet, it's fine. He's upset with me and he has every right to be," Sienna said, taking a step toward Declan.

"That doesn't give him the right to be rude to you."

Declan just stood there with his lips pursed, seemingly itching for a fight. Based on Juliet's demeanor, Sienna thought it was smart he didn't attempt a snappy comeback.

"Declan, could you sit down for a second?" Sienna asked.

"I'd rather stand."

Sienna watched as Juliet narrowed her eyes at him, apparently a look he was familiar with. He threw himself down on the loveseat with an exaggerated sigh.

"You know that your dad and I aren't together anymore, right?"

"I guess."

"I'm not sure how much he's told you, but you have a right to know that we're getting divorced. We had an argument about the divorce paperwork, and he asked me to find my own place. He wasn't wrong for asking that of me. I was reluctant to leave the house because it's been my home for so long, and because you're there. But I should have moved out a while ago. It would have been a cleaner break and it wouldn't have led to so much confusion and unnecessary heartache." Sienna sat next to him on the couch, but Declan made a show of sliding over a few inches.

A lump formed in Sienna's throat. This wasn't how it was supposed to go. She'd wanted an amicable split so she could remain a part of Declan's life, and maybe even someday in the future, Will's. All her ideations about staying a family in one form or another were imploding rapidly.

"Right. So, you're a cheater, and Dad's a liar, and Mom's a liar, and everyone in this family sucks."

Juliet started to intervene, but Sienna held her hand up.

"No, Declan. It's not as cut-and-dry as you're making it seem. There are many things at play here, and it takes time and patience and a lot of sadness and anger before coming to the realization that things aren't going to work. I know you don't want to hear it, but that's between your dad and me. We should have been better at communicating with you, and for that, I'm truly sorry. I never wanted you to be blindsided through any of this."

Declan seemed to relax for a moment, then put his walls right back up. "And you thought hooking up with my mother would soften the blow?"

Juliet walked over to the couch and sat on the coffee table, directly across from Declan. Her eyes were glassy. "This was certainly not how I planned on telling you. But...you were right about what you saw the other night. I have feelings for Sienna. Neither of us meant for it to happen, and we sure as hell tried to make it go away. But we couldn't."

Declan stared at them both incredulously. "Wait, you're serious? This can't be real life right now. You two really are hooking up?" He looked from Sienna to Juliet, his eyes wide with what appeared to be confusion.

"No, we're not 'hooking up,'" Juliet said with a frown. "That's not what this is about."

"Is that why you're divorcing Dad?" Declan turned toward Sienna. "Because you want to be with my mom?"

"No, of course not. When your father and I made the decision to separate, it had nothing to do with anyone but ourselves. I didn't even really know your mother at that time. Just here and there through you and your dad, but not in any meaningful way. We're divorcing because we're unhappy with each other, and that's the *only* reason. I promise you," Sienna said.

"Sienna and I have grown closer over the last few months. Ever since we took you to your baseball camp over the summer. We had this kind of...connection, and it just got stronger from that point on.

Would you have a problem with it if Sienna and I started seeing each other?" Juliet asked.

Sienna felt like she couldn't breathe as the direct question floated between them.

"Yeah, I would have a problem with that. This is really, really weird. In case you didn't know that. You two were barely friends, and all of a sudden, you're *dating*? I don't even know how to deal with this. Seriously, I don't." His mask of anger had morphed into one of bewilderment.

"Well, you don't need to right now. We're here to talk about it, if you want. I know this is a lot to absorb, and we weren't planning on telling you until we'd sorted through some things ourselves. But this was *not* the plan," Sienna said.

Declan looked hurt. "So, you were just going to keep it from me then? Like everything else?"

"No, Declan. We just wanted to be more delicate with the delivery, and it's still really new to us, too," Sienna said.

"I know this is weird, Dec. But nothing is going to change. Sienna and I have been hanging out, and you knew that. Your dad and Sienna were separated before this, and the only difference now is that she's going to move out of the house. These things would have happened regardless, honey," Juliet told him. "Whatever happens between Sienna and I…well, we'll talk to you about it as things change."

"This is insane," Declan said, shaking his head. "What am I supposed to tell my friends? That my mother is hooking up with my stepmother? It's like some screwed up soap opera that makes no sense."

"I wouldn't tell them anything at this point," Sienna said. "Let's figure things out between us before we bring anyone else into the loop. This is new, and like we said, we haven't even really figured it out ourselves yet. And I don't want your dad to find out like that."

"Well, you better figure out how you're going to tell him. Like today. Because if you don't, I will." His jaw clenched as he stared at the coffee table, tears in his eyes.

"You don't need to threaten us, Declan," Juliet said, her voice taking on the stern lilt that she'd had earlier in the conversation. "We'll deal with this in our own way, the right way."

"Whatever. I have to get to school." He stood up and grabbed his backpack off the chair while shaking his head.

"I'll drive you," Juliet offered.

"No, thanks, I'll walk."

"I'll drive you," Juliet said again. It wasn't a suggestion.

Declan shrugged and stormed out of the house. Sienna heard Juliet's SUV door slam shut, so he had obviously taken the hint.

Juliet covered her face with her hands. "What a mess. Thanks for being so patient with him."

Sienna rubbed her back softly. Nothing like being thrust into a situation while completely unready for it. "I'm not upset with him. He's lashing out, which is totally normal. I'll find a motel with a room available. If I have to drive a ways, then so be it. Not sure that me staying here while this is happening is the best idea. It will just make him angrier."

Juliet nodded, though it did seem reluctant. "Yeah, that makes sense. I'll help you. But we do have to figure out the Will thing. He can't hear it from Declan," Juliet said.

"I know." Sienna checked her phone, which chirped from the kitchen table. "I have to go over to Gretchen's. Do you want me to call Will and set up a time for us to talk, or just wait?" The thought of talking to Will made her want to throw up. Their last encounter had been acrimonious at best. Telling him she was seeing the mother of his child probably wouldn't go over well.

"No, don't call him. I'll go over there later on today. This one is on me."

"It doesn't have to be," Sienna said.

Juliet nodded. "I know. But I feel like it's something I should do. He's my friend, we have so much history. If he's going to feel betrayed by anyone, it'll be me. I know we're being forced into opening up about this before we're ready and I don't want you to think there's any pressure."

Sienna smiled a little and pulled Juliet into a tight hug. "The only pressure I feel is your body against mine. And I like it."

The horn blasted from Juliet's SUV. She dropped her head and gave Sienna a quick kiss on the lips. "Call me if anything happens."

Sienna watched her rush out the door, wondering what kind of whirlwind she'd been swept into. Twenty-four hours earlier, they'd agreed that it was best to distance themselves from each other, and now Declan knew, and they were determining the best way to tell Will about their relationship, which they'd only decided to have last night. Sienna could still feel the tingle of Juliet's fingers on her from earlier that morning, so she wasn't able to muster up *too* much anxiety about it all. That would come later.

CHAPTER THIRTY-TWO

"Good morning," Juliet said as she burst through the doors of the police station. Celeste was sitting at her desk, and so were Officers Leland and Deagle. Her smile faded a bit as she noticed they were all staring at her. "Everything going okay so far today?" she asked.

Leland spoke up first. "Yes, Lieutenant. Just working on a break-in that happened at Dr. Prichard's office last night. The thieves took some of their computer equipment."

"That's unusual. Let me know what you find out."

"I'm heading over to Main for traffic duty. The electric company is working on a busted streetlight," Deagle said, adjusting his hat.

"And I'm going to pick up a dozen doughnuts. Can I speak to you in your office for a second?" Celeste asked. She followed Juliet into her office. "What is wrong with you?"

Juliet turned to her, completely confused. "What are you talking about?"

"You came in practically singing. And the big smile was a nice touch. Did you see Kellie last night?" Celeste narrowed her eyes.

She hadn't thought about Kellie in ages, and that most definitely wasn't who she was with last night. "No, don't be weird," Juliet said, busying herself with her stapler.

"You're all flushed and glowy. Who was it?"

Juliet pointed to her door. "Okay, you need to get out and go back to work. Get me a Boston cream."

Celeste gasped. "Oh. My. God. You didn't."

"Didn't what?"

"You slept with Sienna." Celeste nearly shouted.

"Shh!" Juliet yelled and shut her door. "What is wrong with *you*? Do you want me to lose *all* sense of authority?"

"I'm sorry, I'm sorry. How did it happen? Does Will know? Are you freaking out? Was it good?" Celeste sat on the edge of the chair across from Juliet's desk.

"Yes, I'm freaking out. Will doesn't know, but he will soon, because Declan knows. He walked into the house and he'd pretty much already worked it out anyway. And it happened because I'm pretty sure I'm in love with her and everything else is going to shit. And yes, it was fucking amazing. Does that clear things up for you?"

"Wait. You're in love with her? Is she even divorced from Will yet? Is Declan pissed off at you?" Celeste couldn't seem to get the questions out fast enough.

"Not legally divorced yet. That can take up to ninety days. But the paperwork has been filed, as far as I know. Yes, Declan is pissed off at all of us. Will's been downplaying the whole thing, making it seem like he and Sienna were just going through a tough time and would eventually work it out. It really wasn't fair to Dec," Juliet said.

"Poor kid. Do you want me to talk to him?" Celeste asked.

Juliet shrugged. "I don't know that it would do much good. He feels like all of the adults in his life are liars and not telling him anything."

"Exactly. I'm his pal. He has no reason to be angry at me, so maybe it would help."

"True. If he'll let you in, go for it. Just make sure he knows we all love him and even though everything is fucked up right now, we're still a family and we always will be. In one form or another." Juliet sighed and straightened the picture of baby Declan she'd had on every desk she'd sat at for the last fifteen years.

"So, you're going to do this? Like, actually be in a relationship with Sienna? Not just screwing around?" Celeste seemed perplexed.

"Yeah, I think so. It's definitely not just screwing around for me. I haven't felt this way about anyone in a very, very long time. I'm scared shitless, if you want to know the truth. She does things to me that I thought were a thing of the past. You know, all the butterflies in the stomach, feeling like I might have a heart attack, fantasizing about her all the time. All of it." Juliet exhaled loudly. "I just wish it wasn't so controversial. You know?"

"I do. Have you come to terms with the idea that Will might not accept this...ever? Even if things go south with you and Sienna, he may still feel so hurt and betrayed that he might not want you in his life anymore. I mean, not in any meaningful way, anyway. Not like it is now," Celeste said.

Even the idea of it hurt. Juliet had thought about what seeing Sienna would do to her relationship with Will in the short term. But since realizing the depth of her desire to be with Sienna, she hadn't let herself do a deep dive on what their future relationship could look like. Celeste was right. Will would probably never forgive her. Even though things hadn't worked out between him and Sienna, the fact remained that she was his *wife*. Some lines weren't meant to be crossed.

"I know," Juliet said softly. "I just feel like if I don't give what I feel for Sienna a real shot, I'll regret it for the rest of my life. I don't want to have a 'one who got away.' I know how selfish this all sounds, trust me, I do. I'm hurting my son, and I'm hurting my friend. And he's more than just a friend, you know that. He's my kid's dad. We've been through a lot of shit together over the years. Does that mean I just let her go? Tell her I'm sorry, but she's not worth it to me? Do I really have to choose my son and friend over the possibility of a great relationship?"

Celeste looked down at the ground, silent for a moment. "I don't think that's the right answer, either. I wish I could be more helpful. I've been with Brooke so long, I forget what it's like to be in the early stages. Not that I'm complaining. But if I was in your situation twelve years ago, when Brooke and I met, and I was facing the same challenges you're facing now...I wouldn't have been able to walk away from her. For what it's worth." Celeste gave Juliet a fleeting smile.

"Thank you. That actually does help." Juliet walked around the desk and gave Celeste's shoulder a tight squeeze. "I don't look forward to that conversation though, I can tell you that."

Celeste nodded and stood up. "I don't envy you, my friend. The heart wants what it wants."

"Hey," Juliet called, as Celeste made her way back out to her desk. "Don't forget my Boston cream."

The phone on her desk lit up that she had a call parked on line two. She tried to get into the right headspace and reminded herself she had an actual job.

"Mitchell," she answered.

"Good morning, Lieutenant. Dr. Marron."

"Thank you for calling, Doctor. How did the interview with Tara Wolfe go?" Juliet asked.

"I have a detailed file I'll be sending over later today, but in the meantime, she invalidated her confession. She said that the whole idea of a 'relationship' between her and the victim was blown out of proportion, and that she knew it was something that wasn't based in reality. That night caused her such angst that she apparently blocked out certain events from the evening. She also said that she confessed because she felt as though you had pressured her into doing so."

"What?" Juliet said angrily. "That's not what happened at all."

"I'm sure it isn't," Dr. Marron said. "But until more evidence surfaces, one way or another, we have nothing to hold her on. She was free to go."

"Do you think she's guilty?" Juliet asked, drumming her fingers on the desk.

"I can't say for certain. She changed her story rather quickly, but that might have been because the significance of the situation brought her back to reality. She was convincing in her statement, but she was also calculated. I'm sorry I can't give you a more definitive assessment."

"Okay," Juliet said. "Thank you for taking the time to call me. We'll do a little more digging on her to see what we can come up with."

Juliet hung up the phone and tapped the eraser of her pencil compulsively. Tara had made it seem like Juliet was the one pushing for false arrest in order to make the case go away, which she obviously hadn't done. Her euphoria over the night with Sienna fizzled into her usual, as of late, state of frustration.

Charlie Goodman's garage was still dark when Juliet and Celeste pulled up out front. It was nearly three o'clock in the afternoon, so there was no reason the shop should have been closed. Juliet tried to look through the glass cutouts in the entrance door, but the film of dirt and grease made it hard to see anything clearly.

"He had to have been here recently. The daily calendar on the wall is flipped to yesterday's date. Wouldn't he leave a note or something on the door to let his customers know he'd be closed?" Juliet brushed the dust from the windows onto her pants.

"Can't imagine that customer service is his highest priority," Celeste said, pointing to a sign hanging above the garage. It was a distressed metal sign that read "You can't fix stupid, but you can numb it with a 2x4."

"Nice," Juliet said. In the garage, an older model Ford Taurus was up on the jack with all four of its tires missing. Next to it was a rusted minivan missing a back window. The third bay was empty. "I don't know what Kowalski was thinking, getting into business with this guy. They seem like polar opposites. I don't get it."

"His wife said he loved cars," Celeste said. "I guess he saw the garage as an opportunity. I wish he'd had an accountant or someone vet this thing before he got involved."

Juliet looked into the large trash barrel that sat outside Goodman's side door. Some sort of motor sat at the bottom, and garbage covered it. There was a banana peel, the remnants of an emptied ashtray, and an envelope. Juliet turned the envelope over with the edges of her thumb and forefinger and crinkled her nose in disgust. It was wet with something slick.

"Celeste," she called loudly. "Come here."

Celeste trotted over, and then held her nose. "Ugh, what smells?"

"This address is familiar. Any idea?"

Celeste looked at the front of the envelope. "Yeah. Let me double-check something before we get too excited," she said, pulling out her phone.

Juliet looked at the messy handwriting again and placed the envelope back onto the pile of garbage. She fished her gloves out of her belt and picked it up again, and then slid it into a plastic bag. The words were still clear through the plastic:

Morris Bright
310 Quail's Nest Road
Shell Creek, MA 01994

CHAPTER THIRTY-THREE

Sienna pulled out of Gretchen's driveway, leaving her with the physical therapist. She'd come leaps and bounds since the early days after her accident. Sienna was sure she'd be able to walk again soon without assistance. Though her sadness still overwhelmed her most days, she'd found the tiny voice inside her that encouraged her to fight through the pain and to find out what was on the other side of the heartache and anger.

Her mind was on Juliet and what everything that had happened meant, and how they would deal with it, when her Bluetooth kicked on and announced Gretchen calling. She answered the call with a push of a steering wheel button.

"I'm sorry to bother you, but Monique has my checkbook with her, and I have to make out a check for my copay. Would you mind stopping by her house and grabbing it from her? She's on her way home from the supermarket now and she'll meet you there. I asked her to bring it over, but she told me she has a conference call starting soon. I don't mean to be a pest."

"Oh, Gretchen, you're not a pest at all. I don't mind getting your checkbook for you. Can you do me a favor and text me her address?" Sienna asked.

"Yes, I can do that. Thank you, honey."

Stopped at a light, Sienna clicked on the address Gretchen had sent over and used her phone's GPS to get her there. Thankfully, Monique's house wasn't too far away.

She pulled up in front of it and took it all in. The small ranch home itself wasn't bad, but the monstrosity in her backyard would make anyone do a double take. What was at one time a barn, probably a very nice one, loomed large between some sad looking birch trees. The gray paint was peeling, and the door on the second floor didn't have a balcony. If someone walked through it, they'd fall thirty feet to patchy grass and a couple of untrimmed bushes.

Sienna's car was the only one in the driveway, so she assumed Monique wasn't home from the store yet. She sat in her car for a minute until she heard a faint electric whining coming from the barn out back. It was large enough that Monique could fit her car in there, so it was possible she used it as a garage. Sienna stuck her phone in her pocket and walked through the tall grass toward the old barn.

"Monique?" she called, but there was no answer. The whine continued, so she checked the side door of the barn to see if it was unlocked. It turned easily, so Sienna walked in, calling out for Monique again.

The grille of a pickup truck nearly blocked the entrance. A large, red pickup truck.

Sienna froze for a fraction of a second before turning on her heel to hightail it back to her car.

"Can I help you?" a man with a ponytail asked, walking around the side of the truck. The electric sander was still in his hand. For the first time, Sienna noticed that the back half of the pickup truck was taped and in the process of being painted black.

"I'm sorry, I was actually looking for Monique. I'll give her a call later." Sienna plastered an unassuming smile on her face. Or at least she hoped it was.

"Now, hold on. I can give her a message for you," he said, placing the sander on the hood of the truck. He grabbed a rag from his back pocket and wiped his hands. "Your name?"

Sienna didn't know if she should say that she was from an insurance company, or if she should give him her name, or just run away. She didn't have much time to decide. He leered at her, raking his eyes up and down her body.

"Her mother asked me to swing by. It's no trouble. I'll come back." She followed the ponytailed man with her eyes, noticing he stopped near the right front panel, attempting to obscure it. There was a scrape of green paint to the side of the headlight. The same color as Gretchen Kowalski's Jetta.

Sienna looked up, trying to appear like she hadn't noticed anything, but it was too late. He saw where she'd been looking. She started to back toward the door.

He grabbed her by the wrist. "I said I'd take a message," he said through gritted teeth. "Now who the hell are you?"

"I'm her mother's caregiver," Sienna said, not wanting him to know she had anything at all to do with law enforcement. "Let me go!" She tried to pull her arm away, but he tightened his grip.

"I'd like to see some identification, maybe. You must have something that'll tell me who you are," he said, reaching for her pocket.

Sienna saw an opening and jammed her elbow into his stomach. He immediately let go of her and clutched his stomach.

She ran for the door, grabbing at the wooden frame to fling it open wider. She made her way over the threshold, the afternoon sun greeting her like an old friend.

The momentary feeling of freedom ended when she plowed headlong into Monique Breen, who pushed her back inside the barn. She held a handgun between two shaky hands.

"Monique!" Sienna cried. "It's me!"

Monique raised her gun and pointed it toward Sienna. Realization dawned and she turned back toward the man, who was smiling arrogantly.

"Dumb bitch," he muttered, rubbing at the spot where Sienna had elbowed him.

"Why are you here, Charlie?" Monique asked, still pointing the gun in Sienna's direction. "I told you not to come until the weekend. Now look what you've done!"

"Me? If you'd let me finish this earlier, we'd be in Tijuana right now." He grabbed a wrench from the side table.

Sienna stood slack-jawed, momentarily forgetting the gun pointed at her. This was the man Gretchen had mentioned. "You killed your father? You tried to kill your mother? For *money*?"

"No!" Monique yelled. "I would never hurt my mother."

"But Richard?" Sienna asked. "It was you?"

"Just pull the trigger, damn it!" Goodman yelled, standing off to the side. His arms were streaked with black paint.

"Shut up, Charlie! I have to think. We can't just kill my mother's social worker. Don't you think they'll be looking for her?" Monique shouted.

Sienna just stood there, afraid to move. Monique obviously wasn't comfortable with the pistol she was handling, and Sienna feared that any sudden movement could cause Monique to pull the trigger.

"Monique, you don't have to do this. Just put the gun down. I'm sure the whole thing was a misunderstanding," Sienna said, hoping to convince Monique that she wasn't too far gone.

"Of course she has to do it," Goodman said. "You know as well as I do that if you walk out that door your first stop will be the cops. And that's just not going to happen."

"We could tie her up, Charlie. We could tie her up and drive to Mexico and never look back." Monique's voice had taken on a sense of desperation.

"Nope, that's not going to work either. As of right now, no one knows we were involved. When we leave this one tied up, some hero is going to come and untie her and she'll spill everything. It makes a lot more sense to cut the loose ends now and take a leisurely drive south instead of being hunted down and chased by a dozen Feds. Hand over the gun. I know you're squeamish about these things," Goodman said.

Sienna tried pleading with Monique with her eyes. Obviously, if she was going to get out of this alive, it was through Monique and not Goodman.

"It wasn't supposed to be like this," Monique shouted, the gun still pointed at Sienna. It was shaking uncontrollably. "Why did you make me do this?"

"You're your own person, Mo. I didn't make you do anything." Charlie folded his arms across his chest. "You brought this whole thing to me. You thought it would be a good idea to 'expand' the business off the books, not the other way around. Getting Daddy's money was the only way we could walk away from this with our heads intact. If it makes you feel better to blame me, go ahead. But that doesn't change anything. What's done is done. Give me the gun."

He took a few steps toward Monique, who turned and pointed the gun at him instead. Goodman raised his hands and stopped in his tracks.

"Whoa, whoa, whoa. I'm not the enemy here. She is." He pointed to Sienna. "And he *was.* So, we took care of it. We did what anyone else would have done."

"We shouldn't have done it, Charlie. I tried to undo it, but it was too late. It wasn't worth it. When she finds out, she'll never forgive me. I told you to stay away from her, but you didn't listen. And now she'll find out everything," Monique said. She was hysterical, tears streaking down her cheeks, her eyes wild.

Sienna used their private conversation as an opportunity to assess her situation. She took a tiny step toward the door, gearing up to push Monique into Goodman and escape during the chaos. But Monique turned as soon as Sienna did, and the gun was back in her face.

"Don't move, damn it!" Monique yelled.

Goodman dove forward and knocked Monique to the ground, sending her flying into Sienna. Sienna's back exploded with pain as her spine collided with the tool bench. The gun tumbled out of Monique's hand and landed next to her. Goodman jumped on it, and again the pistol was pointed directly at Sienna.

"I don't want anyone else to die," Monique whimpered. She was still curled in the fetal position on the cement floor.

"Well, that's too bad. If you'd only—"

The garage door flew open, whacking loudly against a metal bucket of wrenches. Goodman whipped around, and came face-to-face with Juliet, whose gun was drawn and aimed directly at him. Celeste plowed in behind her, her firearm pointed at shoulder level.

"Drop the gun to the floor, Goodman!" Juliet demanded, her gun steady and cocked, her voice deadly calm.

"You two." He chuckled humorlessly. "I should have taken the shot when I had the chance."

"Drop it or I'll pull the trigger. I have no problem shooting you, and I suggest you don't test me."

"Just drop it, Charlie. It's over for God's sake. It's over," Monique said, sobbing into the floor.

Goodman's nostrils flared with rage. "I'm not going out like that, Mo. And neither are you. This isn't some Bonnie and Clyde bullshit." He pivoted and aimed the gun at Monique's back.

"No!" Sienna screamed, but she was interrupted by the deafening crack of a gunshot. She covered her ears with both hands and closed her eyes, bracing for some sort of ricochet.

When she opened her eyes, she was being enveloped into Juliet's arms. She clung to her, crying and gasping, as Celeste handcuffed Goodman. His shoulder was bleeding onto the cement floor, and he was swearing at her. Juliet had taken her shot before he'd been able to kill Monique, who lay sobbing in the dirt.

"Dispatch, this is Lieutenant Mitchell. We need an ambulance at 310 Quail's Nest Road. Chief is en route. Please send Officer Leland to the scene," Juliet said into her shoulder radio. She turned back to Sienna. "Are you okay? What the hell happened?"

Sienna nodded, tears still streaming down her cheeks. "They killed Rich," she said, her voice barely more than a croak. "How did you know?"

"We found that Morris Bright was getting mail at this address. Morris Bright and Monique Breen are apparently the same person." Juliet glanced at Monique, who still hadn't moved.

"You saved me." Sienna let the tears fall. "He was getting ready to shoot me when you arrived. You saved my life." She grasped Juliet's hand, squeezing it tightly.

"I'm sorry I didn't get here sooner," Juliet whispered. She squeezed just as tightly to Sienna's hand.

"I didn't know he was going to do that to my mother. I never agreed to that. We just needed Rich's life insurance money to hold off some people who were after us. There was no other way." Monique sat up and wrapped her arms around her legs.

Juliet scoffed as they heard the sirens approaching. "You *killed* your stepfather for twenty-five thousand dollars, and you think there was no other way? Really?"

"They would have killed us. I was searching around online and there was a post on a message board, some businessmen looking to use parts from certain cars on other cars and sell some of the parts and make a profit and it sounded like it was too good to pass up," Monique said. She looked like she was going to pass out.

"So, a chop shop?" Juliet asked. "You thought that was a good idea?"

"I was just tired of this town and tired of being a filing clerk and I told Charlie about the opportunity and he said we'd be fools not to take it. He tried to get Rich involved, but he didn't want to do it. It worked well for a while, and then it didn't. And then we got deeper and deeper and had to steal more cars for parts, but we never seemed to get the right things, and Charlie said we could make the money back but we couldn't, and we had to do something! We tried to tell them that certain parts were mislabeled and that someone had messed with our goods and it was all just a big mistake. They didn't go for it. Charlie said it was the only way and Rich's heart wasn't very good anyway, so it wasn't like we were really doing anything that wasn't going to happen soon, and I wish I could take it back. All of it. I tried to stop it. I'm so sorry," Monique said, swiping at her tears with the arm of her sweater. "My poor mother."

"How did you get involved with Charlie, anyway?" Celeste asked, cuffing Monique from the front. She'd already put Goodman in the back seat of the patrol car.

"He's my boyfriend." Monique looked miserable. "Sort of. We got together after I met him when Rich first went into business with him, but my mother always hated him, and Rich would've thought he was beneath me, so I never told them. Keeping it a secret made it more exciting. We've stayed apart since this whole thing happened."

❖

The EMTs arrived, pulled Charlie from the patrol car, and secured him onto a stretcher. They took Monique as well, since she seemed unable to stand on her own without someone beside her for support. Juliet asked if Sienna wanted to get her back checked out, but she just wanted to go home. Wherever home was these days.

"How are we going to tell Gretchen that her daughter killed her husband? And that her daughter's boyfriend tried to kill *her*?" Juliet asked. She continued to hold Sienna's hand as the ambulance pulled away.

"I don't know. But if it hadn't been for Monique, Goodman would have killed me for sure. She tried to stop him, but he wasn't having it. He wanted me dead," Sienna said, and a shiver crawled up her spine.

"Maybe she'll get a few years taken off her life sentence for that," Juliet said. She put her arm around Sienna and pulled her in close. "When I saw your car parked in the driveway, I panicked. I'd texted you a few times to call me, and when I didn't get a response, I assumed the worst when we pulled up to the house. I couldn't imagine…" Juliet shook her head and took a shuddery breath.

"I'm okay," Sienna said, touching Juliet's face. The warmth of her cheek felt like heaven. *I love you*, she thought, but didn't say. It was too soon and too weird and nothing made sense.

"How scared I was, the emptiness that I felt, the rage that took over. I think it just proves what I already knew. I love you, and I know it's way too early to say that, and I'm sorry. But there it is." Juliet looked out at the swarm of first responders that filled Monique's yard. She couldn't seem to bring herself to meet Sienna's eyes.

Sienna's heart swelled and her stomach lurched. "It is. It's way too early. But I love you too, and I don't think that the timing of it really matters to anyone but us. So, we can wait a few months until we say it again, or we can throw caution to the wind and say it whenever we want to." She turned her head toward Juliet and met her gaze. "I love you."

Juliet leaned down and kissed her. Sienna was about to stop her, to remind her that there were people around and it would be out there in the universe, and then there would be nothing they could do to stop it. But she didn't. She kissed her back instead, relishing the soft comfort of Juliet's lips.

"Okay, lovebirds, we have a crime scene to bag and tag." Celeste snapped on a pair of gloves. "Sienna should probably sit down with the chief sooner rather than later to go over everything that happened."

They broke apart and Sienna nodded. The mixture of emotions made her light-headed. The fear had subsided, but the comedown still made her tremble. She smiled at Juliet and sought out Chief Quinlan while Juliet remained in the barn with Celeste and Officer Leland. The twinge in her back didn't hurt nearly as much as the conversation with Gretchen was going to.

CHAPTER THIRTY-FOUR

Back at the station, Juliet leafed through her notes on Monique. She had no priors, no real motive of her own, and a valid reason to have been at the library that day. She'd brought her dad a cup of coffee. It had all seemed so innocent at the time. Juliet slammed the drawer of her filing cabinet shut. There had to have been something, some clue she'd overlooked.

"Hey, Mitchell," Quinlan said, stopping in front of Juliet's open door. "Just heard from the officer stationed at the hospital, one of County's guys. Goodman is going to be fine. He'll be hurting for a while, but that's it. No lasting damage. You did good, Juliet."

Juliet gave him a tight-lipped smile. "Thanks, Chief. I'll be glad to get back to the town's usual business. You know, parking violations and rowdy teenagers. I have to go over to Gretchen's a little later with Sienna. I'm not looking forward to it."

"No, I can't imagine you would be. You don't think anyone filled her in yet, based on the spectacle at the daughter's place?" Quinlan asked.

"I highly doubt it. No one wanted to touch this. She's going to be heartbroken, Chief. When this is all said and done, she'll have lost a husband *and* a daughter. Can't even imagine." Juliet swallowed hard. She couldn't help but picture Gretchen and Monique at the town benefit, sitting together while Kowalski was honored by his friends. The gall of the woman, to sit beside her mother knowing she'd killed Rich. "She left Sienna a message telling her to forget about the checkbook. I guess the PT guy said he'd grab it next time."

"I just finished up with Sienna. Seems like the daughter wasn't keen on her mother being targeted. Maybe that'll be something. Not much, but something."

"Yeah. Maybe."

Quinlan shrugged. "Either way, they're both going away for a long time. It's too bad Goodman won't get as much time as Monique, since he didn't *actually* kill anyone. But we'll make sure justice is served."

Juliet nodded. Quinlan dropped a booklet on her desk before he went back to his own office. She looked down and shook her head. There was a sad-looking police officer sitting in an office chair with his head in his hands. The title was *A Practical Approach to Addressing Police Trauma*, and on the back was a sticky note with the number for one of the police psychologists. Quinlan's scribbled note indicated that she needed two sessions of counseling because she shot someone, and they needed to make sure she didn't have lasting issues because of it. Juliet didn't feel like she needed much of anything based on Charlie Goodman having a sore shoulder for a while. Richard Kowalski was dead, and Gretchen Kowalski was still in physical therapy, a widow now. Juliet didn't feel any guilt at all.

Her phone sitting on the desk vibrated. It was a text from Declan.

Is it true? Were you involved in a shootout?

Well, that was disconcerting. Maybe they should head over to Gretchen's earlier than they'd originally planned.

Not a shootout. I'm fine, Sienna's fine. I'll be over in a little bit to tell you about it.

The response bubbles appeared and disappeared a few times, but nothing came through. Juliet wondered if Declan was going to ask about Sienna being there with her, and then decided against it. She needed to talk to him again, alone.

With two uncomfortable conversations ahead of her, Juliet sighed loudly and closed her laptop. Monique's statement meant everything had been dealt with, and the case was officially closed. They'd hand off the chop shop element to the city authorities since Monique said that's where they were based. She texted Sienna to ask her to meet her at Gretchen's. Sienna responded in the affirmative and added a sad face.

Juliet parked the police car in front of Gretchen's house, behind Sienna's Volvo. Sienna was standing on the front porch, her hands firmly in her jacket pockets.

"Hey," Juliet said.

"Hey."

"Let's do this." Juliet rubbed Sienna's back in a light circle. "Waiting won't make it easier."

Sienna nodded and knocked on the door. After a few minutes, the door opened, and Gretchen was standing there using only a cane.

"Pretty good, huh?" she asked, holding it out for them to see. "Lieutenant, to what do I owe the pleasure?"

Seeing Gretchen smile at her presence made it all the worse. Juliet stepped forward. "We have some information about Rich's death, Gretchen. Can we come inside for a minute?"

"Of course." Gretchen limped back to the couch. "Did you catch who did this? Was it a gang initiation? I've heard about those."

"No, it wasn't." Juliet sat in the armchair across from the couch. "It was something a little closer to home than that."

Sienna sat next to Gretchen and held her hand. Gretchen looked at Sienna, confused, then back to Juliet.

"What was it?" she whispered.

"Well, you remember when you told Sienna about Charlie Goodman? The business partner Rich had for a short time?" Juliet asked.

"Yes, did he have something to do with this? I never liked him."

"He did, yes. But it wasn't him, exactly. He was close with Monique. I'm not sure if you knew that."

Gretchen looked disgusted. "What do you mean, close? I didn't even know they knew each other. Not well, anyway."

"They were seeing each other romantically." Juliet paused, while a pall cast itself across Gretchen's face. "I'm sorry, Gretchen. Monique was the one who poisoned Rich. It seems to have been under duress, but we don't know anything for sure about that. Charlie was the one driving the truck that ran you off the road. They coordinated poisoning Rich together, but Charlie appears to have been on his own when it came to you. I'm so sorry."

Gretchen was silent. She was looking down at the carpet, and when she looked up her eyes were glass. "How do you know this? She wouldn't have done such a thing. She loved Rich."

"She confessed, Gretchen. She held Sienna at gunpoint and confessed to killing him. They were caught up in some bad business and wanted to collect Rich's life insurance money. And Charlie wanted to collect yours, too. I don't even know what to say to you, Gretchen. I'm just…sorry."

"I think she was probably coerced into this. Monique was never a warm and fuzzy type of daughter, but she got along with Rich just fine. It had to be a false confession. Charlie Goodman threatened her, I'll bet," Gretchen said. She was surprisingly calm, which Juliet took as a very bad sign.

"We found the red truck in Monique's garage. It appears to be *the* red truck. I'm sure once everything is processed and the dust has settled, you'll be able to talk to her," Sienna said, rubbing her arm.

"Why did he try to kill me? What have I done to him?" Gretchen ignored Sienna.

"Same reason. You both had life insurance policies, and Monique had access to your checkbook and your online banking info. Goodman thought it would be better to collect two payouts instead of one. He's a bad man and we'll make sure he doesn't get away with anything that he's done." Juliet looked over at Sienna, who gave her a helpless shrug. It probably wasn't the time to convince Gretchen that her daughter was the one who'd set the plan in motion.

"Well, I'm glad we have some resolution, I suppose. I told Rich time and time again that he wasn't a person to get tied up with. He didn't listen," Gretchen said. She let tears spill down her cheeks. "I was so happy when he told me he'd cut ties with that man. He told me that he was involved in something shady, and Rich didn't want to be a part of it. Funny how one bad choice can ruin so many lives."

"If you want to talk about it, I'm right here," Sienna said. "I'll answer any questions that I can, and what I can't, I'm sure Juliet will tell you whatever she is able to."

"No, I'm okay. My nephew is here from Ohio, and he should be here any minute now. He's staying in the area for a few nights. I think I might just need a little family time. Once Monique is released, I'm sure she'll want to see him, too. I have to use the restroom. I'll be right back."

Sienna stood to help her, but Gretchen held her hand up. She made it to the bathroom by herself and left her cane against the wall.

"Should we leave her like this? In such denial?" Juliet asked quietly. It would have been terrible for Gretchen to accept that her daughter was a murderer, but it almost felt worse that she was pretending like Monique was wrongfully accused.

"We don't really have a choice. My services are optional, so if she doesn't want me here, then I need to go. Unless we think she might hurt herself, which doesn't seem likely at this point. We can wait until the nephew gets here," Sienna said.

"Okay." Juliet covered her face with her hands. "This whole thing really, really sucks. I can't believe that Rich's stepdaughter and that scumbag Goodman did this to her. It's so unfair."

Moments later, the doorbell rang, and a man in his thirties entered with a bag full of take-out. Gretchen greeted him warmly, and they held each other for a few minutes. He looked at them questioningly, but Gretchen shook her head and told him they needed to have a talk. When Juliet felt like it was safe for them to leave, she and Sienna left with a promise to return the next day.

"Well, that was awful," Juliet said on their walk to the cars.

"Understatement," Sienna agreed. "This is awkward, and I'm sorry, but I'm not really sure where I'm supposed to go right now. Should I go to your place? The motel? I know what we said earlier, but I don't want to assume anything."

"Of course, you can go to my house. You should. I have to go see Declan and Will, but I'll be home right after that. We can figure things out later. Tomorrow. Next week. All I know is that I want you next to me, and everything else is just a matter of semantics," Juliet said. It was the truest thing she'd said all day. They hugged briefly, Juliet handed Sienna her key, and they went their separate ways.

Juliet couldn't remember feeling much worse than she did as she pulled up to Will's house. His car was in the driveway, which made her heart sink. She had no idea what she was walking into, or what Declan had or hadn't told him.

She tried the front door and found it was unlocked. As she was about to call out for Will or Declan, she was nearly barreled over from behind.

"I'm still pissed at you, but I'm glad you're okay," Declan said, wrapping his arms around her.

Juliet turned and folded him into a hug, relishing the affection. "I'm fine, honey. We brought down a couple of bad guys today, so I guess it was a good day, all things considered. I know you're pissed at me, but I would like to talk to you about it."

He turned away, petulant. "I don't want to."

"Come on, Dec. You know I love you, I love your dad, and now I love Sienna, too. So, it's not that much of a stretch, right?" Juliet asked.

Declan wasn't biting. "You know it's different."

"I do, yes. Have you told Dad anything? I need to know how to approach him."

"No."

"Thank you for that. I appreciate you giving me the opportunity to talk to him myself," Juliet said, straining to see around the corner. She was putting on a brave face, but the truth was that she was filled with dread at the idea of telling Will.

"Whatever, it's fine. I see that Sienna bagged out, huh? Disappointing." Declan shook his head

"She didn't *bag* out, Declan. I told her that I wanted to be the one to talk to your dad. I don't want him to think I'm hiding anything from him, or that he doesn't mean enough to me to have a face-to-face conversation about something that concerns us both."

"Except that you *are* hiding something. Something pretty huge. How could you let this happen? Maybe she would have gotten back together with Dad, but now that will never happen. Everything could have gone back to normal, but you screwed it all up." Declan leaned against the counter, crossing his arms. He seemed to have quickly forgotten that hours earlier, his mother and stepmother were involved in a shooting incident.

Juliet shook her head vigorously. "No, Dec. They weren't getting back together, regardless of what happened between the two of us. Maybe she would stay close by, maybe she would go. Staying married was never an option."

"So, what am I, then? Her acquaintance? Dad's baggage from when he was just a stupid kid?"

"No! She loves you very much. You were one of the only reasons she stayed as long as she did. She wanted you in her life no matter what happened between her and your father. But she also knew you'd be very angry with her. She didn't know if you'd forgive her, or even want her in your life anymore. Sienna was heartbroken over the thought of losing you."

Declan seemed to soften. "Yeah, well. I wish none of this ever happened. Just want to go back to normal."

"This *is* normal now. Dad and Sienna living apart, you still seeing all of us. Hopefully. Do you still want to see her?" Juliet asked. She was afraid to hope.

"I guess. But not now. And not with you two being all kissy face or anything."

Juliet chuckled softly. "That, I get. You don't like your parents being kissy face with anyone ever, so I suppose it makes sense in this situation, too."

"What situation?" Will asked, toweling off his hair with a too-large bath towel. He walked over to Juliet and hugged her tightly. "So glad you're okay. I still can't believe it. I've driven by that guy's garage a million times on my way to the city."

Who the hell had already told Will what had happened? She supposed at that point it was irrelevant. She hugged him back, feeling like a traitor. Maybe she was being paranoid, and he would understand. Highly unlikely, but maybe.

"It was crazy. Definitely not used to that kind of thing in our little oceanside slice of heaven," Juliet said. She tried to sound as nonchalant as possible.

"I saw Celeste at the Mobil station," he said. Ah, that explained a lot. "She said Sienna was there too, because of Gretchen, and almost got shot? Is that really how it went down? I know Celeste likes to embellish a little."

"A little?" Juliet laughed. "But in this case, she's right. If we'd been a few minutes later...I don't even want to think about it."

"I know," Will said. He looked thoughtful. "I shouldn't have told her to move out. I was angry and acted hastily. It wasn't fair to her."

The pit in Juliet's stomach continued to grow.

Declan scoffed.

"What?" Will asked.

"Nothing," Declan said. He shrugged. "I have homework to do."

Juliet was torn watching him run up the stairs. On the one hand, she needed to talk to Will alone. On the other, a buffer would have been nice.

"What's his problem?"

"I don't know," Juliet said. And then wondered why she lied. She had to gear herself up, not just blurt it out. She wanted to be thoughtful and considerate of his feelings.

"Anyway, I'm just glad she's okay. I was thinking of asking her to come back, even for a little while. She might just need that sense of home, instead of being holed up in some hotel. I got a call from my lawyer this morning, funny enough. Apparently, she wants to 'expedite the process' as he called it," Will said, sarcastically. "You'd think she was already in another relationship." He smirked and shook his head.

Sweat began to form on her forehead and her stomach churned. She didn't smile back at him.

"What?" His smile faded. "Do you know something? Jules, tell me. Is she already seeing another guy?"

He looked so vulnerable and afraid of the answer that Juliet nearly wept. She cleared her throat. "Will, I have to tell you something."

His eyes widened. "Juliet, if she has already moved on, I will freak the fuck out. She told me that there was no one else, that it had nothing to do with why we were splitting up. You've been spending a lot of time with her, has she told you anything?"

"Will, I promise you that there was no one else. She wasn't lying about that."

"There *was* no one else? What does that mean?" Will asked. His face clouded over. "What are you not telling me?"

Juliet cringed. He sounded desperate, and the longer she took to spit out the words, the worse it was going to get.

"I know this is hurtful, and I am so sorry. But…yes. She is seeing someone." Juliet swallowed hard, willing herself not to cry. She didn't think it would help the situation at all.

Anger flushed Will's face. "Who is he? I'll kill the sonofabitch. She's my wife, goddam it. Even if it wasn't working right now, that doesn't mean we couldn't have reconciled sometime in the future."

"No, Will. No. You weren't going to reconcile, *ever*. I don't mean to crush your hopes and dreams, but she told you time and time again that she was done. I don't know what else she could have said to make you understand. It was over. Over. It *is* over." Juliet inhaled deeply, realizing that she was angry as well.

Will just stared at her, and slowly, it was clear he understood. "Is it you?" he whispered.

Juliet's silence was all the answer Will needed.

"You need to go," he said, looking down at the counter.

"Will, it was never supposed to happen. You know I would never—"

"You know what, Juliet? I don't know anything anymore. You were my friend, probably my closest friend in the world, and when I told you Sienna needed a friend, somehow you interpreted that as an invitation to fuck my wife."

"Don't say that. That's not what this is about, believe me when I tell you that I tried to push it away, I didn't mean to fall in love with her," Juliet yelled, furiously wiping at her eyes.

"In *love* with her? You're in *love* with her? Get the fuck out, Juliet. I mean it. Go."

"Please," Juliet said. She was desperate for something she didn't know how to articulate. It was too early to ask for forgiveness, but she didn't want him to shut her out completely.

"Go!" Will shouted, slamming his fist on the marble countertop.

Juliet looked up and saw Declan peeking at them over the railing. His eyes were red, and his lip quivered, like it had when he was a toddler.

She let out a broken breath and headed for the door, not knowing what she'd expected to come out of the conversation. She knew how Will still felt about Sienna, so it wasn't as though he was going to pat her on the back and wish them well. She'd known that starting something with Sienna was going to upend everything. She'd known but decided it was worth it. Juliet drove toward home in a daze, talk radio droning on in the background. Everything hurt.

CHAPTER THIRTY-FIVE

Sienna finished wiping down the counters and organizing the silverware drawer when she heard Juliet's car pull into the driveway. She was anxious, and her back hurt, and she was afraid that Juliet would change her mind about the two of them when she was alone with Will and Declan. Maybe Will would sour her on Sienna and make her feel guilty for even entertaining the thought of ruining their lives. She took a hefty swallow of wine as she heard Juliet open the front door.

"Hey," Sienna said softly.

"Hey," Juliet said.

Sienna could tell she'd been crying. Her eyes were puffy, and her cheeks were flushed. "Didn't go well, I assume?"

"No, it didn't. I knew it wasn't going to, but I had it in my head that I could make it all make sense and Will would see the light. Or some bullshit like that. But no, it didn't go well."

Sienna stiffened. What did that mean, exactly? "What did he say?"

Juliet poured herself a glass of wine and leaned against the refrigerator. "Just that I basically flushed our years of friendship down the drain and ruined everyone's lives. You know, the usual."

"Oh, Juliet, I'm sorry. I should have been there with you," Sienna said.

Juliet shook her head. "No, I think that would have made it worse, honestly. He was just so *angry* at me. I've never seen him like that. Toward me, anyway. He gets all ragey at business stuff and things like that, but never toward me. I expected it, but I wasn't prepared for it, if that makes any sense," Juliet said.

"It does."

Sienna contemplated walking over to her, putting her arms around her and telling her that everything would be okay, but that was probably a lie.

"Where do we go from here?" Juliet asked, swishing the wine around in her glass.

"Has anything changed? Do you think we should put the brakes on so you can figure things out with Will and Declan before we go any further?" Sienna asked. Her heart was on the verge of being torn in two, but she didn't want Juliet to resent her. Ever.

Juliet hesitated. "That's probably the smart thing to do." She sighed and put her glass on the counter.

Sienna's heartbeat began to quicken. They'd come so close. She tried to tell herself that it was probably for the best.

"But no, that's not what we're going to do. I love Will. I love my son, and you know I would do anything for him. But this is for me. This is what I need, and the only thing that I want." She moved closer and took Sienna's hands in hers. "We don't have to flaunt it or talk about it in front of them, but I'm not about to lose you, Sienna. What I said earlier, I meant it. I love you."

Relief flooded every one of Sienna's senses. "I love you, too." She pushed forward and brought her lips to Juliet's. They were soft against her own, but firm in their persistence. Juliet's hand found its way to the nape of Sienna's neck and pulled her tightly against her. Possessive, almost. Sienna melted beneath her touch and her body reacted in kind.

As things were starting to progress, there was a soft knock at the door. Sienna pulled back, giving Juliet a questioning look. Juliet shrugged, straightened her shirt, and went to open it.

"It's Declan," she called out, opening the door.

"Hey, Mom. Sienna. I didn't want to walk in on anything weird. That's why I knocked," he said, as he walked into the living room. "I can't stay long. I told Dad I was grabbing a pizza from Luigi's. He's really hurt and angry and he's not going to let it go any time soon. Just wanted you to know that."

Sienna didn't know what to say. Maybe Declan just needed to voice it to someone who would understand, she wasn't really sure. She looked over at Juliet, who was frowning.

Declan scuffed at the carpet with the tip of his shoe, his hands stuffed in his pockets. "I just wanted to come over because I know you were upset when you left, Mom. This sucks, what's going on. But I love you both and I'm pretty mad right now, but I'll get over it. Sienna, I wanted you and Dad to stay together because I didn't want things to be different, and I liked our family just the way it was. But if this is normal now, like Mom said, then I'll deal with it. I'm definitely on Dad's side right now, but I'm sure I'll feel differently the more time passes. So, I'm going to go get my pizza, with bacon and sausage and pineapple, because I'm upset too, and Dad said I could get whatever I wanted. So, yeah. I love you guys. But you both still suck a little." Declan nodded at the end, as if to put a period on his thoughts.

Sienna rushed over to him and hugged him, and Juliet did the same. He was mostly dead-armed, but that's how he usually was, so it wasn't a huge deviation from the normal Declan. She could see Juliet crying again and squeezed her hand as it rested on Declan's back.

"That's all we can ask, Dec. Thank you," Sienna said, though her words were garbled. Her face was smushed into his shoulder.

"Okay, okay. That's enough." He wriggled out of their embrace. "I didn't say everything was good. Yet. Now let me go eat."

Sienna backed away and Juliet reluctantly let him go. She whispered something to him on the front porch and Declan nodded before he took off down the street. She came back into the house looking lighter than she had earlier.

"Thank God," Juliet huffed, falling backward onto the couch. "I know he said it will take time, but at least he's open to it. I can't even describe how much better that makes me feel."

"Me too. He really is a good kid. I'm so grateful I get to keep him in my life. That weighed on me more than I can tell you. Seeing his journey from a goofy five-year-old into the man that he's becoming… it's been one of the great privileges of my life," Sienna said. And she meant it.

"I love that you love him," Juliet said, smiling. She patted the couch next to her. "*Alien* is on channel twelve. I could use some mindless entertainment for a little bit. You down?"

"Always," Sienna said and sat next to Juliet. She curled her legs underneath her and rested her head on Juliet's shoulder. Juliet was tracing her fingers over the curves and ridges of Sienna's hand while Sigourney Weaver kicked ass in the background. Sienna hadn't felt as content or as comfortable in as long as she could remember. Even after staring death in the face just hours earlier, Sienna felt peacefully safe.

CHAPTER THIRTY-SIX

"Lieutenant, we have a problem," Chief Quinlan said, dropping a file on Juliet's desk.

Juliet looked up at him curiously. "What problem?"

"Monique Breen finally spoke to the interrogator and told him everything she knew. He noted that he doesn't believe her to be lying, but he's willing to use a polygraph to be sure."

"Why would we need a polygraph for a murder confession?" Juliet asked. She was utterly confused.

"Because what she's saying doesn't match up with what happened. She could be concocting some story so she gets less time or so she looks like a patsy. She says she added one hundred milligrams of strychnine that Goodman had shipped to him from Canada, to a hot cup of coffee. She brought it to Kowalski and then when they were in his office, she panicked and had a change of heart. She purposely knocked the coffee over and it spilled onto the floor. They mopped it up with paper towels, but she left the cup sitting on his desk. She thought that was the end of it, but when she found out he'd died, she assumed there must have been a little left in the cup and he'd drank it, and that the strychnine mixed with the nitro caused his death. I have the lab guys over at the library now testing the carpet."

Juliet stared at him, trying to comprehend what he was saying. "They didn't find any strychnine in his system when they did the autopsy. So that's not possible."

"No, it isn't. So, either Breen is a masterful liar, or our case is still open. I asked her why Goodman went after Gretchen if she'd put the kibosh to their grand plan, and she told me that she'd chickened out of telling Goodman that the plan was off. He thought everything was still a go and decided to take matters into his own hands." Quinlan shook his head. "How is it possible that *two* people were after Kowalski at the same time? Stranger things have happened, but this is really out there."

"You think Goodman could have somehow gone behind Monique's back and used a different poison to accomplish the same goal? This time with Kowalski's meds?" Juliet asked. It didn't make sense, but talking out possibilities seemed like the best thing to do.

"We would have seen him on the surveillance footage. Kowalski never left the building that day and it isn't Goodman's prints, or Monique's, on the bottle we found the nitro in."

Quinlan paused. "There is one avenue we didn't fully explore, due to the circumstances, and I hate to say this, but maybe from a bit of bias as well. Who is the one person who knows where Rich keeps his medicine, his dosage, and who knows his daily routine?"

Juliet looked up at him.

He nodded. "Gretchen."

"Come on, Chief. You really think Gretchen could have done this?"

"No, I don't. But at this point I don't know who we can trust and who we can't."

"Her story has been consistent from the beginning and her alibi is lying in a ditch. That seems pretty solid to me," Juliet said.

Quinlan nodded. "Okay. I'll let you know what the lab guys say as soon as I hear from them. If you need me on this, let me know. Jeffries and Leland are up to speed on the latest as well. Check back once you've spoken with her, all right?"

Juliet nodded. "I will. Are they going to polygraph Monique today?"

"Not sure. Hopefully. They need to get their poly guy out to conduct the test, so it will depend on his schedule, most likely. Apparently, Monique is open to taking it."

"Thanks, Chief."

Quinlan left her office and Juliet just sat there for a minute, stunned. It was clear-cut just twenty-four hours earlier. Monique had poisoned Richard; Goodman had run Gretchen off the road. Murder one and attempted murder, with conspiracy to commit murder one charges.

Juliet rubbed her face vigorously and checked her phone when it pinged a text message.

Heard from my attorney this morning. Will signed everything as is and agreed to an expedited hearing if possible. I'll keep my own retirement fund and my car, and that's about it. Once the judge gives us the okay, it should be wrapped up shortly. I guess the conversation between the two of you is what did it.

Juliet didn't know how to feel. She was happy for Sienna and for herself but sad for Will and sad for Declan, and maybe even a little sad for Sienna, since the life she'd known for the last ten years was officially about to end.

Ok. Let me know if you want to talk about it.

That seemed to be the path of least resistance at that moment, and Juliet wasn't sure she could handle much else.

On my way to Gretchen's. Wanted to check on her after last night. Her nephew is spending the day sightseeing up north, so I'd rather she not be alone.

Juliet didn't think Sienna was in any danger by going over to Gretchen's, but the thought did give her pause. It wasn't something she wanted to text or talk about by phone, she wanted to sit down with Sienna and hash through everything in person. It wasn't like Gretchen Kowalski was a cold-blooded killer.

❖

Two big trash bags and a few boxes were piled up on Juliet's front stoop. She sighed when she saw them, knowing exactly what they were and who had left them there. She peeked into one of the bags and saw a sweater lying on top. She supposed it was better than finding everything strewn all over her front lawn.

She picked up Sienna's things and put them against the wall in the living room. She'd stopped at home to change into a short-sleeved shirt. It felt a lot warmer outside than she'd anticipated that morning and she'd taken advantage of some quiet time to reflect on everything going on.

Her radio squelched to life.

"Looking for 5A-12, Dispatch."

Juliet buttoned her last few buttons and answered, "This is 5A-12, go ahead."

"We have a 10-53, possible homicide, 37 Blanchard. EMS is en route."

Her head snapped up. That was Gretchen's address. Sienna was on her way over there.

"En route."

Juliet flew out of her house, the screen door of the porch slamming shut behind her. She didn't even remember getting behind the wheel and activating her siren. She drove so fast to Gretchen's house that she pulled into the driveway before the EMS vehicle arrived.

Her stomach lurched. Sienna's car was parked across the street and she wasn't inside it.

Juliet drew her gun and kicked open the front door, which was open just a hair. She saw Sienna kneeling on the floor, her hair covering her face. A body was beside her.

"Sienna, are you hurt?" Juliet asked, pointing her gun toward the body.

"No," she whispered. "It's Gretchen. She was like this when I got here. I haven't seen anyone else."

Juliet sprang forward, kneeling next to Sienna on the floor. Gretchen lay unconscious, her eye swelled shut and her bottom lip split and swollen. Blood seeped from a wound in her chest, turning her white blouse crimson. She put two fingers to her neck and breathed a sigh of relief. "She has a pulse. It's weak but it's there."

Juliet stood and drew her gun again as she made her way through the house to clear it. She walked slowly into the kitchen, where she followed a trail of blood leading to the kitchen sink. She noticed the pixie cut first. In a heap, lying next to the sink, was Tara Wolfe.

A carving knife, covered in blood, lay next to her.

Juliet bent down and felt for a pulse. There was none. She had a bright red wound on her forehead, with a swirl in the center of it.

Juliet lifted her head slightly, to see if there were any bullet holes or stab wounds or anything that would make more sense than what would presumably amount to a large bruise. Her temple was fileted open, and blood pooled beneath her head. The disruption to the body caused it to spread in a wide arc around her.

Juliet jumped back to avoid the blood and looked around the sink area where she saw that the corner of the granite countertop had a few droplets of blood on it, and a tiny stream that stopped about halfway down the cherrywood cabinets.

"What the hell happened here?" she whispered, backing away from the body. She did a quick search of the house and didn't find anyone else or anything that suggested there was another person on the premises. EMS had arrived and she gave the all clear.

"Did you see Tara when you got here?" Juliet asked.

"Who?" Sienna asked.

"Tara. She's in the kitchen. She's dead," Juliet said, bracing herself for Sienna's reaction.

"*What?*" Sienna looked like she was about to lose it. It really was too much.

Gretchen gasped for air as she was being loaded onto the stretcher. She looked around, wild-eyed as she regained consciousness. "It was me," she croaked, sounding more like a bullfrog than herself.

"Try not to speak, ma'am," one of the technicians said, hooking her up to oxygen.

"I killed her," Gretchen said, ignoring him. "It was an accident. She came at me with a knife, like a madwoman. She said I kept the only man she'd ever loved a prisoner. I thought I was dying, but I didn't fall down. She seemed to be in shock, so I took my cane and hit her. Hard. I didn't mean to kill her. Poor thing. Must have been having an episode."

"Ma'am, you really shouldn't be talking. We need to get you to the hospital," the other technician said. They wheeled her out of the house, while the rest of the police force arrived. Quinlan was calling in the forensics team, Celeste was calling the medical examiner, and Deagle was taping off the perimeter. It was much too similar to what had happened in late summer.

"Why would Tara Wolfe go after Gretchen? Wasn't she being held for questioning? How was she able to do this?" Sienna asked. She was clearly distraught.

"That was over a week ago. They had nothing to hold her on, you know how that works." Juliet tried to make sense of it along with Sienna.

Quinlan walked back into the living room, stepping around the bloodstain on the carpet. "Tara Wolfe had recanted everything she'd said, said it was due to everything that had happened, and she was overwhelmed with emotion. She must have realized the gravity of what she'd sort of confessed to and decided to walk it back."

"The regional hiring committee actually hired someone new to take over the library. A woman from out of town, I think. Maybe that pissed her off," Deagle said, shrugging.

"How do we know that Gretchen didn't ask Tara to come over, and then Tara stabbed her in self-defense?" Celeste asked.

They all looked at her like she had three heads.

"Gretchen just started walking without a walker about three days ago. Her legs buckle if she tries to move too fast or turn too quickly. I don't think she was under any illusion that she could take Tara Wolfe in a fight," Sienna said.

"I'm sure forensics will be able to sort it out," Quinlan said. "We'll have to question Gretchen, *again*, when she is able to speak with us. How much can that poor woman take?"

The mood was somber as they filed out of Gretchen's house. Sienna leaned up against Juliet's police car and took a few deep breaths.

"I don't know if she'll bounce back this time," Sienna said. "She's tough, and she's a fighter, but come on. You know the first thing she said to me when I walked in and found her like that? 'I told you Monique didn't do it.' And then she blacked out, or passed out, or whatever the hell happened."

Was Gretchen trying to protect Monique, to keep her from going to jail for what Gretchen had actually done? There were still too many questions. "I thought you were in trouble again. This has really got to stop. My heart can't take it. Quinlan wanted me to question Gretchen again. He thought that maybe she was the stone we left unturned."

Sienna shook her head. "Wasn't it Monique? I thought that part was evident."

Juliet hadn't had a chance to catch her up on the earlier events of the day. As far as Sienna was concerned, the case was still closed. "I'll fill you in back at the station. You won't believe it."

CHAPTER THIRTY-SEVEN

Sienna sat at the kitchen table, utterly spent. Celeste handed her the salad dressing while Juliet scooped a pile of lettuce and other veggies onto her plate. Brooke was furiously buttering a dinner roll.

"I'm still in total shock. I know Tara personally. She used to come into my shop all the time for the aloe bars. We would shoot the shit a little, she'd tell me about library gossip, about her boyfriend's antics, and I'd talk about you," Brooke said, nudging Celeste.

"What was her boyfriend's name?" Juliet asked, drenching her salad with Thousand Island.

"She never told me his name. Said she didn't want to say anything until he told his family. Because they…" Brooke trailed off, seemingly realizing what she was saying. "Oh. Huh."

"Why did you never tell me that?" Celeste asked. She looked at Brooke incredulously.

Brooke shrugged. "How would that even come up? I talk to people all day every day. Do you want me to come home and tell you about Elvira Houston's gout? Or Louis Zipp's tomato garden failures?"

Celeste nodded. "Good point. But with what happened to Rich Kowalski, I'd have thought you'd say something."

"You didn't tell me she was a suspect and I didn't think twice about it. Your big line is always, 'I can't talk about an active case, Brooke. It's confidential.'" Brooke imitated Celeste's voice.

"Well, it is," Celeste said. She petulantly stabbed a cucumber.

"What did she say about him?" Sienna asked.

"Not much, really. Just little things about gifts he'd given her and late-night phone calls, and how they had so much in common, that kind of thing," Brooke said.

"I know about the gifts," Juliet said. "Didn't see too many late-night phone calls on his cell records though. A few after the library had closed, but those could have been business related."

"It's really a tragedy all around. She obviously needed help, and Rich paid the price with his life. Monique will still go to jail, and Goodman will too. And Gretchen has so much to deal with. My heart breaks for her," Sienna said. She really was concerned about Gretchen making a full recovery after what had happened earlier. She'd fought long and hard through the last injury, but without any immediate family left to support her, it might be a lot more difficult this time around.

"I know what you mean. It's so sad. Not to change the subject, but I'm still in shock about this." Brooke wagged her finger between Juliet and Sienna. "So, you guys are a thing now? For real?"

Sienna looked at Juliet. She wasn't sure how much they should be saying or not saying, and she didn't want to overstep with Juliet's friends.

Juliet smiled. "Yes. For real."

"I should have known something was up the night we came over to watch the Sox game. You two were all nervous around each other and hyper aware of how close you were sitting next to each other. I can sense these things," Brooke said.

"Oh please, you had no idea," Celeste interjected and rolled her eyes.

"Just eat your salad." Brooke waved her fork. "I did too. Are you living here now?"

Sienna shook her head. "Not exactly. I'm just squatting here until something close by opens up."

"Makes sense," Brooke said. "How's Will taking it?"

Silence fell. Celeste looked down at her plate and Juliet took a long sip of water.

"Not good," Sienna offered. She gave a tight smile and refilled her water glass.

"Hint taken," Brooke said and thankfully, let it go. "Let's talk about something lighter, like religion and politics."

It was so strange yet so comfortable, sitting at the dinner table with Juliet and her friends, doing things that couples did without giving them a second thought. The last time she'd sat down to dinner with Will and anyone else was when her cousin and her husband had flown in from Florida a few years back. Will had left the table to get some work done when the conversation had turned to Sienna's family. If she had to pinpoint a moment when she'd realized that she wanted more out of marriage and companionship and love, and that she had to do something about it, that might have been it.

Juliet seemed to realize that Sienna was deep in thought and reached over to give her knee a quick squeeze. When Sienna looked up, Juliet winked at her in the most adorable way. Sienna hadn't realized how much those little things meant to her. Allowing themselves to be together wasn't just the right thing to do. It was the only thing to do.

"Morning, Nancy," Sienna said into her cell phone. Her supervisor had called her back after she'd heard Sienna's lengthy message, explaining Gretchen's current situation. "I'll be able to check on Gretchen in the hospital, but otherwise my schedule is open at this point."

She was sitting at Juliet's kitchen table, since she couldn't imagine staying alone in a hotel room after what had happened with Gretchen, but she was going to get a room for the upcoming night, come hell or highwater. Her stay at Juliet's could be chalked up to unfortunate circumstances. Juliet walked by and placed a light kiss on Sienna's neck on her way to the kitchen. The sensation brought the previous night's activities into clear view. Sienna needed to ignore the flip-flop in her stomach and refocus her attention on work.

"Sure, I can do that," Sienna said, writing some notes on an old menu she'd found in Juliet's junk drawer. Her next case would begin in the next few days. In the meantime, she had a novel-length report to prepare on Gretchen's accident, recovery, attack, and hopefully her recovery from the attack.

Juliet handed her a cup of coffee, three creams and one sugar, just how she liked it. "Mmm, thank you."

"Welcome. We have to go in and do another top to bottom sweep of Tara's apartment today. Her parents are flying in from Chicago to make arrangements. Sometimes you forget that when the 'bad' guy dies, it still leaves a hole in a lot of people's hearts."

"I see that a lot more often than I'd care to admit," Sienna said. She sipped her coffee. "Not all of my clients are the proverbial good guy, that's for sure."

"Okay, I better get going. We need to figure out Tara's motive for going after Gretchen, and about a thousand other things today. I'll check in with you in a bit," Juliet said, lacing up her shoe.

Sienna stood and opened her arms for Juliet to fall into. They hugged for a full minute and then Juliet kissed her tenderly. Sienna was fairly certain that this was what heaven would be like. Without all of the deceit and murder, of course.

As she was finishing getting ready to head into the office, Sienna's text alert went off. It was a message from Celeste, who had just left the hospital.

Gretchen is awake, sort of. She asked if you could let her knitting group know what happened. She said it's her turn to make the prayer shawl this month, and now she won't finish it. I assured her they would understand, given the circumstances, but she still wants you to let them know. She said the group email is on the computer. If not in inbox, check spam. Password to get in is richgretch37.

Celeste finished it off with a shrug emoji.

She just woke up from being stabbed and that's what she's worried about? Lol. I'll make sure they get word and please let her know I'll be by afterward.

Celeste responded with a thumbs-up.

Driving to Gretchen's felt surreal. Knowing that she wouldn't be there, that she'd been attacked *again*, that Monique was in a prison cell somewhere...it was too much. Though Sienna had never really cared for Monique, she'd gotten used to her being around.

The area around Gretchen's house was still taped off. Sienna pulled her badge out of her bag, but the officer working at the scene recognized her and nodded at her that she was cleared to go in.

Gretchen's laptop was in the same spot it had been when they'd paid her bills the other day. On a tray table pushed up against the family room wall, the mouse sitting on top like an electronic guardian. She opened it up and entered Gretchen's password.

The background of a sandy beach appeared. She opened the webmail client that Rich had renamed "RICH AND GRETCH EMAILS." Sienna tried to ignore the prickliness she felt at seeing 23,668 unread email messages in the inbox.

She didn't see anything that jumped out at her as a knitting group email in the first few pages of the inbox, so she decided to look elsewhere. Sienna let out a groan at seeing 2,335 messages in the spam folder. She'd hoped that the reason Gretchen's laptop was so slow was because of how old it was, and not a virus she'd let in through spam. None of the messages had been clicked on, and since nearly all of the messages had to do with anatomy enlargements and overseas dating, that was a good thing. She went over to page two, where nothing there had been clicked either. Her eyes were drawn to the only message in the folder that didn't have hearts or tongues in the subject line. It was a message from Tara Wolfe dated August 23. The night that Richard Kowalski had died.

Sienna stared at the name for what felt like hours. She brought the mouse pointer over to the message and clicked the subject line, which read, "Good-bye."

At the top of the message, in bright red font, the email client announced that the message appeared to be spam because it was an unrecognized address that had been flagged on other websites. Sienna clicked ignore and proceeded to the message.

Dear Gretchen,

Things have progressed to a point where we can no longer lie to you. I know that this is going to hurt, and I am sorry for that. But Rich and I are in love, and even though we can't be together in this world, we will surely be together in the next. You still have so much—your daughter, your friends, your church groups. Rich is all that I have, and all that I need. But I can't keep pretending that you don't exist and that he truly belongs to me. By this time tomorrow, we'll be in heaven, or hell, or wherever people go when this life is through with them, but we'll be together, as it should be. I can assure you that Rich loved you, and that we never meant for this to happen.

We'll have one last drink tonight, in your honor.

Tara

Sienna's thoughts were moving so quickly she didn't know what to do first. She forwarded the email to Juliet and texted her to read her email, immediately. She went back to the inbox and waded through page after page until she found an email that came from "GRETCH'S KNITTING LADIES." She was able to click on that and compose a quick note to let them know why Gretchen would be unable to fulfill her prayer shawl duties for the month. She was vague and left out most details, but the message would still get across. She slammed the lid of the laptop shut and sat in Gretchen's chair, wondering if life would ever feel normal again.

CHAPTER THIRTY-EIGHT

W hat the fuck is this?" Juliet asked aloud, while reading her email from her phone. She opened it up as soon as she'd received Sienna's text. She blasted it to Quinlan, Celeste, Leland, and Deagle.

Quinlan walked down Tara's stairs reading the email on his phone. "Where did she find this?" he asked.

"She was on Gretchen's laptop sending something to a knitting group. Found it in the junk mail folder. Guess we're lucky she saw this before it was lost in spam hell forever. So, Tara planned on taking them both out that night. She mustn't have been able to go through with it," Juliet said, the hair on her arms standing on end.

"This is un-fucking believable," Quinlan said. "She's been under our noses the whole time."

They all looked at the usually reserved chief, but none of them said anything.

"Make sure the tech guys go through Wolfe's personal computer piece by piece," Quinlan said to Celeste. She nodded. "Didn't we already go through her email? And his?"

"We did, yes. This came from some other account, and definitely didn't originate on her work computer. They looked at her laptop, too, but a lot of people have more than one these days. Rich's email was clean as a whistle. This one seems like an old account that he set up for him and Gretchen, but I'd guess Gretchen used it most. Look, it's an AOL account." Juliet held up her phone. Not that anyone needed to look at it, since she'd sent them all the email.

"So, what ended up as solely a murder was supposed to be a murder/suicide. But I still don't understand why that would make her attack Gretchen after the fact. Was she pissed off that her grand plan didn't work? That she couldn't go through with it?" Leland asked.

"I don't know that we'll ever find out," Juliet said, rereading the email for the tenth time. "She obviously had a lot of feelings toward Gretchen for being the one 'standing in the way' of her and Rich. Maybe she said more to Gretchen before she stabbed her. Thank God she didn't have very good aim."

"This is like a twisted game of whodunit," Deagle said, his face buried in his phone. "And the answer is: everybody done it."

"Collect everything you can," Quinlan said. "If there is *anything* else that points to her being the one to kill Kowalski, we need to find it. I want that whiskey bottle retested. See if they can match Wolfe's print to that partial. Somebody see if Gretchen's awake enough to talk to us."

Juliet volunteered to check on Gretchen. Sienna would probably be there by then, and she seemed to be able to get Gretchen to open up better than anyone.

She drove to the hospital and raced up the stairs to the second floor, where Gretchen was located this time around. Juliet found it hard to believe it had been less than three months since the first time Gretchen was stretched out on a hospital bed, hooked up to innumerable machines and medicine bags. Thankfully, Sienna was sitting by her side.

"Good, you're here," Juliet said. Sienna was the proverbial sight for sore eyes, and she was grateful that she didn't have to see Gretchen alone.

"Hey," Sienna whispered. "She's sleeping. When she was awake a little while ago, I asked her if she'd ever received anything from Tara by email and she was confused by what I meant. She said she didn't think so, and she'd have remembered that email if she'd seen it, especially after he died."

"Yeah, I agree. Did she say if Tara said anything else when she showed up at her house?" Juliet asked. She pulled one of the vinyl chairs over to Sienna and sat next to her.

"Not really. I'm not a hundred percent convinced that she knew Tara was talking about Rich as the only man she'd ever loved. When I mentioned Rich's name in that context, she asked if I was mixed up. I didn't want to keep confusing her, not when she's like this. I figured it could wait." Sienna gently moved Gretchen's hand so that the IV wasn't buckled beneath it. "She seemed to understand that Tara was the one who poisoned Rich, but I don't think she fully grasps why."

"Well, that's awful. I wasn't sure there was anything left to make this whole thing more terrible, but there it is. It'll be fun having that discussion with her, telling her that Rich's co-worker was convinced they were having an affair and that's why he's dead. And if her daughter had gone through with her own scheme, he would've been dead by her hand. I mean, come on," Juliet said. She leaned her elbow on the arm of the chair and massaged her forehead. She was sure it would return to normal at some point, but the town she knew and loved and felt so much a part of, a town that hadn't seen a murder in twenty years, seemed completely tainted. "I suppose in some sense, we're lucky. More than a third of murders go unsolved. We could have been spinning our wheels for the next year and come up with nothing."

"True," Sienna said. She rubbed her hand up and down Juliet's arm. "I have to go to my office for a bit. I have stacks of paperwork to complete. I suppose it's my own fault for letting it pile up. I'm so grateful my boss let me spend this kind of time with her," she said, nodding at Gretchen.

"Okay, go ahead. I'll hang out with her for a little while. I'm picking up Declan tonight for dinner. Promised I'd take him to Casa Mañana for some nachos. You want to come?" Juliet asked.

Sienna smiled. "No, you spend some time with Declan tonight. Maybe I'll take him out over the weekend, and we can just ply him with fast food until he forgives us."

Juliet laughed. "Sounds like a plan. I'll see you tonight," she said.

Sienna nodded and blew her a kiss.

Juliet sat back in the chair, the hum of Gretchen's machines lulling her into a false sense of relaxation. When Gretchen was still out an hour later, and Juliet wasn't sure if she had dozed off in the chair or not, she headed back to the police station to see if anything else had been uncovered. The nurse at the desk outside of Gretchen's room promised to call if and when Gretchen woke up.

❖

Juliet could have beeped the horn or texted Declan to tell him she was outside, but the last thing she wanted to be was a coward. She knocked on the front door and took a step back to wait for someone to answer the door.

Will opened the door, and his face changed as soon as he saw it was Juliet. She started to say hello, but he just walked away, didn't acknowledge her one way or the other. She noticed that he had his suits laid out over the couch, presumably from the closet in the pool house. She just exhaled loudly and looked up at the orange sky. Forcing him to speak to her wouldn't do anyone any good.

Declan bounded down the stairs, his hoodie only halfway over his head. "I'll be back later," he called out.

"Hi, honey," Juliet said as he came outside. "Everything going okay over here?"

Declan shrugged. "It's fine. He has a lot of interesting words he uses when he talks about you guys, but when he finishes his rant, he always says that you're a good mom and I shouldn't let his feelings about you right now rub off on me."

Juliet scoffed. "Well, I guess that's something. They're not, are they?"

Declan buckled his seat belt after he slid into the passenger seat. "Not what?"

"Rubbing off on you. You know, his feelings about me right now."

"Nah. He's mad. I would be too if I was in his shoes. Josh said I need to take advantage of the situation. Everyone's going to feel bad for me, poor little boy from a broken home, so I should stock up on all the electronics and food I want before it goes away," Declan said with a small grin.

"Nice. You can forget it. I'll bring you for Mexican and *maybe* I'll buy you an Xbox game, but that's where it ends," Juliet said.

"I'll take it," Declan said. He popped his earbuds into his ears and that was the end of the conversation until they reached the restaurant.

While Declan was rambling on about a sweet pair of kicks he saw online, Juliet felt her phone vibrate in her pocket. She pulled it out and saw a text from Quinlan.

Lab results in from Kowalski's office. Coffee on rug and traces of strychnine sulphate found as well. Breen was telling the truth.

"Shit. Wow."

"Shit what?" Declan asked.

Juliet stuck the phone back in her pocket. "Shit nothing. And *language.*"

She finished listening about the sneakers that he'd probably forget about before the week was through. Juliet had to admit, it was nice being out with Declan, talking about inane things, while Sienna was at home waiting for her, and Declan knew it. He wasn't ready to talk about it, not in any meaningful way, but Juliet was grateful for the baby steps he was willing to take.

"You ready to come home yet?" she asked as she was paying the bill.

Declan looked down at his empty plate. "Not yet. If it's cool with you, I'd like to stay with Dad for a little longer. I think he can use the company."

Juliet was actually proud of his compassion. "I agree. Of course, that's cool with me. Look at you, being all aware of people's feelings," she teased him.

He just rolled his eyes at her again and popped in the earbuds. All in all, she chalked it up to a pretty successful night of communicating with her son.

CHAPTER THIRTY-NINE

The news was droning on in the background, but Sienna was concentrating on the silkiness of Juliet's hair. She was jealous that even without any product, Juliet's hair always seemed so soft and full. Sienna needed half a bottle of smoothing oil just to keep the frizz away. She never left home without it.

Juliet lay between her legs, munching on potato chips and offering her own commentary on the nightly news. Sienna was only half-listening, but Juliet wasn't really talking to her, anyway. She'd learned early on that Juliet liked to give her opinions on things without expecting any feedback. It was one of the many things Sienna loved about her.

"Hey," she said, knitting her brows. "Did you ever check out those places on the list? I forgot to ask what you thought of them."

Juliet froze. Sienna had given her a list of available apartments because Juliet had said she wanted to vet the area before Sienna committed.

"I, um, didn't go see them," Juliet said and turned to face Sienna. "I totally understand if you think it's too fast, and it is. I'm not stupid, but I was sort of hoping you'd consider just living here. With me. I figured that we'd be spending most of our time together *anyway*, so why add another household worth of bills when we could just split one set? It's actually brilliant if you think of the logistics."

Sienna couldn't help but smile. Juliet's anticipation was painted all over her face. "When were you planning on telling me this brilliant plan of yours?"

"I was planning on telling you tonight. And I just did. So, there you go."

"Mm-hmm." Sienna laughed.

"What do you think? No pressure, I promise. You've been living with someone for a very long time, so if you want to feel what it's like to be completely on your own again, I won't take it personally, at all. It's really up to you," Juliet said. Her eyes shifted nervously.

"I think it's a wonderful idea," Sienna said.

"That's fine, really. Wait, you do?" Juliet looked stunned. "I thought you were going to be super mad at me for not going to the apartments. I wasn't trying to take the choice away from you, I promise. I'm just kind of a chicken."

Sienna laughed. "I know. You're definitely a chicken. I would love to live here with you. If you're sure."

"I've never been more sure of anything. You make me so happy," Juliet said. Her face was lit up like a summer morning.

Sienna felt herself getting emotional, but decided it wasn't the time for it. She leaned in and kissed Juliet, softly at first, and then firmer and with purpose. Juliet responded quickly and maneuvered herself off of the couch.

She held out her hand. "I think we should probably make it official in *our* bedroom, don't you?" Juliet asked, raising her eyebrows.

"I do."

Sienna took her hand and let Juliet lead the way. Once inside the bedroom, Sienna started kissing her again, wasting no time. Her tongue fluttered against Juliet's, a promise, and Juliet buried her hands in Sienna's hair, tugging with urgency. Sienna pulled Juliet against her, wondering if she would ever feel close enough. Juliet broke contact first and slipped onto the bed. She pulled Sienna on top of her, nipping lightly at her earlobes, her jawline, her chin. Sienna sighed, thinking about how good Juliet felt, how right, and how perfect they fit together. She had one hand on Juliet's shoulder, the other stroking the length of her back. She tickled her fingers from the nape of Juliet's neck to the small of her back, eliciting a shiver.

When they were finished, Sienna rolled onto her side and pulled Juliet close, her arm wrapped tightly around Juliet's waist.

Juliet smiled at her, spent and glowing. "How do you feel?" she whispered, tucking a piece of Sienna's hair behind her ear.

Sienna returned the smile and closed her eyes. "I feel like I'm home."

❖

Gretchen was sitting up in the hospital bed, complaining about the mashed potatoes. They were too lumpy and tasted like paste. Sienna was thrilled to see that side of her again.

"I talked to Monique, finally," Gretchen told her, examining the tiny piece of chicken on her plate. "She felt a little less guilty knowing she wasn't the one that put Rich in the ground, but not much. Nor should she. She told me she was pretty snowed by Charlie, and I believe her. But I don't think I'll ever be able to forgive her."

Sienna could think of several responses to that line of thinking, but she didn't feel it was her place. If Gretchen wanted to salvage some shred of a relationship with her daughter, Sienna didn't want to be the one to stop it.

"She knows she's going to prison and she seems at peace with it. Until she actually gets there, I'm sure. County is a cakewalk compared to Federal, or so I'm told. I wish Goodman would get a life sentence, but I know that won't happen. He tore this family to pieces with his greed and bullying," Gretchen said. "And I still don't understand why that Tara wanted to kill my husband. Even if she did think that they were having an imaginary love affair, why would anyone want to kill the person they say they love? Just doesn't make sense."

"I think there was more to it than that, in all honesty," Sienna said. "She snapped, and decided that life without him, in the way that she wanted, wasn't really worth living. She needed help, Gretchen. I hope that wherever she is now, she's at peace."

"I don't. She killed him and she tried to kill me. I hope she's rotting in hell," Gretchen said, digging into her Jell-O cup.

Sienna decided changing the subject was probably the best course of action. Gretchen had similar sentiments when Juliet had told her about Tara's motive. Sienna knew that Gretchen was speaking from a place of hurt and anger, and that she probably didn't mean the things she said. Or maybe she did. Either way, she wouldn't be wrong, though the double standard was interesting. Monique was going to kill Rich for money, for a man who most definitely didn't deserve such unwavering loyalty. But because she hadn't succeeded, Gretchen was willing to overlook it. Family was a complicated thing.

A familiar voice called out a hello and Sienna was happy to see Juliet walk in with a balloon bouquet.

"How's my favorite stabbing victim?" Juliet asked, placing the balloons on Gretchen's nightstand.

Gretchen chuckled and then held her wound. "Don't make me laugh, I told you that. The stitches will pop open and I'll bleed out."

"Sorry." Juliet leaned down and gave Gretchen a quick hug. She turned to Sienna. "Can I talk to you for a quick second?"

Sienna nodded and rose from her chair. They walked to the hallway and stood outside Gretchen's room.

"Everything okay?" Sienna asked.

"Just got preliminary results from the ME."

"Oh, from Kellie? Did she sign them with hugs and kisses?" Sienna teased her.

Juliet ignored her. "Guess what came back in Tara Wolfe's tox report? Nitroglycerin. A good amount of it, too. Looks like she went over to Gretchen's already planning to check out, one way or another."

"Where did she get it? Was it Rich's?" Sienna asked.

"Most likely. She must have been skimming off of his prescription for a while. Cause of death was a lethal head injury, but there was enough nitro in her bloodstream to cause some serious damage."

"Wow," Sienna said. There weren't any other words to adequately describe the situation.

"I know. How is she?" Juliet asked, nodding toward Gretchen's room.

"Good, actually. She'll be in here for a few more days, mostly for observation, and then she'll be able to go home. She'll probably have to start some things over in physical therapy. Setback to say the least," Sienna said.

"That's huge. I hope her nephew comes back, or someone else, so she isn't alone all the time."

"I'm sure they will. But also, she has me. I'm not going anywhere. I might only be a part of her life in a professional capacity for a little while longer, but I have no plans to abandon her after that. She's like my kooky aunt now," Sienna said.

Juliet smiled warmly. "You're so good. Okay, I have to get back to work. Just wanted to bring Gretchen something to brighten her room and tell you what they found."

"Okay, go. See you in a little bit. Love you," Sienna said.

"Love you, too."

Sienna watched her walk down the hallway, a spring in her step. It would be nice to finally put Richard Kowalski to rest. She went back in to sit with Gretchen for a while, maybe to play some cards or watch one of those Halloween cooking shows. And then, when Gretchen was comfortable and relaxed, Sienna would go home. *Home.*

EPILOGUE

One Year Later

Declan poked around the glass tray filled with sweet pickles, a tradition that Sienna had insisted upon. That was how Thanksgiving was done in her family, and her family now had better try to embrace it. The tray consisted of sweet pickles and a few varieties of olives.

"Stop playing with the food, Dec," Sienna called from the kitchen.

Juliet pretended to gag at the weird pickle and olive tray and held her hands around her throat. Declan nodded in agreement and flicked an olive onto the table.

"Really, Juliet? How is our son expected to behave at family gatherings if *this* is the role model he has?" Sienna asked, standing with her hands on her hips.

"You're right. I'm sorry, sweetie. That was rude. These pimento things are delicious." Juliet tried to keep a straight face.

"They *are,* actually," Sienna said. She popped one of them into her mouth and gave them a pointed look.

The doorbell rang and everybody froze.

"I'll get it," Declan said and made a beeline for the door.

"This is the worst idea ever, isn't it? Be totally honest," Juliet said, rubbing her palms on her thighs.

"No, it's fine. It'll be fine. We'll have a nice time, I'm sure," Sienna said, not meeting Juliet's eyes.

"You're lying," Juliet shout-whispered. "I know when you're lying."

"Hey, Mom, Sienna," Declan said, re-entering the dining room with two guests in tow. "This is Ashley."

"Hi, Ashley, nice to meet you." Sienna held out her hand, warm and friendly as always.

Juliet echoed Sienna's welcome and then turned toward Ashley's date.

"Hi."

"Hey," Will said. "House looks nice."

"Thank you. I'm so glad you and Ashley could come. Sienna's been planning the menu for weeks," Juliet said. She was glad that Will had accepted their invitation to spend Thanksgiving with them. She was so surprised when he'd agreed to come, she'd blurted out a flabbergasted "really?" before she could stop herself. When Declan had told her that Will's Thanksgiving plans included staying at home with Ashley and ordering sandwiches, she immediately told him that Will and Ashley could just come to their house. Declan had given her an alien look but seemed genuinely happy about the idea once it had sunk in. Things hadn't returned to normal with Will, and Juliet wasn't sure if they ever would. But she appreciated his baby steps.

"I'm sure she has. The Thanksgiving dinners we hosted were always one step away from a fine dining experience. Did she make you put out that pickle plate, though?" Will asked. He shrugged his coat off and folded it over the back of Juliet's couch.

"Yes! God, it's all so gross." Juliet made sure Sienna wasn't listening.

"Wait until she makes you try one of the black ones dipped in bleu cheese dressing. I almost threw up."

Sienna turned from her conversation and smiled at them both sweetly. "Did the two of you forget that my superpower is listening to two conversations at once? You'll both be enjoying Cheesy Olive Supreme this evening."

Declan laughed and pointed at them mockingly.

Juliet smirked at him and raised her eyebrows. "Sienna? Declan said he thinks it's disgusting, too."

"Then I'll be sure to put out enough for him to enjoy, as well."

"That was shitty, Mom," Declan said.

Juliet, Sienna, and Will all turned to him and said, "Language!"

"Whoa," Declan said, his eyes wide. "That was freaky."

Juliet punched him lightly on the arm and went into the kitchen to help Sienna with the turkey.

"Maybe this won't be so bad, after all," Juliet said, basting the turkey while it was in the oven.

"No, I think it will be good. Good for Declan," Sienna said. She bent down and kissed Juliet on the nose. "And good for you."

"Gretchen's here," Declan yelled from the living room.

Juliet rushed to the door and helped Gretchen in, though she didn't really need the help anymore. The cane she still walked with was more of a crutch than a necessity.

"Smells delicious in here," Gretchen said, handing her coat to Juliet. She took the seat next to Declan and pulled an old, battered, Game Boy out of her purse. "I found this in my attic. I thought you might like to play with it, even though it's about a hundred years old. They say that old becomes new again, so go on and give *Donkey Kong* a try."

The timer finally dinged. They brought out dish after dish, each one more enticing than the last. Juliet was impressed. Sienna had thrown together a magnificent holiday meal, without a whole lot of time to prepare.

Juliet went to get the cranberry sauce and came back to everyone seated at the table, reaching for potatoes and stuffing and corn, talking and laughing over Thanksgiving dinner.

She was flooded with emotion, seeing her family, all of it, celebrating together. She let it overtake her, allowed herself to settle into that overwhelming sense that the pieces finally fit together.

Sienna caught her looking at them and gave her a knowing smile. Juliet smiled back. Somehow, they'd made it through the storm. Together.

About the Author

Nicole Stiling lives in New England with her wife, two children, and a menagerie of pets. When she's not working at her day job or pounding away at the keyboard, she enjoys video games, comic books, clearing out the DVR, and the occasional amusement park. Nicole is a strict vegetarian who does not like vegetables, and a staunch advocate for anything with four legs.

Books Available from Bold Strokes Books

16 Steps to Forever by Georgia Beers. Can Brooke Sullivan and Macy Carr find themselves by finding each other? (978-1-63555-762-6)

All I Want for Christmas by Georgia Beers, Maggie Cummings, Fiona Riley. The Christmas season sparks passion and love in these stories by award winning authors Georgia Beers, Maggie Cummings, and Fiona Riley. (978-1-63555-764-0)

From the Woods by Charlotte Greene. When Fiona goes backpacking in a protected wilderness, the last thing she expects is to be fighting for her life. (978-1-63555-793-0)

Heart of the Storm by Nicole Stiling. For Juliet Mitchell and Sienna Bennett a forbidden attraction definitely isn't worth upending the life they've worked so hard for. Is it? (978-1-63555-789-3)

If You Dare by Sandy Lowe. For Lauren West and Emma Prescott, following their passions is easy. Following their hearts, though? That's almost impossible. (978-1-63555-654-4)

Love Changes Everything by Jaime Maddox. For Samantha Brooks and Kirby Fielding, no matter how careful their plans, love will change everything. (978-1-63555-835-7)

Not This Time by MA Binfield. Flung back into each other's lives, can former bandmates Sophia and Madison have a second chance at romance? (978-1-63555-798-5)

The Dubious Gift of Dragon Blood by J. Marshall Freeman. One day Crispin is a lonely high school student—the next he is fighting a war in a land ruled by dragons, his otherworldly boyfriend at his side. (978-1-63555-725-1)

The Found Jar by Jaycie Morrison. Fear keeps Emily Harris trapped in her emotionally vacant life; can she find the courage to let Beck Reynolds guide her toward love? (978-1-63555-825-8)

Aurora by Emma L McGeown. After a traumatic accident, Elena Ricci is stricken with amnesia leaving her with no recollection of the last eight years, including her wife and son. (978-1-63555-824-1)

Avenging Avery by Sheri Lewis Wohl. Revenge against a vengeful vampire unites Isa Meyer and Jeni Denton, but it's love that heals them. (978-1-63555-622-3)

Bulletproof by Maggie Cummings. For Dylan Prescott and Briana Logan, the complicated NYC criminal justice system doesn't leave room for love, but where the heart is concerned, no one is bulletproof. (978-1-63555-771-8)

Her Lady to Love by Jane Walsh. A shy wallflower joins forces with the most popular woman in Regency London on a quest to catch a husband, only to discover a wild passion for each other that far eclipses their interest for the Marriage Mart. (978-1-63555-809-8)

No Regrets by Joy Argento. For Jodi and Beth, the possibility of losing their future will force them to decide what is really important. (978-1-63555-751-0)

The Holiday Treatment by Elle Spencer. Who doesn't want a gay Christmas movie? Holly Hudson asks herself that question and discovers that happy endings aren't only for the movies. (978-1-63555-660-5)

Too Good to be True by Leigh Hays. Can the promise of love survive the realities of life for Madison and Jen, or is it too good to be true? (978-1-63555-715-2)

Treacherous Seas by Radclyffe. When the choice comes down to the lives of her officers against the promise she made to her wife, Reese Conlon puts everything she cares about on the line. (978-1-63555-778-7)

Two to Tangle by Melissa Brayden. Ryan Jacks has been a player all her life, but the new chef at Tangle Valley Vineyard changes everything. If only she wasn't off the menu. (978-1-63555-747-3)

When Sparks Fly by Annie McDonald. Will the devastating incident that first brought Dr. Daniella Waveny and hockey coach Luca McCaffrey together on frozen ice now force them apart, or will their secrets and fears thaw enough for them to create sparks? (978-1-63555-782-4)

Best Practice by Carsen Taite. When attorney Grace Maldonado agrees to mentor her best friend's little sister, she's prepared to confront Perry's rebellious nature, but she isn't prepared to fall in love. Legal Affairs: one law firm, three best friends, three chances to fall in love. (978-1-63555-361-1)

Home by Kris Bryant. Natalie and Sarah discover that anything is possible when love takes the long way home. (978-1-63555-853-1)

Keeper by Sydney Quinne. With a new charge under her reluctant wing—feisty, highly intelligent math wizard Isabelle Templeton—Keeper Andy Bouchard has to prevent a murder or die trying. (978-1-63555-852-4)

One More Chance by Ali Vali. Harry Basantes planned a future with Desi Thompson until the day Desi disappeared without a word, only to walk back into her life sixteen years later. (978-1-63555-536-3)

Renegade's War by Gun Brooke. Freedom fighter Aurelia DeCallum regrets saving the woman called Blue. She fears it will jeopardize her mission, and secretly, Blue might end up breaking Aurelia's heart. (978-1-63555-484-7)

The Other Women by Erin Zak. What happens in Vegas should stay in Vegas, but what do you do when the love you find in Vegas changes your life forever? (978-1-63555-741-1)

The Sea Within by Missouri Vaun. Time is running out for Dr. Elle Graham to convince Captain Jackson Drake that the only thing that can save future Earth resides in the past, and rescue her broken heart in the process. (978-1-63555-568-4)

To Sleep With Reindeer by Justine Saracen. In Norway under Nazi occupation, Maarit, an Indigenous woman; and Kirsten, a Norwegian resister, join forces to stop the development of an atomic weapon. (978-1-63555-735-0)

Twice Shy by Aurora Rey. Having an ex with benefits isn't all it's cracked up to be. Will Amanda Russo learn that lesson in time to take a chance on love with Quinn Sullivan? (978-1-63555-737-4)

Z-Town by Eden Darry. Forced to work together to stay alive, Meg and Lane must find the centuries-old treasure before the zombies find them first. (978-1-63555-743-5)

Bet Against Me by Fiona Riley. In the high stakes luxury real estate market, everything has a price, and as rival Realtors Trina Lee and Kendall Yates find out, that means their hearts and souls, too. (978-1-63555-729-9)

Broken Reign by Sam Ledel. Together on an epic journey in search of a mysterious cure, a princess and a village outcast must overcome life-threatening challenges and their own prejudice if they want to survive. (978-1-63555-739-8)

Just One Taste by CJ Birch. For Lauren, it only took one taste to start trusting in love again. (978-1-63555-772-5)

Lady of Stone by Barbara Ann Wright. Sparks fly as a magical emergency forces a noble embarrassed by her ability to submit to a low-born teacher who resents everything about her. (978-1-63555-607-0)

Last Resort by Angie Williams. Katie and Rhys are about to find out what happens when you meet the girl of your dreams but you aren't looking for a happily ever after. (978-1-63555-774-9)

Longing for You by Jenny Frame. When Debrek housekeeper Katie Brekman is attacked amid a burgeoning vampire-witch war, Alexis Villiers must go against everything her clan believes in to save her. (978-1-63555-658-2)

Money Creek by Anne Laughlin. Clare Lehane is a troubled lawyer from Chicago who tries to make her way in a rural town full of secrets and deceptions. (978-1-63555-795-4)

Passion's Sweet Surrender by Ronica Black. Cam and Blake are unable to deny their passion for each other, but surrendering to love is a whole different matter. (978-1-63555-703-9)

The Holiday Detour by Jane Kolven. It will take everything going wrong to make Dana and Charlie see how right they are for each other. (978-1-63555-720-6)

Too Hot to Ride by Andrews & Austin. World famous cutting horse champion and industry legend Jane Barrow is knockdown sexy in the way she moves, talks, and rides, and Rae Starr is determined not to get involved with this womanizing gambler. (978-1-63555-776-3)

A Love that Leads to Home by Ronica Black. For Carla Sims and Janice Carpenter, home isn't about location, it's where your heart is. (978-1-63555-675-9)

Blades of Bluegrass by D. Jackson Leigh. A US Army occupational therapist must rehab a bitter veteran who is a ticking political time bomb the military is desperate to disarm. (978-1-63555-637-7)

Guarding Hearts by Jaycie Morrison. As treachery and temptation threaten the women of the Women's Army Corps, who will risk it all for love? (978-1-63555-806-7)

Hopeless Romantic by Georgia Beers. Can a jaded wedding planner and an optimistic divorce attorney possibly find a future together? (978-1-63555-650-6)

Hopes and Dreams by PJ Trebelhorn. Movie theater manager Riley Warren is forced to face her high school crush and tormentor, wealthy socialite Victoria Thayer, at their twentieth reunion. (978-1-63555-670-4)

In the Cards by Kimberly Cooper Griffin. Daria and Phaedra are about to discover that love finds a way, especially when powers outside their control are at play. (978-1-63555-717-6)

Moon Fever by Ileandra Young. SPEAR agent Danika Karson must clear her werewolf friend of multiple false charges while teaching her vampire girlfriend to resist the blood mania brought on by a full moon. (978-1-63555-603-2)

Quake City by St John Karp. Can Andre find his best friend Amy before the night devolves into a nightmare of broken hearts, malevolent drag queens, and spontaneous human combustion? Or has it always happened this way, every night, at Aunty Bob's Quake City Club? (978-1-63555-723-7)

Serenity by Jesse J. Thoma. For Kit Marsden, there are many things in life she cannot change. Serenity is in the acceptance. (978-1-63555-713-8)

Sylver and Gold by Michelle Larkin. Working feverishly to find a killer before he strikes again, Boston Homicide Detective Reid Sylver and rookie cop London Gold are blindsided by their chemistry and developing attraction. (978-1-63555-611-7)

Trade Secrets by Kathleen Knowles. In Silicon Valley, love and business are a volatile mix for clinical lab scientist Tony Leung and venture capitalist Sheila Graham. (978-1-63555-642-1)